OPEN
SEASON

WUNDERFOOL

W P

P R E S S

Brad Whittington

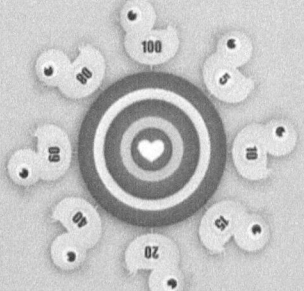

OPEN SEASON

A JAKE AND BERF STORY

ISBN: 978-1-937274-23-8
Published by Wunderfool Press
Austin, Texas

Dewey Decimal Classification: F
Subject Heading: Fiction / Humorous

CONTENTS

What they're saying about Whittington

Whittington spins an enjoyable literary story
and is definitely a novelist to watch.
–Publisher's Weekly

Brad Whittington is an artist with a pen.
–Ethan C. McDonald, DancingWord.com

It is always a joy to find a new writer who knows
what he's doing. –Rick Lewis, Logos Bookstore

Whittington is a welcome new voice in the world of
fiction.
–Cindy Crosby, author of By Willoway Brook

Who can resist a story of someone else's alienated
youth if that someone else is as talented as Brad
Whittington?
–JT Conroe, author of The Blue Hotel

The pacing, humor, honesty, and believable
characters made me turn page after page in rapid
succession until there were none.
–T Leigh

Brad Whittington paints some of the best word
pictures I've seen.
–Cammi Ellis

Cast of Characters

In Order of Appearance

BERF WIGGINS Artist, bon vivant, and man-with-a-Code about town

TOM Itinerant cabbie

JAKE Hair stylist, foodie, hipster photographer, and ex-brother-in-law to Berf

HANK THE JACK RUSSELL Berf 's father's dog

AMELIA BARKER Librarian, engaged to Berf twice

SUMMER HARDESTY Philanthro-tourist approaching forty at the speed of light

BILLY TRENT Estate manager and wannabe film producer

HENDERSON Aging alcoholic herpetologist and ranch hand for his brother-in-law, Dr. Payne

DR. PAYNE Gentleman rancher and proctologist to the stars

CHIP Venture capitalist and significant other to Zoe

ZOE PAYNE Society princess and daughter of Dr. Payne

JL MARTINEZ Buffer pad magnate, serial entrepreneur, and treasure hunter

YVONNE MARTINEZ Cajun queen and wife to JL

ZACHARY MARTINEZ Oldest son and movie buff

JOSIAH MARTINEZ Youngest son and video game addict

MITCHELL LANCE FLOOD Pediatric intern, nickname "Emil" from his initials "ML"

BONNIE HOLLINGSWORTH Eight-time barrel-racing champion and neighbor to the Paynes

For Ian

Who helped build the foundation

"I believe there are two ways of writing novels. One is mine, making a sort of musical comedy without music and ignoring real life altogether; the other is going right deep down into life and not caring a damn."

—P.G. Wodehouse

"We must have reasons for our actions, even when the reasons are not always good ones."

—Louis L'Amour

Chapter One

"When I was a mere tadpole, knee high to a grasshopper, my grandpa Wiggins gave me a Monopoly game. No surprise there. But my grandpa Berford gave me three gifts: a set of watercolors, a print by Remington, and a little book called *Sackett* by Louis L'Amour. Not much, you might say, Tom."

The cabbie said no such thing. Instead he turned east off Exposition Boulevard directly into the rising sun as it peeked above the tree line over Austin.

Berford Oswald Wiggins, riding shotgun as usual, flipped down the visor and continued.

"You may well think of it as not much. You might as well say the same thing about Einstein's first slide rule or Lincoln's first whisker or Stalin's first manic episode. Seemingly inconsequential at the time but monumental in retrospect. It changed the course of my life. Right then, right there."

Berf gestured. "Take a left here. Of course Dad didn't think much of it. Couldn't see how to turn it into money. Plus it came from his father-in-law, so he would have spurned it even if it had been the original plates from Fort Knox."

Tom raised an unkempt eyebrow as they slid through the dawn shadows pooling under the oaks in Tarrytown but otherwise declined to interrupt the story.

"Grandpa didn't know it, but when he handed me that box, he threw me a lifeline. Or maybe he did know. After all, he had a TV, just like every bully in my junior high. He saw the commercials. He must have guessed what I was going through. Pull up right here."

As they coasted to the curb, Berf cracked open the door and set one foot on the street. He handed Tom a scrap of paper and a Franklin. "Here you go, Tom. That's my cell number."

Tom crammed the cash and the note into his shirt pocket, which was already bulging with random scraps of paper and a crumpled pack of Marlboros. "Gotcha."

"Half now, half when you find it." Berf slid out of the taxi. Before he closed the door, he stuck his head back in. "Vintage 1966 Jaguar XKE. Silver with black interior."

"Got it all right here." Tom winked and tapped his forehead with the two fingers that held his cigarette, ashes dropping onto the ledge of his eyebrows.

"Thanks." Berf closed the door, knocked on the roof twice, and watched the cab disappear around the corner. Seemed like a nice guy, even if he did have an unfortunate resemblance to Kid Newton, especially that time in New Mexico when the Kid called out Tell Sackett. It was the eyes. Too close together. Squinty, you might say.

But that wasn't Tom's fault. As Berf had discovered in his twenty-nine years out here in the old west, a feller didn't get to choose his face, only his fate. And his wardrobe.

Confident that he had put his best man on the job, Berf turned toward his rambling, multi-level house nestled under an oak canopy. He breathed in the cool morning air and sighed with the anticipation of a quick breakfast and a solid day's sleep.

Then he caught sight of Jake in the bay window of the breakfast nook and remembered that he wasn't home alone. They locked eyes for a second before Jake slowly lifted the business section of *The Statesman* to block him out.

Berf preferred the sound of "Berf, party of one" when he returned to his Tarrytown fortress following a night of revelry. But when Jake showed up on his doorstep last month after disappearing into the jungles of Borneo for a year or so, Berf saw his duty and stepped forward.

It had been years since he had shared his campfire with a fellow drifter, and they were still working out the kinks. Jake was of the "early to bed, early to rise" school of thought, and this difference had caused a bit of domestic tension. Berf could appreciate Jake's philosophy, at least on a theoretical basis, but sometimes a feller had to bust loose from the traces and raise a little sand.

Berf checked his watch. Friday, 7:47 a.m. Just over an hour before Jake had to be at the salon. Well, Berf could manage a few minutes of awkward conversation, especially if supplied with a stiff cup of coffee. He sampled the breeze. And a slab of bacon, if he wasn't mistaken. You could always rely on Jake to scratch up a little grub in your hour of need.

He moseyed up the sidewalk to the front steps, across the sitting porch, and into the foyer. His reflection in the hall mirror pulled him up short.

His face was smudged, as if he had been shoveling coal in a locomotive, and his normally sleek black hair looked more like two mangy coons fighting. The ruffle on his shirt hung as limp as a haberdasher's handshake, and his bow tie circled his head like Willie Nelson's bandana. Not bad, considering.

These days Berf's bag of undomesticated oats was half empty. On any given evening he was more likely to be at home sitting by the fire with an improving book than out on the tiles running rampant and pilfering traffic signs.

But despite his sedentary and reflective nature, he did feel a certain obligation to set an example for the younger generation. After all, things should be done a certain way, and if a guy was going to paint the town red, tradition dictated that he at least get the hue right.

Berf glanced at the framed 1965 first-edition cover of *The Sackett Brand* hanging in the foyer and pushed open the swinging door to the kitchen as if daring Kid Newton to draw on him.

The only evidence of Jake's presence was a set of fingers curled around the wall of newspaper that hid his face. Berf let the door swing shut and dropped onto the chair opposite Jake. He draped an elbow over the back of the chair and snagged a slice of bacon. "Coffee?"

A hand slid a teapot from behind the newspaper. "Oolong tea."

Berf stared at the teapot as he would at a rattlesnake with a chip on its shoulder. He munched the bacon while considering whether to expend the effort to grind beans or to just cash in his chips and head off to the bunkhouse.

Jake's voice floated from behind the paper. "What happened to the Jag?"

"In the course of the evening festivities, I somehow became separated from my trusty steed."

"You must be heartbroken."

"I figure it was somewhere along the trail of the pub crawl that broke up at the Scoot Inn. But fear not. I have deputized a reliable confederate to locate the little filly and repatriate her to the Wiggins corral."

As Berf delivered this bit of information, a jingle and a few clicks sounded from under the table and a Jack Russell terrier sprang into the third chair.

Berf frowned at the dog and studied his back trail, paying particular attention to the driveway. "How does Hank come to be here?"

"Roger dropped him off."

Berf half rose from the chair. "Dad? Is he still here?"

"Gone to take Trixie to see the Great Wall of China."

Berf settled back in the chair and regarded Hank the Jack Russell with the reservation that a cowpoke fresh off the trail from Durango might regard a bottle of rot-gut whiskey. Both offered certain entertainments, but the chances of an unwelcome ending were practically inescapable.

"Do me a kindness, then. Mark the date of Dad's return on the calendar so I can make arrangements to be in Tucumcari for the week."

Wherever Hank the Jack Russell was, Dad would eventually turn up, and through the years, Berf had taken strong measures to place as many miles of dead air as possible between himself and his father without having to forgo the sybaritic pleasures the greater Austin metropolitan area offered.

To say nothing of Trixie, Dad's new wife. Berf shuddered and scratched the dog behind the ears. "Is Hank *persona non grata* in the People's Republic?"

"Roger was afraid he would become an entrée." Jake folded the paper. "You know how them Chinese are," Jake said in a surprisingly good impression of Roger. "They'll cook anything,"

Berf gave the wiry dog an appraising glance. "More like an appetizer."

Jake set the paper aside and slid a stack of twenties across the table.

"What's that?" Berf asked after wrapping himself around another slice of bacon.

Hank the Jack Russell probed the air with a quivering nostril, but remained silent.

"Rent," Jake said.

Berf made no move to take it. "That's a lot of hairdos."

The money lay next to the jelly in the no-man's-land between them, silently reproaching Berf. He drew another bacon slice from the plate and poked the cash back toward Jake.

"Jackson's the accountant. Give it to him." Berf nibbled the bacon. "I'm the silent partner. Very silent. Think of me as Tell Sackett, riding beside you on the cattle drive from Laredo to Dodge City without saying a word. Wrapped in a Navajo rug, staring into the—"

"Not for the salon. For the room."

"Oh." Berf glanced at the pile of cash with even less enthusiasm. "Has it been a month already?"

Jake nodded at the newspaper. "November first."

Berf glanced at the paper and back to Jake, but his head snapped around for a closer look. Under the headline "Halloween Gala Is Scary Good," a large photograph featured Berf on one knee before a bevy of luscious debutantes, microphone in one hand, the other outstretched in song.

"'I Did It My Way?'" Jake asked.

Berf shook his head. "Probably 'Crazy.'" He pushed the paper aside with the bacon slice and gestured at the twenties. "You're going to need a deposit to get your own place." He bit off a chunk of bacon. "Plus it's mostly my fault. I introduced you to her. Although, in my defense, I was drunk at the time and—"

"There's plenty of blame to go around."

"Yes, but she's my sister. I knew better. Shoot, half of Austin knew better."

"And now I know better."

"That cinches it." Berf shoved the cash back to Jake's side of the table. After everything that had happened in Cancún, he owed Jake a lot more than one month's rent.

Jake picked up the twenties and fanned through them, pulled a brochure from the bottom of the stack, and set it on the table. "Or we could use it to drown our sorrows in Aruba for the weekend."

Berf snorted. "Aruba's great. If you want to go missing and end up with your driver's license photo in the tabloids."

"That lady disappeared almost ten years ago."

Berf shook his head. "Only one of many. You obviously haven't been keeping up with your tabloid reading."

The doorbell rang. Hank the Jack Russell leapt from the chair with a single yap and dashed to the swinging door, where he awaited a doorman to do the honors.

Berf picked up the brochure, glanced at the idyllic tropical scenes. "What next? Cancún again? Umbrella drinks?"

The bell rang again, this time in an urgent staccato that indicated a lack of good breeding. Berf tossed the brochure aside and looked at Jake. "You expecting someone?" Unlike many of the modern generation, Berf didn't allow bad manners to instill a sense of urgency. Let them ring was Berf's motto.

Jake shoved the money into his pocket. "I'll get it."

Berf glanced over his shoulder at Jake's retreating back and slurped down half the tea in Jake's cup. He took another look at the newspaper photo. He didn't have a recollection of that moment in the evening, or many other moments, for those keeping score at home, but providing amusement for the masses was just one of the many services he offered.

He turned the paper around to see it straight on. Not that he was the type of man to expect others to take notice, but he had to admit the photographer had captured something of his essence. Maybe he would clip it for his scrapbook.

Jake's overly loud voice interrupted his reflections. "Amelia! What a surprise!"

Despite the bolt of electricity that sizzled through Berf's nervous system, he had to smile. Setting aside Jake's questionable views on circadian rhythms, he was a good 'un and could be relied upon to give a feller a heads-up regarding an impending crisis.

In less time than it took Tell Sackett to snatch that kid from the wigwam in the Sierra Madres, Berf shot up from his chair, turned toward the door, hesitated, and then grabbed the last few slices of bacon before lighting a shuck to the safety of his bedroom suite.

Amelia was a jewel, practical and sympathetic, if a bit horsey around the face. The flower of good old pioneer stock, always ready to rescue a stray or do a good turn to those in need. But the unvarnished truth was that on such a morning as this, what a feller wanted was fewer Amelia Barkers and more closed shades and warm blankets pulled up to his chin as a vintage requiem on the iPod lulled him to the shores of Lethe.

But the hesitation for bacon had cost him. When he pushed through the swinging door, he ran into Amelia.

"Oh!" Amelia staggered back.

Jake, who was right behind, steadied her. Hank the Jack Russell sprang out of the way without a sound and stood by with wagging tail for further instructions.

"Well, Amelia Barker," Berf exclaimed. "If that don't beat all. We were just wondering what you were up to these days. Why, just a second ago I said to Jake, 'I wonder what Amelia Barker is up to these days.' Didn't I, Jake?"

Then he realized she was staring at the bacon strips in his hand. He held them out to her. "Bacon?"

Amelia selected a slice cautiously, as if expecting a trick, and held it in front of her like a candle at a memorial service. Her gaze wandered to his forehead.

Ah! The bow tie! He snatched it off his head and tossed it into the umbrella stand. Then he toasted her with a bacon strip and took a bite. Crunchy, yet chewy, just the way he liked them.

"So, Amelia, what brings you to Chateau Berf at this unlikely, if not ungodly, hour?"

She stood before him in the gloom of the hallway, a rangy woman with reddish-brownish hair and the expression of an assayer inspecting an unconvincing sample of iron pyrite. "You invited me to breakfast."

Chapter Two

"Breakfast," Berf said. "Of course."

He ignored the exasperation emanating from the general vicinity of where Jake stood. It was entirely possible that Berf had invited Amelia to breakfast at some point in the past. She was a reliable trail hand and he had no reason to doubt her word. "What I meant was that we were wondering when you would get here. Right, Jake?"

He backed through the swinging door and held it open. "We're fresh out of cornflakes. How about flapjacks and cowboy coffee?"

Amelia hesitated. Hank the Jack Russell darted through the door and assumed his former position in the chair that backed to the bay window. Amelia took the seat facing the door.

"Come along, Jake, let's rustle up some grub for our guest."

"I have to get to the shop," Jake whispered.

"Where are your manners, pardner? Besides, we both know that place runs on autopilot and Suzie never schedules your appointments before noon."

Berf gestured him in. Jake snorted a sigh like an annoyed bull and pushed past him into the kitchen. Berf let the door swing closed.

"Amelia, you remember my ex-brother-in-law, Jake?"

"I was China's maid of honor," Amelia said. "As the best man, you escorted me down the aisle at their wedding."

"Of course I did." Berf had done his best to smooth out that little wrinkle in his hippocampus, with spotty results. He stepped to the pantry and rifled through the packages. "What are you in the mood for? Cheese toast and baked kale? Vienna sausage and biscuits? Sautéed asparagus with capers and salsa?"

Jake pulled Berf out of the pantry and extracted an onion from a net bag. "I'll make a Denver scramble."

"Say what you will about Jake, but he can sure put the groceries together. I'll whip up some coffee." Berf put on a kettle and poured beans into the hopper of a burr grinder.

He had to admit that seeing Amelia here, fresh as a mountain meadow and soft as a morning sunrise, unsettled him no little bit. They had a history, and though he had no desire to restore her to most favored nation status, he was not indifferent to her finer qualities. A sentiment that had landed him in her web when he was young and had not yet learned the value of caution when dealing with the gentler sex.

"I was just wondering when was the last time I saw you," Berf shouted over the grinder. "I said to Jake not ten minutes ago, 'Jake, when was the last time we saw Amelia?' Right, Jake?"

Jake declined to answer.

Amelia gazed at Berf with an expression that filled him with a vague sense of unease, like Tell Sackett noticing a broken branch on a trail where no branch should have been broken. An ambiguous expression, like she couldn't choose between annoyed and amused.

"It was last night. When you invited me to breakfast."

Berf masked his faux pas by dumping the grounds into the French press. "Ah, yes, at Justine's."

"At the gala." She glanced at the paper. "Just before you sang that song."

"Of course!" Berf poured the water over the grounds and set the timer. Then he looked for tasks that would save him from sitting down across the table from Amelia and looking into her eyes. He retrieved a carton of half-and-half from the fridge, set it on the table, and cleared away Jake's breakfast dishes.

"Are you still painting?" Amelia asked. "I loved the ones you did back in college. What was it? Space aliens sitting around a card table?"

"Mutants," Berf said.

A lot of people had liked those paintings. He'd paid cash for this Tarrytown house from the prints he'd sold on eBay. In the past few years he had moved on from photo unrealism, as he liked to call the genre he had invented. The new stuff didn't have the broad appeal of mutants playing poker, but had attracted the attention of galleries and collectors. In the words of the great philosopher Anatole, Berf could take a few smooths with a rough.

Amelia turned the newspaper so she could see the photo. "I always loved that song."

Berf moved the travel brochures to the buffet and tried to remember which song he had sung. "It's a good 'un."

Amelia smoothed the crease and hummed a melody. She sang a few lines softly. "When I'm alone with my fancies, I'll be with you, weaving romances and making believe they're true."

Ah, that was it. Berf suppressed a smile. Old Satchmo and "Kiss to Build a Dream On." That song used to reel them in by the dozens back in the day. In fact, Amelia was the first he had reeled in. Or was it the other way around?

Amelia glanced over at the stove where Jake sautéed onions, bell pepper, and ham, and lowered her voice. "I didn't realize Jake would be here. I mean, when you came back from Cancún you said he ran off to Bali or Java or somewhere with some nurse—"

"Borneo. He showed up on my doorstep last month."

"No wonder he's back," Amelia breathed. "It was too soon after your sister and he . . . well, they say you should give it a good year after a breakup before you try again."

"Very wise." Berf stepped to the counter and pushed the filter down on the French press. He poured three cups of coffee, left one for Jake, and took the chair opposite Amelia.

Rather than talk, he took a long, slow sip. Even black, like any good trail hand preferred, it was darkly rich without a hint of bitterness. He watched Amelia doctor hers until it looked more like hot chocolate.

Such was ever the way of the gentler sex, smoothing the rough edges, soothing the troubled waters, taming the wild things, blunting the red tooth and claw of nature.

It warmed the heart when you thought about it, this civilizing force in the world. After all, what was the point of man blazing trails through uncharted lands, carving out a patch in the wild places, if not for woman to come along behind and transform the wilderness into a paradise?

But that kind of civilizing took a special kind of woman. Someone who was about more than picking curtains and planting window boxes and keeping sensible hours. Someone who could flourish inside a paradox, who could see both sides of the coin without feeling the need to call heads or tails, who could embrace the tension of the philosopher-warrior.

A woman who could break a wild stallion without breaking his spirit.

Berf had found a woman like that once. Or thought he had, but in the end he came back to Austin without her.

"Just like old times," Amelia said.

Berf blinked at her, startled from his ruminations by the sentiment in her voice. He had let himself relax, like staring into the campfire until you lose your night vision and become unaware of the threats lurking in the shadows.

Amelia sat with her elbows on the table, the "Don't Mess with Texas" mug cradled in her two expertly manicured hands, and gazed at him through the steam.

"You and I," she said. "Together. Sipping coffee at sunrise."

He took another sip, reminded of one particular sunrise they had shared over breakfast. She had pulled an all-nighter studying for her finals in library science. He had stumbled into the diner after a dusk-to-dawn painting session fueled by martinis. It was the morning when he had . . .

"You put a quarter in the jukebox and played that song," Amelia whispered.

That song. The one he sang last night, if she was right, and she usually was.

Amelia's eyes flared. "And when it finished, you said—"

"Ah, yes." He remembered what he had done. Hit her with the one-two punch of Satchmo and Browning.

Grow old along with me! The best is yet to be, the last of life, for which the first was made.

And the next thing he had known, he was engaged to Amelia Barker, although he didn't remember actually saying the words. It just sort of happened. And not for the first time. There was the time when they were freshmen, just after they had watched *Big Fish* in the theater. It was a life lesson. Be wary of Tim Burton movies.

"And now here we are again," Amelia said. "Three's a charm." She reached across the table and took Berf's hand, the one that wasn't holding the coffee. "The best is yet to be."

This sounded disturbingly familiar. "Ah, well," Berf said. "Twenty-nine is hardly the last of life. More like the first, I should have thought."

"And it will only get better," Amelia said.

Berf studied her. Perhaps he was wrong about Amelia. Could she be that rare woman, the one in a gazillion? Maybe the first two times around he had been too young, too raw to recognize her mettle. One thing was for sure, she wasn't short of perseverance.

"I knew what you were thinking last night as soon as you started that song. The time has come." Amelia squeezed his hand.

"It has?" Berf glanced at the clock. "Oh, is that the time?" He jumped to his feet, pulling his hand from hers. He needed space to think. A lot of space. "I hate to cut this short, but I have a . . . thing. I was just headed out when you arrived."

Although the possibilities might be boiling around in his brain, he was not prepared to pull the trigger over a Denver scramble.

To Berf's surprise, Amelia smiled. "Oh, Berf, you haven't changed a bit after all these years. Too shy to show your true feelings. But I want you to know the answer is yes."

Berf stared at her, his mind racing for some way to unask a question that hadn't been asked. Was this how it had happened the first two times? "Well, the experts say one shouldn't rush into these things. Give it a year, you know."

Amelia stood just as Jake arrived at the table with a skillet full of breakfast goodness. "That looks wonderful! Since Berf has to go, could I take a doggie bag?"

Jake looked from her to Berf.

"Me too," Berf said. "I have this thing, but just roll it up in a tortilla and I'll have it on the way."

Jake shrugged, set the skillet on the stove, and pulled out some plastic containers.

Berf turned to Amelia. "Sorry, have to change. For this thing." He indicated the one-sleeved tux jacket. "But I'll catch up with you later."

"I'll come by this evening," Amelia said. "We can get drinks at Annie's and dinner at Bess Bistro."

Berf heard the last bit faintly because he was already through the swinging door and halfway down the hall-way.

On the way up the stairs and down the hall, he discarded the amputee tux jacket, the tired ruffled shirt, the scuffed shoes, and the wrinkled pants in a sartorial trail that led to his bedroom.

She would be back in twelve hours. Could be ten. Either way, it was hardly enough time for him to process this notion, the possibility that what he had been looking for had been in his own backyard all along.

This type of thing was best pondered on the trail, wandering among the lonely places, maybe with a laconic partner off whom he could bounce the odd thought or conjecture. At any rate, the operative phrase for this moment was "somewhere else."

Berf barely looked up when Jake entered and held out a Denver scramble taco. "One for the road."

"Make one for yourself too."

Hank the Jack Russell scampered in and immediately began chasing Berf around the room as he dashed about in his undershirt, boxers, and socks, cramming clothes into a suitcase.

Jake leaned against the door and took a bite of the taco. "It's only Amelia."

"Only? You've met her, right?" He made room for a bottle of Bulleit bourbon. "It's only the slippery slope, the nose in the camel's tent, the gentle boiling of the frog. She has this way, this . . . thing where you think you have her just where you want her, and the next thing you know, it's the other way around and you're buying rings. And maybe . . ."

He stood and faced Jake. He couldn't explain, not here, not now, not even to himself. He'd deal with that when the time came. First the logistics. "You got those flight times for Aruba?"

Jake froze in mid-bite. His eyebrows flickered a good centimeter. "Don't toy with me, Berf."

"Someone can cover for you at the shop, right?"

"I can make some calls." Jake finished off the taco in two bites and stepped to the phone by the bed. As he reached for it, it rang.

Berf convulsed like he'd been jacked into the mains, scattering underwear around the room. "If it's Amelia—"

Jake calmly swallowed and picked up the phone. "Yes?" He glanced at Berf. "Hold on. He's right here." He held out the phone. "It's for you."

Berf took the phone and held it to his head like it was a gun. "Hello?"

"Berfman!" a voice blared from the receiver.

Berf pulled the phone away, shook his head, and then held the receiver somewhere in the proximity of his ear. "Chipster, are you vertical?"

"How's the head?" Chip asked.

Berf put his hand over the mouthpiece and turned to Jake. "No worries. It's just Chip."

Jake looked back with a weary stare. "I—"

"Since when do you care about my head?" Berf said into the phone and resumed his packing one-handed.

"You were feeling no pain last night. That's why I waited so late to call."

"Late? It's barely nine a.m."

"I'm already in the second hour of my tai chi routine. Look, I need a favor."

Berf hated to disappoint an old fraternity brother, but this was a clear case of every man for himself and devil take the hindmost. "Can it wait until next month? I have a flight to catch."

"I'd do it myself, but Zoe rushed me out right after your karaoke act. By the way, you still got the old special sauce."

"I aim to please."

"When are you going to lasso a filly of your own and settle down? You could have had your pick last night."

This comment hit a little too close to home for Berf's liking. "Don't start. Besides, when you snagged Zoe, you got the pick of the litter."

"That's why I'm calling." Chip's voice suddenly dropped to a whisper. "Can you pick up a ring at Langstrom's? I'm popping the question tonight."

"Chip, you old horse rustler! Congrats." Berf wasn't too surprised that things had come to this despite the fact that Chip and Zoe had been back together for maybe three months at most. Chip was known throughout the territories as a fast worker.

"It's a big decision, Chipmeister, but you won't regret it. Zoe Payne is a fine woman. Good old prairie stock, that one." And Berf was one to know. He'd been engaged to her three times himself.

"Thanks. Now about that ring."

"Any ring of yours is a ring of mine."

"Can you pick it up?"

"Why can't you get it? I'm in desperate straits. I can't go changing horses in the spur of a hat."

"I'm down at Payne's ranch."

"El Rancho del Bolero?" Berf straightened up in mid-pack, a stray sock dangling from his right hand. The tumblers realigned in his mind, unlocking a better exit strategy. A Hill Country retreat. Long western vistas. A well-stocked bar.

"I know it's a three-hour drive," Chip said. "But you wouldn't abandon a Sigma Chi on the big day, would you?"

A three-hour drive was three times better than a ten-hour flight, and a lot cheaper. And unlike Aruba, at the Payne ranch, Berf faced considerably less risk of becoming a record in the FBI missing-persons database. Plus if things really got desperate, it was halfway to Laredo and the border.

"How long will you be there?" Berf glanced at Jake, who regarded him with narrowed eyes as he leaned against the door.

"A week or two," Chip said.

Berf smiled. "Your legendary luck is sprouting in spades. I'm in the market for a remote getaway. How are you fixed for spare rooms?"

Jake pushed away from the door and took a step toward Berf.

"Got a house full of them," Chip replied.

That was all Berf needed to hear. "Where did you say this ring was?"

Jake waved his hands and mouthed an emphatic "No!"

"Langstrom's on San Jacinto. Paid for. An obscenely large diamond."

"One obscenely large diamond coming faster than you can say 'obscenely large diamond.' Book two rooms for the duration. Jake will ride shotgun to safeguard the cargo."

Jake threw up his hands and turned away, shaking his head.

Berf hung up the phone and tossed it on the bed. "Before Amelia can say 'prenup,' we'll be sipping Mexican martinis poolside in Bolero."

Jake spun around, pulled the cash out of his pocket, and waved it at Berf with such force that Hank began barking. "I said Aruba. Bolero is nothing like Aruba."

"True. For one thing, you can save all that cash for a bottle of premium tequila, because the rooms and meals are provided courtesy of Dr. Payne, proctologist to the stars. And the sunsets are spectacular."

Jake shoved the money back in his pocket and picked up Hank. "This doesn't solve anything. Amelia will still be here when you get back."

"If I get back," Berf said as he resumed packing. After all, he didn't yet know what fruit his cogitations would yield. "Remember my motto: take life one disaster at a time." He redistributed the boxers in rows rather than piles. "Also we'll have to take your Volvo. I'm short one car at the moment."

Jake turned without a word and walked out.

"Another bonus," Berf called after him. "Payne's ranch is on the southwest corner of the Hill Country. You'll feel like you just walked into a Sackett novel."

CHAPTER THREE

Summer Hardesty looked down on the endless monotony of gullies and hills from the copilot seat of the two-million-dollar turboprop owned by the Trent Corporation and regretted ever telling Billy Trent that Zoe's ranch looked just like a scene out of a Louis L'Amour movie.

In fact, she suspected that it was probably her fault that he had decided to take another stab at the movie business. After he lost three mil of the Trent estate on his pet project *Don Quixote: The Movie* a few years back, she figured he had learned his lesson. Apparently not. After all, three mil was a rounding error for his family. Not that the rest of them saw it that way.

Summer couldn't decide which she would rather do: push Billy out of the plane or jump out and leave him alone with his precious shot list for his new movie, *The Lonely Men*.

"Over there." Billy banked the Cessna Caravan into a slow turn and pointed. "Those arroyos would be perfect for the opening scene."

Summer released a sigh from her inner depths and tried to balance her chi. "They don't look any different from the last ten arroyos we buzzed. And that's not counting the ones before breakfast in Fredericksburg."

Billy flashed the smile she had found so charming three years back when they met at the Austin Film Festival, but now it felt condescending. "This is the first arroyo. Before it was a wash, two buttes, three gullies, a mesa, and a box canyon. Have you ever read a Louis L'Amour novel?"

"I'm more of a Tom Robbins kind of girl." She left the rest of the sentence unsaid, that he was giving this cowgirl the blues.

Billy checked the GPS. "Write this down. 30.238112, -99.83771."

As he reeled off the numbers, Summer grabbed the clipboard from the seat pocket and started writing.

"No," Billy said. "On the shot list." He reached over, flipped back a few pages, and stabbed at a page with his finger. "For the first shot."

Summer tossed the pen at him. "You do it."

"Here." Billy punched a button on the GPS. "Just write down 'user waypoint number twelve.'"

Summer dropped the clipboard in his lap, pulled off her headset, unbuckled her harness, and squeezed between the seats to the passenger cabin.

It was a rare day that she took a drink before five p.m. in whatever time zone she found herself. She liked to stay in control. Plus at her age, she couldn't maintain her runner's figure by drinking high-calorie cocktails like they were shots of wheatgrass.

But this definitely qualified as a rare day, and as Tom Robbins said, B is for Beer. Or in this case, S is for Screwdriver.

Summer plopped down in a passenger seat, opened the cooler, and extracted the necessary tools and ingredients. Then she envisioned the shaker as Billy's neck and shook it like he was on the menu for dinner.

When her hands started hurting from the cold, she poured the result into the aluminum travel mug and glanced up at Billy in the left seat. He'd been in decent shape when they met, but he'd grown like a tumor since his wife left, the poor goober. Must have put on at least ten pounds.

As she took a healthy swig, she felt the plane bank again.

"This looks like a good place for the Indian camp," Billy yelled. He held the clipboard out toward her. "Shot one-fifty or thereabouts."

Summer eyed the clipboard a few seconds before taking it. This whole thing felt too much like déjà vu all over again for her liking. She climbed back into the right seat, buckled in, and pulled the headset back on. "Are you sure this film thing is a good idea?"

"I'll have to see these spots from the ground, but they look good. If we can work out a reasonable deal with Payne, we're set for all our outdoor locations." He pushed a button on the GPS. "User waypoint number thirteen."

She flipped through the pages until she found the shot for the Indian camp and made a note. "I mean, you remember what happened last time."

"Well, of course the horses were emaciated. You can't have Don Quixote riding some fat, sassy mare, can you? I tried to get the numbskulls at PETA to understand that they were rescues we were nurturing back to health, but you can't reason with those people. In their minds, you're either doing it their way or you're torturing the things."

"You'll have a lot more horses on this project. What's to keep them from shutting you down with another demonstration?"

"No skinny horses. I've already told Caleb I don't want a single rib showing anywhere, not even in craft services."

Summer slipped the clipboard back into the seat pocket. "What about financing? You burned a lot of bridges last time."

Billy rolled the plane back into level flight with an exasperated sigh. "How many times do I have to apologize? It's not like that hundred K sunk you."

That was hardly fair, seeing as how she had never complained about losing the money she had invested in the film. "No, but it could have provided pure drinking water to a fifth of the villages in Kenya."

Besides, the lost three mil didn't sink the Trent estate either. Under Billy's management, they had made hundreds of millions just in the last few years alone. But that didn't stop his family from crucifying him over the movie at every board meeting, holiday, and family reunion for the last two years. Not everyone was as forgiving as she was.

And she wasn't about to mention that it didn't stop his wife from moving to California, taking the kids and half his assets along with her, citing excessive moping as grounds for divorce. Summer knew better than to go there. Any mention of moping became a self-fulfilling prophecy.

"I'm just saying that your old backers are probably gun-shy, and you can't expect any help from the board of the Trent estate. What if we just forget about the movie and enjoy a nice, relaxing weekend on the ranch? We can ride some horses, go quail hunting, shoot some pool."

"This time it's different," Billy said. "This isn't just a movie. It's a deconstruction of the doctrine of American exceptionalism and of superficial interpretations of rugged individualism. Think *Apocalypse Now*, but without the sex, drugs, and rock and roll. Or the assassinations or the insanity."

"Sounds like a blockbuster." Summer watched the glint in his eyes as he warmed to his exposition and did her best not to roll her own eyes. "You want a solid investment, why not call Matt McConnaug-honey and do a nice little rom-com? He's making a comeback."

Unlike Summer, Billy made no effort to avoid rolling his eyes. "We're not producing a big-studio fluff piece. Sure, back in the day, Hollywood used to take a stand, put something out there with a message, but now indie films are the only place left with the guts to rip the scab off the festering sore that is the industrial-military complex."

"You're going to stick it to the man? You *are* the man. And how does Louis L'Amour come into it?"

"Don't be facile. You of all people should know that you have to change the system from within. And I know you think Tom Robbins hung the moon, but you can't beat L'Amour for reducing life to the essentials. Survival. Honor. The Code of the West."

Summer took a heavy sip of her screwdriver. She loved to spar with Billy about philosophy and politics, but she hated it when he spoke in capitals. Although that usually didn't happen until he was a few drinks into the evening.

"What would you know about survival?" she said. "You've never been more than ten minutes away from a martini or a sirloin in your life. You wouldn't last two days in the mountain jungles of Peru."

"Are you kidding? I survived a month in a snow-bound cabin in Alaska."

"Right. Let's see. Hot showers from solar-powered utilities with a backup generator and two months of fuel?"

"You had a cabin in Peru."

"A bottomless liquor cabinet and a library of over four hundred DVDs? And an in-house gourmet chef with supplies flown in weekly? Is that the snowbound cabin we're talking about?"

Billy pretended to find a strange reading on one of his instruments. Summer could tell from his expression that he now regretted ever bragging about his Alaska hunting trip. With a twinge of repentance, she brushed the hair over his ear with her fingernails. "You're getting a little shaggy. Should I set up an appointment with Jake?"

Billy brushed her hand aside and banked the plane.

As she leaned back in the leather seat, Summer realized she had allowed herself to become complacent. Two years without a project, beyond rescuing Billy from himself after the divorce.

She glanced at her partner in the left seat. Here she was, approaching thirty-nine at the speed of light but still able to turn the head of any man in the room, even the twenty-somethings. Or at least she thought she could still turn heads. It had been awhile since she tried. But she had somehow allowed her altruistic nature to be hijacked by this man on the wrong side of 45 with a receding hairline and an expanding waistline.

And when was the last time she had thought about the world outside of Austin, beyond the comfortable west campus house her aunt had left her years ago? Now that she thought about it, perhaps her work with Billy was done. He had recovered his confidence to the point that he had taken on another film project, a feat neither of them could have envisioned after *Don Quixote* imploded and his wife left.

True, she thought it was a mistake, but she could be wrong. Maybe everything would turn out fine. Maybe he didn't need her anymore. And if she was right and the wheels did come off, could she find the energy to spend another two years getting Billy back on the rails?

Or would her limited time on this broken planet be better invested in at-risk kids in some developing country? It had been two years since she went to a mountainside in Peru and blanketed the villages with industrial-grade laptops and Wi-Fi internet access via satellite, all solar powered, of course.

Summer's reflections were interrupted by Billy banking the plane.

"There's Payne out there by the barn. Look at the size of that thing!"

A thousand feet down in a corral, a bull the size of a Hummer dwarfed two men standing outside the fence.

CHAPTER FOUR

Henderson leaned an elbow on the top rail of the corral fence and rubbed the gray stubble on his jaw to steady the tremor in his hands. He didn't like being this close to an animal with the physique of a rhino and sporting twice as many horns. It was one reason he'd become a herpetologist instead of a veterinarian. Not counting the crocs and gators and dragons, you could fit most reptiles into a shoe box and still have room for the shoes.

His brother-in-law, Dr. Payne, glared from the Brangus bull to the neglected heifer and nudged Henderson with an elbow. "What's wrong with him?"

Henderson flinched, turned away from Payne, and spat into the dirt. He'd lived every day of the last ten years on this ranch with the intention of leaving as soon as he got a little scratch together, but the older he got, the harder it seemed to scratch it up.

And he knew Payne would like nothing better than to see the back of his bald head on the way out of the security gate. But the good doctor had made a fatal mistake. He had gone and made a death-bed promise to his wife that he would not throw her brother out once she was gone. The way Henderson saw it, the only good thing about the arrangement was that Payne spent most of his time in Austin getting insider-trading tips from his high-dollar patients.

"It's like she's not even there," Payne said. "Not testosterone. I checked that."

Henderson glanced at the heifer pacing the corral with obvious anticipation. "Maybe she's not ready, Doc."

"I'd say she's ready." Payne gestured to the other bulls crowding the fence enclosing the back forty.

Henderson twisted open a can of Copenhagen and slipped a pinch in his cheek. "Maybe Tiny can't perform with an audience." Who could when it came down to it? He wiped his fingers off on his faded jeans and shoved the can in his back pocket.

"Got any ideas at all?"

"Prostate?"

Payne snorted louder than the bull. "You're supposed to be an animal expert."

"I know about certain animals." Like reptiles. Henderson had told him that ten years ago, and ten times a year since then, but the man refused to remember anything that didn't directly result in positive cash flow. Considering his expertise, seemed like Payne would be staging rattlesnake roundups instead of buying bulls with performance anxiety.

Payne turned his back to the cattle and squared off at Henderson. "Well, Martinez is coming up from San Antonio to buy this certain animal, that's for certain. And he has certain expectations."

In the corral, the heifer also seemed to have certain expectations. She looked back at Tiny and mooed insistently. The other bulls answered from the pasture. Tiny nosed a stray clump of hay he had found in a corner and munched on it. As far as Henderson could tell, that was Tiny's primary activity.

Payne shook his head. "He looks great on paper. Champion line. The records show hundreds of calves that bring top dollar at auction."

Tiny wandered over to where they stood by the rail fence and gazed at Henderson expectantly. Henderson looked back warily. Tiny blasted out a disappointed snort.

Henderson jerked back a few yards from the fence. "He's a stunner all right."

"I'd settle for ugly and a little more action. But after this weekend he'll be Martinez's problem. If, that is, we can lead him by the nose to the dotted line. That's where you come in."

Henderson eyed Payne without turning his head. "How exactly, Doc?"

"From what I can tell, Martinez isn't a cattle man. He made his money with floor buffers or something. But he also has a ranch with a flock of emus. You see what I'm getting at here?"

Henderson frowned. What part of herpetologist did Payne not understand, the herpe or the tologist? "How do I fit in with emus?"

Payne waved his question aside. "It means he's no investment wizard and probably doesn't know beans about cattle. An impulse buyer, which is just the kind of buyer we need. I can lure him in on the strength of the history and one look at Tiny should make him strike, but we might require a demonstration to set the hook."

As Henderson tried to divine how he could be expected to orchestrate such a demonstration, Payne put an arm around his shoulder.

"Now see here, Henderson. You'll get a nice bonus, a percentage of the selling price. You'd like a bonus, wouldn't you? A big chunk of cash in one lump sum?"

"Yeah, but—" What did the man think he could do? Flip some invisible biological switch?

"A bundle like that, it could get a fellow like you back on your feet. Set you in the right direction. I think you get my drift."

Like he thought that the promise of a hunk of walking-around money in Henderson's pocket would somehow change Tiny's perspective on one-night stands. "But how—"

Payne gave his shoulder a squeeze. "I've put him through the paces, run every test I could think of, but I've come up dry. But you." Payne squeezed again. "You've been around the block a few times, all over the world, met a lot of people, seen a lot of things. Surely you've picked up a few things along the way."

"Sure, but—"

"Smart guy like you, you'll find a way. I mean, they don't just hand out herpetology degrees to every passing idiot, do they?"

"Course not."

"Good. Then I'll let you get to it." Payne got about halfway to the pool, stopped, and turned around. "And I don't want excuses. I want results."

Henderson watched Payne walk back toward the house. It was the same with all doctors, and Payne was one of the worst. Thought he could just snap the slender little fingers that made him so popular with his patients and things would just happen. But as far as Henderson could tell, no amount of finger-snapping would make Tiny snap to it.

Tiny! Henderson wheeled around, suddenly aware that he had turned his back on the black beast. There he stood, one-ton of very rare steak barely ten feet away, only a flimsy rail fence between them, saliva dripping from his massive lips, two improbably small, beady eyes staring with mindless concentration.

What could he possibly do to persuade this monstrosity to follow the most basic primal urge in the book? Provide mood lighting? Arrange scented candles around the corral? Put on a Barry White album?

He smoothed his bristle-brush mustache with a shaky hand and turned to the barn. Inside, he bypassed the empty stalls and rows of equipment, navigated around a stack of hay bales, and stepped to a work bench with two large cages on it. One contained an appreciable collection of rats of various colors and sizes. The other was a glass case the size of a refrigerator on its side, containing a *python curtus brongersmai*—a blood red python—that would not fit into even the largest of shoe boxes.

She was a long way from the Burmese jungle where Henderson had acquired her on his last species-gathering excursion a decade ago. It had been the perfect profession for a man of his disposition, a lean country boy with a taste for whiskey and a distaste for humans.

Unlike Payne, who had never been outside Texas, Henderson had been in every hemisphere, every time zone, every tropic and subtropic latitude, braving creatures much more cunning and deadly, if less massive, than the hunk of stupid that was slobbering in the corral.

Take Lolita, for example. In the past ten years she had grown to the point she could actually kill a grown man if she had the mind to. But she had no such inclination. She was really just a big old sweetie pie.

Henderson flipped open the lid of the larger cage and stroked the python's head. "How's my girl?"

A forked tongue flickered out in response.

Leaving the lid open, Henderson moved to the rat cage, snagged a victim by the tail, and dropped it into the cage with the snake. "There you go, darlin'. How about a little hair of the rat, eh?"

The coils of scales stirred, unfolding and disentangling as Lolita regarded the rat with murder in her heart and dinner on her mind. Henderson waited, his eye twitching with impatience. As Lolita closed in on the rat, she exposed a trap door on the bottom of the cage. Henderson flipped it open and pulled a bottle of whiskey from the secret compartment.

He snatched off the cap, took a long, slow pull, wiped his mouth with the back of his hand, and settled down on a hay bail to watch the show. He'd worry about Tiny's performance anxiety later. In fact, if this Martinez character was as dopy as Payne said, the whole thing might take care of itself.

Chapter Five

Berf checked his watch again. Chip had failed to mention that Langstrom was a bespoke jeweler who operated by appointment only. He'd called the number on the front door at ten. He checked again, but the closed sign remained as constant as the pole star.

"How much time left on the parking meter?" Berf asked.

Jake didn't even check his watch. "Three fewer minutes than the last time you asked."

"Did I ever tell you how time is a funny thing? Here we are, waiting for old man Langstrom for two hours, feeling like Tell and that black-eyed woman meandering through the desert to escape the Button brothers, and last night twelve hours went by in a blink. Half a blink, if you're keeping score at home."

Jake offered no comment.

Berf settled back into the leather seat of Jake's Volvo and contemplated the verities, trying for the hundredth time to puzzle out this thing with Amelia. At a time like this, a man had to reach down deep, to plumb the depths of his essential nature.

It would be easier if they were ten thousand feet up on a Colorado mountain astride a mountain-bred Appaloosa, scouting out a trail or cutting sign for a pack of Tonto-basin Apaches who could come sweeping down at any moment and force a man to show his color. But angled-in parking on a downtown side street was not an environment conducive to pondering the timeless questions of life.

After a while, he decided to set it aside until he was on the ranch, where nature lent a hand to the troubled mind. Under such circumstances, compartmentalization was the key to avoiding a free fall into the slough of despond.

However, the urban wasteland offered opportunity for reflection of a certain sort.

"You know what I'm thinking, Jake? No, wait, I'll tell you. I'm thinking a jackalope hot dog sounds pretty good right about now, and Frank's is just around the corner. We've got a bit of a drive ahead of us, and it wouldn't hurt to pack a bait of grub for the trail."

Jake made no move to supplement their provisions.

Berf continued unperturbed. "Did I ever tell you how fate is a funny thing? I know what you're thinking, but hear me out. You think you know what's coming, but you never do. That's how fate is. Take the Greeks. Did Daedalus know that when he fashioned those wings to escape that tower, it would cost Icarus his life? I dare you to say yes."

Jake said no such thing.

"Did Oedipus know he had married his own mother? I submit to you that he did not, and we see what that got him."

Jake didn't contradict this statement, and how could he?

"And when I found myself engaged to Zoe as a freshman at UT, did I suspect that one day I would be sitting outside Langstrom's waiting to pick up an engagement ring to grease the skids for my old frat buddy to tie the knot with that selfsame woman?"

"Were you engaged to Zoe before or after you got engaged to Amelia?"

"Both . . . Well, actually before, between and after, but that's not the point, which is—"

"The point is, why are we in this car, fleeing Austin like Sherman's army is just across the river?"

"We're delivering a ring."

"No, you were packing before Chip called."

Jake was usually quicker off the line than this question would leave the causal observer to suspect. "I hardly need to draw you a diagram," Berf said. "You were there. You saw how it stood."

"No, I saw how you ran. Why is it that you draw all these women to you and then pull a Houdini when they respond?"

"I don't exactly draw them to me, per se. There seems to be some magnetic property that emanates from the essential Berf nature that acts as a flame to the moth."

"So you don't do anything to lead them on?"

"Do you even have to ask? I do have a code, after all. No, it's a bit of a mystery, I'll stake you that point, but what woman worthy of the name isn't a mystery?"

"You sang a song to her."

"I sang a song, that much I'll grant you. There were many women within earshot who didn't come a-calling this morning."

"How many of them did you invite to breakfast?"

Berf didn't cotton to the general direction of this line of questioning. Such an interrogation was unlike Jake, who was usually as impassive as the Buddha and twice as pithy. "I can't rightly say. I would say none, but it seems there was at least one."

"And how many of them did you have a history with?"

A tough question. He hadn't surveyed the entire crowd, but given the usual suspects it could range up into the double digits. Either way, he'd rather not say. "Define 'history.'"

"Engaged to."

"One, at least, and that's what I was trying to say before you interrupted. Back when I was engaged to Zoe, I didn't know that fate would bring me here to pick up this ring. But I submit to you that I would not have objected then, and neither do I object now. Any fool can see that Chip and Zoe are as suited for each other as Russian matryoshka dolls. A full set. Gift wrapped."

After having been cut off like that, a lesser man might have been moved to speechify at this point, but Jake was made of sterner stuff. From the moment Berf met him at a Sigma Chi function back in the day, he had suspected Jake had gypsy blood in him, like the Tinker, who had traveled from the Smokies to the bayous to the Rockies and had said maybe three words for the duration.

But Berf didn't require a constant stream of feedback to sustain the conversation. In fact, feedback often caused unwanted speed bumps on the trail to a pleasing punch line. And it seemed that Jake had abandoned his enhanced interrogation techniques for the moment.

"Now, you see," Berf said. "On the one hand, we have Zoe, sixth-generation Texan and a true daughter of the republic. Whatever else we could say about her, one thing is as plain as paint. She's as cute as a three-month-old fawn and twice as clever."

He glanced at the door of the shop, which still declared the complete and total absence of all Langstroms, and launched into the second half of his argument.

"Then we have Chip. We all know he is as sharp as a whip, especially when it comes to turning a small stake into a respectable spread on the eastern foothills. When I tell you that the man could sneeze at a nickel and turn it into a dollar, well, that's just a peek at the monetary muscle he can use to bring the hammer down when it comes shouting time.

"But I'd bet dollars to doughnuts that you couldn't nose out the bloodline that is responsible for his devastating looks. I know what you're thinking, but the real story will rock you back on your heels and make you reflect on the grandeur of the melting pot that is these United States."

Berf paused to allow Jake to reflect, and from all indications, he did just that.

"His grandfather was an African-American GI in the Korean war who fell prey to the irresistible charms of a local maiden. His father, the issue of this unlikely union, married an Italian woman, and Chip is the good-parts version of this great American mosaic, both in physiognomy and temperament."

The sign on the door of Langstrom's suddenly flipped over and an old man with eyebrows like two hedgehogs peered through the flyspecked glass. Berf popped his door open but paused to tie a bow on the saga.

"Chip is handily the most pleasant, easy-going sidewinder in a three-state radius. Except, of course, when provoked, at which time the Italian roots kick in, and then let every man look to his own, for Texas hath no fury like a Chipster scorned."

Then Berf sprang from the car and dashed into the jewelry shop. At first old man Langstrom refused to entrust the ring to Berf, but a phone call soon cleared that up, and a few minutes later he was back in the car. He popped the ring into the glove compartment and belted himself in.

"You can cut another notch in your gun, Jake. Now it's heads down and ears back all the way to Bolero."

"After we stop by the shop to take care of a few emergencies."

Berf was anxious to slip the surly bonds of Austin and feel the wind blowing back his ears, but when it came down to it, they weren't on a timetable. "Divert if you must, but the dinnertime spread at El Rancho del Bolero is not something I'd care to miss if I could."

"Duly noted," Jake said.

"With that in mind, drop me off at Max's. I'm feeling a mite peckish."

A few minutes later Jake pulled the Volvo up to the entrance at Max's. Berf got out, but as he was closing the door, Jake called out.

"Say, whatever happened with Rita?"

Berf paused. He could have asked the same thing about Maggie when Jake turned up on his doorstep last month, hollow-cheeked and broken, but there were some things a guy just didn't talk about until he was ready. If ever.

"I wish I knew," Berf said, and closed the door.

Chapter Six

It seemed like every other day JL Martinez boasted about being a self-made man. And Yvonne thought it was decent of him to take all the blame instead of trying to shift it onto someone else.

She squinted into the sunset and filed her nails as JL drove the Lexus LX 570 west on US 90. With the Friday rush hour traffic, it had taken over an hour to get out of San Antonio as far as Hondo.

The boys sat silently in the back, absorbed in their electronics, and JL was about to get on her last nerve with his lectures about how she should behave in respectable company.

"And no stories about your Uncle Thibodaux and growing up on the bayou. It may look like we're headed out to the middle of nowhere, but we're spending the weekend on a seventy-thousand acre ranch, not in a trailer park."

Yvonne smoothed out a jagged spot on her pinkie nail. "Maybe I should just wait in the car with the AC running."

JL slapped the steering wheel. "That's just the kind of smart aleck comment I don't need this weekend, Yvonne. The important thing is to stay positive. Upbeat! Grease the wheels and close the deal. We aren't driving all the way to Bolero so you can spend the weekend boring everyone with your personal problems."

Of course not. JL never wanted to talk about problems, personal or otherwise, in company or alone. He built his own business from the ground up, starting when he was still an undergrad at UTSA, tackling problems left and right, but ask him to talk to the boys about a problem at school and prepare to have your head taken off.

Yvonne opened a bottle of nail polish, Pole Dance Red, and pulled the brush out. Only half a bottle left. She made a mental note to buy more. "What exactly am I here for anyway?"

"God bless America, Yuh-vonne!"

She hated it when he called her that—the pronunciation she had left behind when she left the bayous for Texas. It meant he thought she had done something stupid.

JL rolled down all the windows at once with the push of a button, turning the car into a wind tunnel that undid two hours at the hair salon in two seconds. "Are you trying to gas us all?"

Yvonne cut her eyes over at JL. Built like an oil drum with a crew cut, forest green polo pullover, and khakis, what did he know about the effort required to put your best foot forward after two kids and a lifetime of pleasing everyone except yourself?

Sometimes she thought that if it wasn't for the kids, she'd just beat a trail back to Louisiana and let JL see how long he could last without her. That would fix his wagon right good. Wouldn't be forty-eight hours before he'd be on the phone begging her to come back.

The only reason she didn't was because she knew it wouldn't be twenty-four hours before she'd be clawing the screen off the door of her parent's house to escape. That was the reason she'd hooked up with JL in the first place. Back when he was thinner and nicer.

She screwed the top back on the polish, tossed it in her purse, and threw it to the floor. "Tell me again why you dragged me out here. I don't know the first thing about cows."

"It's a bull. Champion line."

Yvonne rolled up the one window she had control over. "Good for him. Why couldn't you just drive up by yourself and pick him up?"

"It's how these old-timers do business. Bring in the family, wine, dine, soften them up for the negotiation. Plus the boys could use some good country air. Right, Zachary?"

Of course he would try to get the kids to gang up against her, but she knew it wouldn't work. "Sure, if you can peel them away from their toys for half a second," Yvonne said.

Zachary glanced up from a Will Ferrell movie long enough to deliver a wordless sneer.

"Payne's got thousands of acres to explore. Canyons, arroyos, mesas, buttes. Sounds fun, right, Josiah?'

Josiah just grunted without missing a lick in the game he was playing.

"The trick is to play along, keep Payne happy, thinking his tactics are softening us up, and then at the end, you close in for the kill. That's the secret. Create the climate for success. Negotiation skills."

"Sure, José. Like that deal on the emus?"

She saw him wince but knew he wouldn't say anything. He hated being called José as much as she hated being called Yuh-vonne.

"What? I got a good deal on those emus. Fifty-percent of market value."

"Market? What market?"

"Who knew the emu market would tank?"

"Duh, I dunno. Maybe the guy who dumped them on you right before it tanked."

"Never mind that. The beef market has been stable for centuries. Tiny is a grand champion from excellent breeding stock. All we have to do is get him down on the price."

"Just what we need, a bull to frolic about with our emus."

"It's a no-brainer."

"Then you're the right man for the job."

Zachary snorted, which amused and surprised Yvonne. Who knew he was actually listening? She tossed a small smirk at him and he returned it.

JL took the turn north up TX 127 practically on two wheels, which was just plain crazy even if he wasn't pulling a cattle trailer. "That's just the kind of—"

"The kind of comment you don't need." Yvonne grabbed the armrest for support. "Tell you what. If I promise to behave, will you promise not to kill us all before we get there?"

Chapter Seven

Mitchell Lance Flood, Emil to his friends, banked his Triumph Bonneville T100 off the blacktop, punched in the security code,` and gunned it through the gate onto the Payne ranch.

It was a nice five-hour bike ride straight up from Pharr to Bolero, half of it at eighty-five miles per hour, but the last three miles were the longest. The gravel road wound around and up and down the edge of the Hill Country to the circular drive in front of the Payne manse.

It was impressive, perched on the edge of a mesa that cascaded away to the west to a landscape straight out of a spaghetti western.

The sun was just kissing the horizon and the massive, multilevel limestone house spread out in front of Mitch like an Italian villa designed by Frank Lloyd Wright and erected by pioneers from available materials. Recessed fixtures bathed the faces of the various sections and wings with indirect yellow light, and solar stake lights illuminated the xeriscape along the sloping serpentine walk to the massive oak mission doors.

Mitch pulled his bike in front of the garage, entered through the kitchen, and opened the fridge, confident there would be a pack of sausages in the usual place. He grabbed one, and then he stuck his head into the study to say hey to Dr. Payne before navigating out to the massive patio in search of the rest of the gang.

Just as he expected, Chip was down at the poolside bar, which was done up like a cabana with bamboo walls and grass roof. Unlike Mitch, whose shocking red hair and bristling mustache announced his Irish roots, Chip's ethnicity defied deduction.

Mitch called out as he stepped down the terraced patio to the pool. "Where is everybody?"

A voice answered from behind him.

"I'm right here." Zoe emerged from one of the sliding bedroom doors that opened onto the patio. Her black hair was cut in a bobbed, tapered kind of thing with a tousled look. She was wearing some kind of flowy, clingy white linen outfit, either a short dress or a long shirt over loose-fitting calf-length pants. In other words, she looked too perfect to appear in actual nature, or anywhere outside of a fashion magazine cover.

She flowed down to the level just above Mitch, which still put her a head shorter than him, and stood on her toes to give him a peck on the cheek. "Emil, when did you get in?"

Emil was the pet name Zoe had called Mitch since they were in middle school, based on his first two initials, ML.

"Right now."

"Oh, Chipper, could you make drinks for me and Bonnie?"

Chip grabbed the cocktail shaker. "Who's Bonnie?"

"That's Bonnie." Zoe pointed to a woman rounding the corner of the house on horseback.

The white coat of the horse was tinted a faint rose by the setting sun. The woman on the horse wore boot-cut jeans and a white, long-sleeved, button-down shirt. Her strawberry-blonde hair was pulled back in a ponytail. She steered the horse around the landscaping to a stop at the edge of the patio and took in the threesome with an appraising gaze.

She nodded a greeting at Zoe and raised an eyebrow at Chip, but when her eyes came to rest on Mitch, she studied him for a second, and then her expression softened. She pulled off the hair tie and shook out her hair until it fell over her shoulders like a Scandinavian waterfall.

Mitch self-consciously smoothed out the wrinkles in his PROPERTY OF PHARR CHILDREN'S CLINIC scrubs and checked his hair in the mirror behind the bar. Red tufts jutted out in random directions, like a jester's cap constructed by a spider monkey with a short attention span and rudimentary psychomotor skills. In other words, a typical Mitch hair day. He smiled an apology for his appearance.

Henderson appeared around the corner, long, lanky, and grizzled as usual. Mitch had been a senior in high school when Henderson was introduced to the ecosystem of the ranch. From the first, the old man fascinated him—the slow, sly grin, the occasional under-the-breath sardonic remark, the perennial quiver of his hands.

Mitch waved, but as usual the proximity of a large beast rendered all other things invisible to Henderson. Bonnie swung down and held out the reins. Henderson took them gingerly, as if they were connected to the pin of a grenade.

"Bonnie has the next ranch over," Zoe said. "She raises horses and runs camps."

"Camps?" Chip asked.

Mitch ignored the conversation. Like Henderson, he was focused on one thing, but in his case, it was the woman walking toward them across the patio.

"Barrel racing camps," Zoe said. "Bonnie is a six-time world championship barrel racer."

Bonnie stepped up to the bar. Chip held a drink out to her. "Barrel racer? You could outrun a barrel on foot. Why would you need a horse?"

"Ha," Bonnie said.

"The stand-up comic is my boyfriend, Chip," Zoe said.

"How fast can a barrel roll?" Chip asked. "Is it like a downhill race?"

Zoe turned to Mitch. "And this is Mitch Flood. He's a pediatric intern down in the valley. Mitch, Bonnie Hollingsworth."

Mitch held out his hand. "Miss Hollingsworth. I'm very pleased to meet you."

Bonnie took his hand with a strong grip. She glanced at Mitch's left hand and back at Mitch. "The pleasure is mine, Dr. Flood."

"You bought the next ranch over? The Mortimer place?"

"The fence line is just a mile south."

"I'll have to visit Dr. Payne more often," Mitch said with perhaps more gusto than he should have. He had a tendency to start out too strong and scare them off. Or at least, that's what Berf told him. And when it came to women, Berf was the expert on keeping them on a string.

"Mitch practically lived here when we were kids," Zoe said.

"Dr. Payne is a great man," Mitch said. "And his taste in neighbors seems to be improving."

Chip choked on his drink. "Anybody for a round of insulin?"

Zoe set a hand on Bonnie's shoulder. "We can't stand here chatting all day, boys. Bonnie and I have work to do."

"Right now?" Mitch asked. "You just got here."

"We have to plan the first annual Bolero Christmas Gala."

"How about your drinks?" Mitch said.

"Sure. Bourbon and branch," said a voice.

Mitch turned. A slender, tanned guy with a pronounced widow's peak approached from one of the poolside bedrooms in a peach polo shirt and khaki shorts that looked like they'd been ironed. A trim, attractive woman dressed in Austin bohemian chic emerged from the sliding door.

"Coming right up, Billy." Chip reached for a bottle. "And you, Summer?"

"Mojito," the woman answered.

"Did y'all get settled in?" Zoe asked. She held out a hand to Summer. "Come on, you can help me and Bonnie plan a party."

Mitch watched the women walk to a table on the next level up. Or, he watched Bonnie. The rest were just background noise. Mitch wasn't completely insensitive to the attractions of women as a rule, but for the past nine years he'd been focused on his career largely to the exclusion of anything else, including romance.

But that had changed when Bonnie rode up on her white stallion like a princess in a fairy tale. No, more like a valkyrie in a legend. His mind, up to now completely dominated by organic systems and pathogens and antidotes and pharmacological interactions, had been taken hostage by this vision from another world. A world of equestrian prowess, dust and sweat and competition.

"Mitch, have you met Billy?" Chip asked as he set three drinks on a tray. "He manages his family's money by not investing it in any of my schemes."

"Wise man."

"As the youngest, if aging, member of the Trent clan," Billy said, "It is my lot in life to do the job others cannot or will not do, and then listen to them complain about how I do it."

"Get this man a drink stat," Mitch said. He looked across the bar at Bonnie deep in conversation with Zoe and Summer. "And maybe I should take the drinks to the wimmenz."

CHAPTER EIGHT

Bonnie followed Zoe and Summer up a few steps to an umbrella table above the pool, glancing back at Mitch, who was looking back to see if she was looking back to see. She'd take a slice of that on buttered toast any day of the week.

Given her impressions of Zoe after a single phone conversation, Bonnie had almost turned down the invitation based on the assumption that she and Zoe went together about as well as eggs and battery acid. Plus there was the thing about the land.

Last month when Bonnie got the call from a lawyer saying she had inherited a small ranch from her Uncle Mortimer, she was within an inch of saying, "I don't have an Uncle Mortimer." But she decided that if a ranch came with it, she could find it in her heart to accept dear Uncle Mortimer as part of the family. Besides, she had soft spot for rich uncles.

Along with the land came an offer from the neighboring ranch to buy her out. An offer well above market value. But in the twenty seconds that she had owned the ranch, she had already laid out plans for it down to the last stable and white fence rail.

When she turned it down, the lawyer said that Payne had been trying to buy the place for over a decade and would probably raise the offer, but she turned him down flat.

So she had ridden Barnabas over, a little dubious of the wisdom of the whole thing, but now she was glad that she changed her mind. Mitch was clearly smitten, and a cowgirl could do a lot worse. In fact, she had done, more than once.

True, he was built like a champion steer and she could fit three of herself inside his salmon-colored scrubs, but there was something about that Medusa-like red hair and the nineteenth-century boxer's mustache that just made her want to wrestle him to the ground and hogtie him. He reminded her a little of that bull rider in Tucson a few years back. Corey. The one with the Airstream trailer and the Beanie Baby collection.

They sat down, and Zoe opened a large coffee-table book that lay on the table.

"Summer, I've decided to throw the best Christmas party that Bolero has ever seen," Zoe said. "We'll make it an annual event, the Bolero Christmas Gala, to raise money for charity."

"Oh, that sounds perfect," Summer said. "What's the charity?"

"The Browning Art Museum."

Exactly the kind of thing Bonnie thought would happen when Zoe invited her to plan some kind of unspecified social event. "Why would people in Bolero donate money for an art museum two hundred miles away?"

"Well." Zoe drew it out as if she were about to explain the obvious. "There's no need to expect that just because they live in Bolero, they don't appreciate culture."

"Then why not raise money for an art museum in Bolero?"

"There is no art museum in Bolero."

"That's not the—"

"Zoe," Summer interjected. "Let's think about this. If it's a Christmas event, perhaps a humanitarian charity would be more appropriate. Think about the children."

"Even better," Bonnie said. At least somebody at the table had sense.

For a second Zoe's face registered shock. She composed herself before turning to Summer, but Bonnie could see the sense of betrayal in her eyes.

"Peter wants to bring in the Bosch collection, and I promised him I would help."

Bonnie returned to the most relevant point. "Christmas. Children. It's an unbeatable combination, Z." She saw immediately that Zoe hated being called Z. Good.

Zoe focused a laser-beam glare on Bonnie. "Let's table the issue of the exact charity for the time being. In the interest of keeping it local, we'll get Flo's to cater. Now, as to the theme."

She turned the book so Summer could see it. "I've settled on an Art Deco theme for the first event. As you know, retro is hot."

Summer flipped through a few pages. "I like it. Something old-fashioned for Christmas."

Bonnie spun the book around and scanned through half a dozen pages of fashion from the Twenties and Thirties. Rail-thin models wearing silk dresses that hung in straight folds with nary a bulge on the way down, stopping several latitudes above the knees. Dresses that would look great on the two women across the table, and even on Bonnie, if she would stoop to wearing such a ridiculous outfit, but definitely not on a typical Bolero rancher's wife.

"Honey, let me tell you right now, you'll never get the locals into one of these."

"The designs can be altered for a more generous figure if necessary."

"Z, this ain't Dallas or Houston. These women won't spend that kind of money for something they'll wear only once."

"There will be other events," Zoe said with a little more snippiness than was warranted.

Bonnie smiled. The Z was working.

"Good point," Summer said.

"With other themes, no doubt?" Bonnie slammed the book shut. "We'll do a Western theme."

"How original," Summer said.

"You don't live down here. You don't know how we think." Bonnie had lived in rural Texas all her life. These two women were blue-dot city folk in a sea of red.

"Perhaps *think* is too strong a word, dear," Zoe said.

Bonnie stood so abruptly she knocked her chair back. "If you can get two hundred Austin snobs to drive four hours for a party in the middle of nowhere, go right ahead. But if you want Bolero to show up, it's Western."

She whirled to leave and ran into Mitch, who was coming up the steps with a tray of drinks. Orange juice and vodka soaked the front of her white shirt.

"Perfect," she blurted and stormed off toward the barn for her horse. Halfway there she called out for Henderson, but before the old man appeared, she heard someone call her name.

She ignored it and continued toward the barn, then felt a hand on her shoulder and spun around. It was Mitch, the shirt of his scrubs soaked from the drinks.

"I'm sorry," he said. "I'll pay for the dry cleaning."

"It's just a cotton shirt and Wranglers."

"Well, I'm still sorry. I was hoping you'd stay for dinner."

"Like this?" She gestured to her sopping clothes.

"Maybe you could change and come back?"

Bonnie took a deep breath and dialed her heart rate down into double digits. This thing wasn't his fault. Perhaps she could endure the company of Z and her hippie friend for the sake of dinner with the doctor.

"I'd have to ride back and change."

"I could pick you up in, say half an hour?"

"Tell you what. Give me your shirt and I'll wash it for you."

Mitch looked from her to his shirt. "I can just rinse it out and hang it up."

"Don't be silly." She gestured to her own soaked shirt. "I'm running a load anyway." She snapped her fingers. "Hand it over."

Mitch studied her for a moment, then pulled the shirt over his head and handed it to her.

Bonnie sucked in a quick breath. She had been sincere about washing the shirt, not playing some trick to see him with his shirt off, but now that it was done, she wasn't sorry about it. She didn't know how a resident in a children's clinic found time to work out, but this one obviously did.

"Let's make it forty-five minutes." On this occasion, it would be worth the trouble to take a little more time.

Mitch shrugged "Sure. See you then."

With an effort, Bonnie wrenched herself away from the doctor and continued to the barn, stopping at the door to look back. Mitch still stood in the same spot, watching her. She waved, stepped inside, and found Barnabas in a stall contentedly munching hay. As she opened the gate the old man rushed out from a back room.

"Are you leaving already, miss?" he asked, but hung back well clear of the stall.

"Yes." She led Barnabas out of the barn, mounted, and pointed him south toward her spread as the old man watched with a relieved expression.

Bonnie's Bolero ranch was a small thing compared to the Payne spread, but it was the culmination of her barrel-racing career. All those long hours training, all the miles and rodeos and living on beans and the occasional steak, all the trophies led to this. The parents of the next generation of barrel racers would pay a premium to learn the secrets of the sport from the legendary Bonnie Hollingsworth. Once she got the camp schedule established, she would branch out into breeding horses for racing and hit them coming and going.

It was a foolproof plan and all it needed was a little more capital to set up the infrastructure. In that regard, Bonnie had decided to avoid banks and go for private financing. There was plenty of money in these hills, and once she had established herself as one of the locals, she had no doubt that the old-family money that infested the ridges would step up with funds to establish Bolero as the epicenter of barrel-racing expertise, with everyone sharing in the rewards.

And in the larger scheme of things, Zoe's harebrained scheme of an Art Deco Christmas extravaganza was a disaster. Bonnie had no doubt that it would alienate the locals, so she could not afford to be associated with it. But if she distanced herself from it and then it succeeded, she would be marginalized.

She had no choice but to control it or kill it. Mitch was the key, her inside connection. He knew the family, practically grew up here on the ranch. And the fact that he was cuter than Corey didn't hurt her feelings any.

CHAPTER NINE

Meanwhile, back at the other ranch, Chip looked up in time to see Bonnie storm off and Mitch follow her in the direction of the barn. Gone to challenge a few barrels to a race, no doubt. He shifted his gaze to Zoe and Summer, who were halfway down to the poolside bar.

"What happened?" Chip asked as they arrived.

"Party foul." Zoe slid onto a barstool. "We'll need a new set of drinks, minus one."

"I'll pass," Summer said. "I had one on the plane."

Chip placed a finger alongside his nose and nodded sagely. Summer was always one for keeping her wits about her. Smart girl.

Billy leaned on the bar and picked up his tumbler. "What happened to the cowgirl?"

"I'm afraid she won't get a mark on her card where it says, 'Works and plays well with others.' Thanks, Chip." Zoe grasped the glass with both hands and sampled it. "Just what I needed."

"She'll get over it," Summer said.

Billy rattled the ice in his glass. "Have you been taunting the locals again?"

"If she can't run with the big dogs, she should stay on the porch," Summer said.

Chip, steady on the mark when it came to signs of a glass half full, provided Billy with a generous pour of bourbon and a splash of water.

Billy took a sizable swig of his drink. "What did you do, read her horoscope and make her reschedule the party?"

Chip glanced from Summer to Billy to Zoe. It looked like a storm was brewing under the grass roof of the cabana, and he liked his guests plump and pleasant. He reached to make Summer a drink in the hopes that it would calm the waters, but it was too late.

Summer bristled. "Billy, why don't you just stick to what you know—debits on the left, credits on the right. You're out of your depth when it comes to society."

"Depth?" Billy rolled his eyes toward Chip. "Says Miss Petri Dish 1989."

Chip had the drink mixed and was sliding it toward Summer when she jumped off her stool, crossed the patio in long strides, and disappeared through the sliding door into their poolside bedroom.

When the door slammed shut, Billy grabbed his glass in one hand, the bourbon in the other, and stalked off in the other direction.

Chip shrugged and sipped the drink he had mixed for Summer. Sometimes you are the bat, sometimes you are the ball. He glanced at Zoe. "So what really happened?"

Zoe picked up the paper lying at the end of the bar and flipped it open. "Creative differences. I'm not sure Bonnie is the right person for the job."

Chip found himself assailed by a fit of logic, as some-times happened despite his better judgment. "Isn't it a party for the locals?"

Zoe nodded, turning pages slowly as she skimmed them.

"And isn't she a local?"

Zoe shrugged.

"Then maybe she knows what the locals like." After all, it wasn't rocket surgery. As an investor, he made his best money when he had local intel rather than bulldoz-ing into a deal with preconceived ideas on how a deal would go down.

"Chipper, use your brain," Zoe said impatiently. "If the locals knew how to plan a Christmas gala, then they already would have done so, and I wouldn't be stuck do-ing it."

Before Chip could point out that maybe the locals didn't care to have a Christmas gala at all and that was why they hadn't done so, Zoe set the paper down and smoothed out the creases to reveal a photo of the Hallow-een gala, where Berf—center frame—serenaded a flock of debutantes who wore a variety of expressions ranging from delight to disdain.

"Did you notice Berf last night?" Zoe asked.

For a nanosecond, Chip frowned at this non sequi-tur, but a few years at Zoe's side had schooled him in the art of zigging instead of zagging. "He was hard to miss."

Zoe sighed in a zagging sort of way, and Chip frowned again, wondering in which direction she was now headed and if he would be able to get there without pulling a tendon.

"He's so sweet, the little nubbin. It's so sad."

"Sad?" She must not have seen the performance he had seen. "Berf was at the top of his game last night. Killing it." Chip finished off Summer's rejected drink and set it on the bar, warming to the subject. "It was like seeing Michael Bolton in his prime."

Zoe seemed to not hear him as she stared off into the west at the last few rays of the dying day. "He's still not over me. I could see it, even though he tried to hide it. After all these years, it's sad."

This was a zag for which Chip was not prepared, despite a half-decade, on and off, of hitting Zoe's change-up pitches. He looked at her as if she had just announced that Tommy Lasorda had switched to the Giants.

His reaction finally drew Zoe's attention. "'Kiss to Build a Dream On,'" she said defensively and gestured to the photo. "It was our song."

Chip picked up the paper and took a closer look at the photo. Berf was indeed crooning with a wistful expression that seemed to be directed to the teenage girls at the front of the crowd. But in the corner of the photo, behind the ridiculously young debutantes, a face appeared faintly. A familiar face watching Berf with a matching wistful expression. Zoe.

He set the paper down and looked across the bar at that same expression on Zoe's face this very moment. A switch flipped in his brain and suddenly he saw it all spread out in front of him like a map. How could he have been so blind? "You and Berf?"

She locked eyes with him. "Didn't I just tell you? He's not over me. After all these years."

Chip's eyes narrowed. "Maybe he's not the only one."

That snapped her out of her dreamlike state. "What?"

Chip picked up Zoe's drink and finished it off. "You think Berf's not over Zoe. I'm saying that maybe Zoe's not over Berf." He poured a double vodka into the glass, threw in some ice, splashing some on the counter, and drank half of it at a single go. "I'm saying that maybe you wish you were still with him."

Zoe looked at him through lidded eyes. "Oh, Chipper. Are you a hinky-binky bit jealous?"

Chip blew out a dismissive lungful of breath. "Ridiculous. It's just that it's all Berf this and Berf that. I can't get a word in edgewise with all this talk about Berf. Enough Berf. He's a slacker."

"He's a sensitive soul with a heart of gold."

Chip had heard all he wanted to hear about Berf, in any hemisphere or time zone. "His portfolio is highly overvalued. I mean, what does he do? Sit in his attic a few hours a month painting pictures of things that don't exist in nature. What kind of job is that? Have you seen those paintings? A monkey could do it while gargling tequila."

Not that he begrudged Berf his livelihood. A Sigma Chi is a Sigma Chi, and he'd take a bullet for the guy, but sometimes you just had to lay it out. It was like comparing the Hill Country Middle School Spring Frolic to the Olympics.

Zoe's eyes flashed and she sat up straight on the stool. "I wouldn't expect someone like you to understand Berf. He didn't have everything handed to him on a platter. You've met his father. You saw the Lawn Arranger commercials in the nineties."

"Most kids would kill to be on TV."

"In a raccoon suit?" Zoe waved her hand, knocking over a martini glass, which shattered on the floor behind the bar. "And then he turned his back on the family fortune to make his own way as an artist. When was the last time you stood up to your dad?"

Chip ignored the broken glass. "Oh, sure. Berf is fine if you like to sit around all night drinking exotic cocktails and talking art, but where is he when you need to pull together an IPO on a week's notice? Riddle me that!"

"He's with the ones he loves instead of off at some all-night business meeting over drinks and who knows what else."

Zoe jumped off the stool and stormed up the levels of the patio into the house.

For a good minute, Chip stared at the spot where she used to be, then cleaned up the broken glass, cleared away all the bottles for lesser drinks, and created the signature Chip martini. The drink that every drink wished it could be when it grew up. Thus fortified, he strolled aimlessly, scrolling through his options for a Zoe-free location in which to nurse his drink and his wounds, when a sudden thought poleaxed him.

Berf was on his way to this very location bearing an engagement ring that would cause Warren Buffet to request a defibrillator, and he was planning to take a room for the duration. The situation required the lightning decisiveness and incisive action for which Chip was justly famous. He whipped out the phone and hit the button. In a tight spot, Chip could stare down a CEO and double his percentage of equity in a troubled startup. Berf would be putty in his hands.

Berf answered on the second ring and began talking immediately. "A few delays. Had to wait for old man Langstrom to open, then verify our bona fides and take care of a few other matters, but we're closing in on your twenty as we speak. Before the hour is up you will be holding the aforementioned obscenely large diamond in your twitching fingers to present to the woman of your dreams."

"Change of plan," Chip said.

After a brief pause and perhaps a quick intake of breath, although over the phone Chip couldn't be sure, Berf said, "Don't taunt me, Chipmeister. I'm a desperate man."

"Bring the ring around midnight."

"Didn't you want to propose tonight?"

Chip turned toward the house and caught sight of Zoe on the balcony of her bedroom. She locked eyes with him, spun on her heel, and disappeared through the French doors, jerking the curtain closed behind her.

Chip headed toward the barn. "I'm not worried about me. It's you."

"Me?"

"Old man Payne would as soon shoot you as look at you."

"That's not news, my man. But it's a big house. I can steer clear of him. Plenty of practice."

"No. He saw the paper. Zoe described your performance in Technicolor."

"And he decided to adopt me?"

That was Berf. Ever hopeful. "I won't repeat the exact words, but I would say shares of Berf Preferred are in the tank."

"That bad?"

"Worse. Zoe agreed with him."

"Impossible. She's crazy about me."

Aha! There it was. Chip hadn't imagined it. He must keep them apart at all costs. "Just slip into my room through the pool entrance and drop off the ring. I'll leave the door open."

"No dinner from the chuck wagon? No bunk for a weary traveler and his faithful companion?"

"I'm heartbroken. What can I say?"

"Say no more, old friend. I will deliver the goods as quietly as Jubal Sackett stalking a deer."

Chip released a sigh of relief. "There's my man. I will make it up to you. How about a nice round of Longmorn 16 before you slip off into the night?"

"Chipertino, my man, you have got to me right down where I live. Midnight's the word."

"So let it be written. So let it be done."

Disaster averted, Chip disconnected and strolled into the barn in search of Henderson. He was always good for a drink and a story of the old days in the Amazon rainforest searching out new species. And maybe he would have some advice on how to deal with Zoe.

Chapter Ten

Berf pocketed his phone and turned to Jake, who was driving.

"The doors of El Rancho del Bolero are closed to us. We must take evasive action until midnight, deliver our cargo, and then fold our tents and slip into the night. No, no, I know what you're thinking, but out on the trail, a man has to learn to read the sign and play it as it lies. By my rough reckoning, we're halfway to Mazatlan, where the climes are fair and so are the señoritas."

Berf glanced at Jake, who proceeded without comment up TX 127. "In the meantime, there is a little Moroccan restaurant nearby where we can hang our spurs for a few hours. Just swing a left at Andy's onto 83 and head back down to Uvalde."

Jake gave up a grudging nod. Hank the Jack Russell snored in the back seat.

Berf looked down at the ring he had retrieved for the betterment of his fraternity brother. "You know, when you think about it, it's inspiring, isn't it?"

Jake didn't answer. Berf took this as a cue to continue.

"Did I ever tell you how love is a funny thing?"

Jake glanced toward Berf without actually looking at him, but said nothing.

"I know what you're thinking," Berf said. "No, I do, really. You're thinking it won't last, that the Wild West is hard on dreamers. Well, maybe it is, but you got to have hope, Jake. No, don't interrupt. Let me say my piece."

Berf paused, but Jake didn't interrupt, so he rolled up his sleeves and set to. "I know you've been chewed up in the machinery a bit—okay, a lot. We both have, but you can't give in to cynicism. That's no way to live. The way I see it, a man can lie down and give up, or he can keep on plugging because nobody taught him how to quit."

Berf snapped the ring box closed. "Did I ever tell you how Chip and Zoe got together? No? Well, pull up your socks and settle in. You might want to keep a hanky handy." He placed the ring safely in his pocket.

"You might remember back in the day when Zoe and I were on-again, off-again, like a left-turn blinker. Ancient history, actually, back before I introduced you to China. Back then Chip and Zoe had met but had never Simonized their watches, as they say.

"Then came the fateful day. This was one of those times when Zoe and I were off again. She and Chip crossed paths on the Congress Avenue bridge at the Bat Festival. As the moon rose, millions of bats fluttered into the night. As you know, Zoe doesn't like spiders and snakes and all that."

Berf spread his hands out toward the windshield. "Picture it. To suddenly find herself in the dark surrounded by rats with wings, well, it drove her over the edge. Not literally. She didn't jump off the bridge or anything. Instead she clung to Chip like a tenderfoot on a bronco. She buried her face in his chest. He consoled her, petting her hair and whispering comforting nonsense. A lot like Tell Sackett and Ange Kerry on that mountain in Colorado before the blizzard. At any rate, love was born in a moment, much like a desert flower after a flash flood."

Berf assessed his audience, wondering if he had laid it on too thick for present company. The twilight had deepened into darkness. Jake's face glowed in the green light of the dash, impassive, but with a hint of the pathos of the narrative. Thus encouraged, Berf pressed on.

"It makes you wonder, don't it. We are just pawns in the hands of fate. Take two strangers, stir in a million bats, and you get true love. Who woulda thunk?"

They topped a rise, and the lights of Uvalde, such as they were, spread out before them like a thousand fireflies in a halftime show. "It doesn't take much to change the course of a life. A flying mammal. A chance invitation to breakfast. A missed phone call. Take me, for example.

"First hundred or so dominos: a childhood so eaten up with absurdity that it would make Edvard Munch scream. Next hundred dominos: a set of watercolors for Christmas and a decade of hiding from the world behind a canvas. And then a chance sighting of a little item on the back pages of the internet, two paintings in the *Dogs Playing Poker* series going for over half a million dollars at auction."

Berf shook his head at the cosmic intersection of chance and fate. "A light came on, a domino was flicked, and the next thing I knew . . ."

He couldn't fit it into words. It wasn't just a Tarry-town house, a vintage Jaguar, or any of the other stuff, paid for with cash. It wasn't anything you could hold in your hand.

It was liberation. Freedom from the insanity of his family. A chance to be his own man, go his own way, like the first Sackett turning his back on an inheritance in England and crossing the sea decades before the pilgrims to build a new life in a new world.

All this from such inconsequential, seemingly random events. Berf stared out into the darkness down US 83, the lights of Uvalde glowing over the horizon.

"And now here we are, you and I, unlikely companions on a selfless quest of romance and exile. What strange chance event awaits us, lurks out there just past the edge of the firelight, to mold our lives?"

His mind drifted back to a chance meeting in Cancún with an extreme-sports junkie named Spider, the random appearance of a bee through the driver's window as he backed a trailer down a slope, and all the other dominoes that had fallen a year or so back to land him on a Caribbean beach with a local girl named Rita who had a way about her that set a man to thinking thoughts best kept to himself.

When it came to an appreciation of Rita's more obvious talents, Berf had taken the bit without hesitation and pulled like a mountain-bred Appaloosa, but with the unspoken understanding that it was not for the long haul. How could it be, considering the circumstances?

Now that he thought about it, he realized that he never would have even suspected her mettle, much less realized they shared a common code, the kind they could build a life on, had he and Jake not found themselves in the crosshairs of an assassin.

Berf took a deep breath and shook his head. He had let his mind wander into places that it was best to keep clear of. There were some things that a man had to leave go or he would founder in a wilderness of second-guessing, alone and helpless.

The point that occurred to him now was whether he had made the same mistake with Amelia Barker. She shared many obvious talents with Rita, in her own way, but with her own parcel of red flags. Now he wondered if his preconceptions had blinded him for the past decade. If he should tell Jake to turn around and head back to Austin.

But a hasty judgment in the past could not be cured by a similarly hasty judgment in the present. It was better to study on it for a spell. He dug into his pocket, pulled out a long, thin bit of processed beef, and turned to Jake.

"Slim Jim?"

Jake declined with a single shake of his head.

Berf munched the Slim Jim and pondered these things in his heart. Down in Mazatlan he would have plenty of time to ferret out the truth while staring at the Pacific Ocean and sipping fruity concoctions.

Chapter Eleven

JL punched the code Payne had given him into the keypad and the gate trundled open. The old doctor had done well for himself. Based on his research, JL knew that the ranch covered ten square miles of Hill Country and rugged desert. And somewhere in that expanse of wasteland lay the true object of his visit.

They had done the drive up from the turn at Sabinal in silence, which was fine with him. The less of Yvonne's whining the better, and the boys had their electronics to occupy them, sparing him their own juvenile brand of conversation.

Halfway down the three-mile driveway, Yvonne broke her aggrieved silence. "Is there really a house down here or are you just driving out into the desert to dump us and start over with a newer model?"

JL didn't dignify the remark with an answer. She'd change her tune when she saw the house. Mansion, actually. Payne's house covered more square feet than one of JL's warehouses. He couldn't wait to watch her jaw drop.

Which it did when they pulled into the circular drive. JL opened his door without comment and got the bags out of the back, corralling the boys to serve as pack mules.

The door opened as they navigated the winding path to the house, and Payne appeared. "Martinez. Good of you to come. And this must be your lovely wife . . ."

"Yuh-vonne," JL said, knowing it would infuriate her. It worked.

"Yvonne," she said, cutting her eyes at her husband.

"Hello, hello," Payne said and rushed them inside.

JL made note of the old man's aversion to social awkwardness. It could come in handy during negotiations.

"And the boys," the old man said.

"Zachary and Josiah," Yvonne said.

The boys, burdened down with suitcases, looked at Payne without comment, already bored. That would change soon.

A redheaded guy built like a delivery truck lumbered into the room. "Can I borrow your car, Dr. Payne? Just going to pick up Bonnie."

"Who?" Payne asked.

"Next ranch over. Barrel racer."

"Of course. Keys on the pegboard."

The guy nodded at JL on his way out. The slam of the door echoed in the cavernous room, which seemed more like the great room in a ski resort than a living room. Artisan rugs and furniture formed from leather and rough wood littered the space.

Payne shook his head at the closed door and then gestured for JL to follow. They walked to the end of a long hall in one of the wings of the absurdly expansive home. Payne directed the boys to the last door on the left and led JL to the last door on the right.

"As soon as you get settled, come on down to the den and we'll have dinner," Payne said.

"Looking forward to it."

Payne disappeared down the hall. JL dropped his bags in the bedroom, left Yvonne to unpack, and stepped to the boys' room. He closed the door carefully and turned around.

"You can unpack later. Sit down."

The duffle bags lay untouched in the corner. The boys, who were already sitting on the edge of the bed with their respective devices, looked up as if disturbed while studying in the library.

JL motioned to their earbuds. "Turn those off."

The boys set aside their electronics. JL took a broad stance in front of them. At one time, they had thought that JL invented cool, had wanted to grow up to be like Daddy, but for some reason, he had ceased to be cool years ago, long before they turned thirteen. In a few minutes, he would turn that all upside down.

"Listen up and keep your mouths shut. I'm going to tell you why we're really here. I am the only one in the world who knows this. You can't tell anyone else what I'm going to tell you." He leaned toward them. "Got it?"

The boys exchanged glances, rolled their eyes, and turned toward him. JL didn't bother to reprimand them. He pulled a chair from a desk and sat down on the edge of it, leaning toward them.

"In 1896, when he was only eighteen and a heck of a lot smarter than either of you, Pancho Villa masterminded the looting and burning of a ship off the coast near Mazatlan, Mexico containing twenty-four million dollars in gold coins. Most of the treasure was buried near Durango, but one of Villa's lieutenants smuggled two million dollars into South Texas for safe keeping."

Zachary yawned.

"Keep awake. This is where you come in. After years of research, I have put together hundreds of clues from dozens of sources." JL pulled out a Moleskine and wiggled it at them. "I'm the only person in North America, shoot, in the whole world, who knows where Villa's treasure is."

Josiah frowned and glanced at Zachary, who shrugged and turned back to JL expectantly.

"It's somewhere on this ranch. And you're going to find it."

Zachary turned to Josiah, who punched him in the shoulder. Zachary knocked Josiah off the bed.

"Behave yourselves," JL said. He stood and pointed the notebook at them. The notebook full of clues that had taken him two decades to gather and decipher. "Meet me at the car after dinner."

Then he shoved the Moleskine in his back pocket and walked out.

CHAPTER TWELVE

Mitch figured that the way most women did things, he'd have time to shower, change, and drive over to Bonnie's ranch before she'd even decided what to wear. He took his time picking out a shirt and finally settled on jeans and an old-school western shirt, plaid with pearl-inlay buttons. He bypassed the Mephistos that saved his feet during long hours in the clinic and went directly to the snakeskin boots. This was no time for half measures.

He wrestled his hair into a vague semblance of submission and declared victory.

On the way out the door, he passed the doctor and a nuclear family that seemed to be on the verge of meltdown. He reflected how it was ever the way of things as he pointed Dr. Payne's Cadillac down the driveway. Why was it that people who were totally incompatible gravitated to each other?

Sure, opposites attracted, but it was that very principle that made the nuclear bomb possible, wasn't it?

Folks like his dad, a diamond-in-the-rough Irishman who had chased a tight-lipped Irish Catholic woman like a dog chased a car. And like the dog, he didn't know what to do when he caught her. He alternated between walking on eggshells and putting his foot down, and she managed him with a passive aggression passed down for generations unnumbered.

The last of seven kids, Mitch grew up in a home where pretense had worn as thin as a lab coat. His parents weren't fooling anyone, not even themselves, but the roles had been laid out over the decades, and everyone played their part, afraid to dislodge the indelicate balance.

As he approached Bonnie's driveway, his thoughts turned to her. There were women, and then there were women, and Bonnie was definitely of the second variety. A woman who knew her mind. A woman to be reckoned with. You could tell by the way she came visiting on a horse. I mean, a woman who does that isn't trying to impress anyone. She is what she is and you either take her or leave her. And he was inclined to do the former.

Life with a woman like Bonnie, well, it wouldn't be a passive-aggressive stalemate of passion and prohibition, would it? No, it would not. No games. All the cards on the table. What you see is what you get, and he liked what he saw.

He pulled in front of a bunkhouse-style home, the porch running the full length of the first floor with a matching balcony above, both populated with rocking chairs like a Cracker Barrel restaurant. He got out of the car, but before he made it to the porch, the front door opened and Bonnie stepped out.

She had transformed her appearance with an off-the-shoulder dress that seemed a mix of cowboy, gypsy, and

Indian, completed with a wrap that was either a serape or a lace shawl or both.

The combination stopped him like a bull confronted by a picador. He thought she couldn't have been more cute than the moment she slipped off that white horse in boots, jeans, white hat, and white shirt. Now he could see that he'd been seriously mistaken on that point. She was obviously a woman of many talents.

"You're early," Bonnie said.

"You're ready."

"You're right."

"Now that's been settled." Mitch held out his hand. "Shall we?"

"Let's." She reached past his hand to take his arm.

Through the fabric of the western shirt, he felt her small, strong fingers settle on his bicep. He led her to the car, opened the door, and allowed her to pull in the shawl before he closed the door. The short walk around the back of the car to the driver's side seemed an eternity of separation and anticipation.

He tried to remember the last time he'd been on a date. He was embarrassed to discover it had been over a year. Until that moment, he hadn't realized how much his career had consumed his attention.

As Mitch turned back up the driveway, he tried to puzzle out how he could continue that career while making regular five-hour drives up from the Valley to Bolero. He would have to find a way.

"You've been friends with Zoe for a long time?" Bonnie asked.

"Oh, yeah. Since middle school."

A fortuitous concourse of events had offered the young Mitch a release from the tumultuous life of his Houston home. Through the years, his dad acquired just enough polish to leverage his longshoreman legacy into a position as a lobbyist for the union. As such, he kept a house in Austin for when the legislature was in session, and his house just happened to be next to the Payne house. Mitch had grown up considering Zoe his sister and Dr. Payne an uncle.

The ranch had been his refuge since he was a kid, a bastion of calm where he spent summers. During those long months in the isolation of the pristine West, the influence of Dr. Payne had led him to break with the generations of longshoremen in his family and pursue a more noble profession.

"How much time does Zoe spend in Bolero?" Bonnie asked.

"I've been busy the last five years. We used to spend summers here. Now I think she's here mainly on holidays. Weekends in the summer. Maybe more in the winter."

"Does she spend much time in town? With the locals?"

"Zoe?" Mitch laughed. "What would she do with the locals?"

"Maybe dinner parties out here with some of the other ranchers?"

"Let's put it this way. Did you see any locals out at the pool for drinks before dinner? Besides you, of course."

In the silence following his question, Mitch studied Bonnie from the corner of his eye as he negotiated the winding two-lane blacktop road between the two ranches. She appeared to be deep in thought, and the slight frown of concentration bathed in the blue light from the dash brought to mind something Michelangelo might have teased out of a particularly choice bit of marble. He pondered on the capricious hand of fate that had lured him from his monomania at the clinic to this place and this moment.

What if he had turned down the invitation, too busy or too tired to bother with the drive? He shuddered at the thought.

Then she turned to him and froze him with those eyes rendered doubly blue by the light of the dash. "So tell me about this children's clinic down in the Valley."

Chapter Thirteen

Payne surveyed the dining room table with satisfaction. He had the situation well in hand. If Henderson could step up to the plate, Payne would exit the weekend minus one white elephant of a bull and a few thousand dollars to the good.

He had placed Martinez on his right, the better to prepare him for the fleecing. He could rely on Chip, placed strategically on the other side of Martinez, to keep things on an even keel. Beyond him, Zoe's friend Summer, and then Mitch.

To Payne's left, the new barrel-racing neighbor seemed a solid choice. Easy on the eye for Martinez and not likely to talk nonsense. The rest of the lineup on the left served to fill out the table but were positioned too far away to interfere with the true purpose of this dinner.

First that Trent fellow, Summer's partner, seemed sound enough, if obsessed with this cowboy movie he wanted to shoot.

He had placed Martinez's wife next, as far away from the action as possible. His first impression, and he was good at first impressions, told him she could prove to be problematic. If anyone could queer this deal, she would be the one. Martinez wanted Tiny bad enough, but a disaffected wife was bad business. She could derail a locomotive without even trying. He would have to take special measures to keep her separated from Martinez until the ink was dry. Then let her kick all she wanted.

And he had placed the two odious teens in the back forty, as far away as possible, of course.

Zoe rounded out the foot of the table, where she could quell any riots from the tadpoles.

Payne turned to Martinez. "How's the steak?"

Martinez nodded with a thumbs up, his mouth too full to answer.

"Yvonne?" Payne asked.

She cut the steak and sumptuous red juices flowed out. Perfection on a plate.

"I don't think this one is done," she said in a barely audible voice.

Martinez washed down his steak with a gulp of wine. "It's fine, Yvonne. People who know quality meat don't blast it to a cinder. This ain't your blackened jambalaya gumbo étouffée po' boy."

Yvonne watched the blood drip from the cut she had on her fork and set it down.

Trent sliced the outside of his steak and offered it to Yvonne. "Try the outside edges. They're not as rare."

"Thanks," Yvonne said.

Payne had half a mind to confiscate the steak from her plate and preserve it for someone who could appreciate it, like himself. Maybe a nice cold steak sandwich for lunch tomorrow. He took a deep breath and looked beyond her. "Boys, what do you think?"

The boys sat with their heads together, obviously plotting to murder them all in their beds tonight. They had that weedy, dissipated look that characterized the mug shots of serial killers on the news. No doubt they both had a middle name of Wayne.

To Payne's way of thinking, Twain had been right. When they turned thirteen you nailed them into a barrel and fed them through the bung hole. At sixteen you plugged the hole.

The boys looked up, burst into spluttering giggles, and resumed their clandestine murderous scheming.

Payne ignored them and held up a tender red slice. "This is the kind of meat that can only be produced by good breeding stock. Commands top price at market." He chewed it with unfeigned satisfaction.

The cowgirl nodded. "This is the best steak I've ever put in my mouth. And after ten years in the rodeo, you can bet I know when it comes to meat." She looked across the table at Mitch and smiled.

"I bet you do," Mitch said.

In the silence that followed, Summer leaned in toward Chip. "I bet she does," she muttered just loud enough for everyone to hear.

That obviously meant something, but Payne couldn't figure out what, exactly. He eyed Summer as he reached for his wine. Perhaps he should have placed her farther down the table.

Then the taller of the juvenile delinquents said, "You got any ketchup?"

Payne froze, a glass halfway to his mouth. Did he really say that?

The entire table fell silent and turned toward the kid.

"What?" the boy said, looking around self-consciously.

In the silence, the fatter kid let out a snorting laugh, Diet Coke spurting from his nose.

Payne set his glass down and drilled him with a glare that could have peeled the bark off an alligator at fifty yards.

Martinez erupted. "Yuh-vonne, can't you control the boys?"

"Josiah," she blurted out. "Behave and eat your supper." She looked an apology around the table and, finding no sympathy, stared at her plate.

"Insanity is inherited," Trent said. "You get it from your kids."

Yvonne smiled weakly at him. He smiled back and raised his glass. They clinked and drank a toast.

Payne continued to stare at the urchins at the other end of the table, unsure if he could enjoy dinner with them infesting the same decade. Perhaps they could be packed into a crate with a box of Frosted Flakes and a case of Mountain Dew and FedExed back home.

Zoe came to the rescue with a change of subject. "Daddy, you should have seen Berf at the gala last night. He was incorrigible."

Chip's head jerked up from staring at his plate, which he had been doing since he sat down, and turned toward Zoe for a second before he very deliberately turned his attention back to his plate and began sawing at his steak like a lumberjack behind in his quota.

There seemed to be a rift in the wagon wheel, but Payne couldn't say he was sorry. Zoe seemed to have a knack for picking dingbats. The Reynolds boy was only slightly better than Roger's boy, Berf, who rated half a notch above compost in Payne's estimation. At least compost served a useful purpose.

Payne pulled his calculating gaze from Chip and focused on Zoe. "So I noticed in the paper."

"It was just like old times." Zoe smiled like she had just been accepted into a sorority for the first time. "Right, Mitch?"

To Payne's surprise, Mitch seemed to be under the spell of the cowgirl and completely insensible of anyone else. This was not the Mitch of his experience, the sober-headed boy who had taken the daring step to break with his family and forge his own path with a clarity of focus that could be a lesson to a few others he could name.

Summer nudged Mitch and he jumped.

"What?"

"The gala," Zoe repeated. "Berf. It was just like the good old days."

Mitch shrugged. "I wasn't there."

Of course he wasn't. He was hundreds of miles away paying his dues in the trenches. Like any self-respecting member of the medical profession.

"Oh, it was wonderful," Zoe said. "They had a dance orchestra. A mirrored ball. They did it right."

"Experience makes the difference when planning a society event, don't you think?" Summer said.

The cowgirl drew in a slow breath. "Sounds nice. We'll have to go next time, right, Mitch?"

A smile broke across his face like a sunrise in the desert. He shoved a hunk of steak in his mouth. "Absolutely."

Payne eyed Mitch and then the rest of the crowd. Something was going on here, and he wasn't sure he liked it. They seemed to be talking in code, but he would be hanged if he could decipher it. He studied Zoe, but she just looked back with the over-earnest smile that she always adopted when she was up to no good. Bad business is what it was.

He shifted his inspection to Summer. She was watching her partner, Trent, who was engaged in earnest conversation with Yvonne, who listened with all the intensity of a paid escort. More bad business. Martinez had better watch his flank or there could be trouble.

Next to Trent, Bonnie seemed to be sending coded messages across the table to Mitch with her eyes. Payne glanced back at Summer and saw a smile creep into her expression. A smile that would have given Machiavelli pause.

Bad business was breaking out across the entire table. Payne needed to take control of the silent room before some kind of society revolution erupted. He turned his attention to his two weekend clients.

"Martinez. Trent. Dove hunt tomorrow morning. We'll meet at the barn half an hour before sunrise."

"Try and stop me," Martinez said.

"Works for me," Trent said. "I want to see as much of the ranch as possible. I have a few locations marked out on my shot list that look ideal."

Payne nodded and looked to the other side of the table. "How about you, Chip?"

Chip flinched at the sound of his name and looked up. "What? Oh. No, not for me."

"Mitch?" Payne said.

"What?" Mitch said, as if from a long distance.

"Dove hunting tomorrow at sunrise."

"No, thanks. Dr. Flood has prescribed extensive bed rest for the weekend."

Payne glanced at the two teens at the other end of the table and shuddered, barely daring to ask. "And the boys?"

Martinez spoke up immediately. "They're going hiking tomorrow to collect samples for a botany project. Native species."

Payne settled back in his chair. Perhaps he had turned the tide. "Excellent!"

"What botany project?" Yvonne asked. She turned to the boys. "You didn't say anything about a project. When is it due?"

"Extra credit," Martinez said.

"Extra credit," the taller one said.

"Yeah, extra credit," the fatter one said.

"Mitch," the cowgirl said. "Could I pick your brain after dinner? I'm putting together a fundraiser for the volunteer fire department right after Thanksgiving. Maybe a fish fry and some games for the kids, like a roping dummy, a rodeo clown, dunking booth, maybe a greased pig chase."

"Sure," Mitch beamed, then frowned and glanced at Zoe. "But isn't there another fundraiser planned for December? Should you have two in the same month?"

The cowgirl smiled. "Oh, I wouldn't worry about that. I'm sure it'll be fine."

There it was again, the feeling that there was more here than met the ear. Annoying and downright disturbing. Bad business. Measures must be taken. Payne cleared his throat.

"How about dessert? Peach cobbler, anyone?"

CHAPTER FOURTEEN

Bonnie had consumed many an excellent steak dinner in her illustrious career, but none as satisfying as this evening. Foremost, of course, was the world-class filet, tender and decadent, paired with a pinot noir that defied description.

Running a close second, the constant thoughtfulness of Mitch, who had a way of making a woman feel like she was the only person in the room. After enduring years of ardent but fleeting pursuit by rodeo cowboys, such concentrated attention was more intoxicating than the pinot.

But almost as satisfying was the expression of muted rage on Zoe's face when Bonnie unveiled her plan to host a fundraiser two weeks before the absurd Art Deco Christmas Gala.

After the dishes were cleared away and everyone had their fill of cobbler and coffee, Bonnie slipped her arm in Mitch's and they sauntered to the den where they settled on barstools. Chip leapt behind the bar and pulled out a promising collection of bottles. But before Bonnie could place her order, Zoe appeared at Mitch's side.

"Emil, can I borrow Bonnie for a moment? I must hear more about this fireman fundraiser."

Bonnie scanned the room for a newcomer named Emil. Zoe grabbed Bonnie's arm and pulled her off the stool. "Let's take it outside, shall we?"

Bonnie abandoned her search for the mysterious Emil and joined Zoe on the patio. In her not very humble but highly accurate opinion, this woman was ripe for a takedown of at least a few notches, and Bonnie was first in line the do the honors.

The moon rose above the roofline of the house. The undulating landscape falling away to the west became an abstract painting of silver knolls and black shadow. A slight breeze rustled the excessive folds of the overstated bed sheet Zoe had chosen to wear for dinner.

Bonnie pulled the shawl tighter around her shoulders. She followed Zoe past the pool to a gazebo that was illuminated by a ring of tiki torches around the perimeter.

"Now, Bonnie," Zoe said as she settled on a bench. "Let's talk about this little idea of yours. Surely you can't be serious."

It was obvious that daddy's little princess was used to getting her way with the bat of an eye or the flounce of a skirt. It was also obvious, to Bonnie, at least, that Zoe was primed for a new experience. Disappointment. "Serious as a rattlesnake in a bedroll, Z."

No more than a slight flicker of annoyance crossed Zoe's face at the nickname. "Oh, I think that would be ill advised. It's always so disappointing when you throw one of these things and nobody shows up."

"They'll show up. You might say I'm in touch with the target demographic."

"Bless your heart, that's not the problem."

"Oh, you're thinking they'd rather save their tax-deductible dollars for your Christmas fashion show instead?"

"Here, this might clear up the confusion." Zoe pulled a sheet of paper from somewhere in the folds of her ridiculous outfit and fluttered it in the space between them.

Bonnie snatched it from her hand and held it up to a tiki torch. It appeared to be some kind of medical report. "What is this?"

"It's a little thing about how you got those trophies."

"I won those races fair and square."

"Of course you did. I remember Lance telling me the same thing. He was very convincing."

"The difference is that this is a fake." Bonnie looked up from the paper.

Zoe sat on the bench with her hands in her lap, Indian style, legs hidden beneath the flowing white outfit, like some kind of guru. Shadows from the flickering light rippled across the folds of the fabric, giving it the appearance of movement. Her tan complexion was rendered a warmer tone from the yellow flames. The woman certainly knew how to stage a scene.

Bonnie focused a glare filled with all the menace she could muster on the evil woman. She'd broken wild mustangs, faced down one-ton steers, fought off over-amorous cowboys by the dozen. She could deal with this society snake.

Locking eyes with Zoe, Bonnie leaned the paper into the flame of the tiki torch and held it there until everything but the corner she was holding had burned. Then she flicked the singed corner away like she would flick a gnat from a plate of ribs.

Zoe shrugged. "That's okay. I have it all here." She held up a memory stick. "And other documents of interest, such as the sworn affidavit from the veterinarian who doped your horses."

"Horse, not horses. I'm a one-horse woman and Barnabas is a one-woman horse. And I can tell you, sure as you're nothing more than a lily-livered snake in the grass, Barnabas has never been doped."

"I have a vet who says different."

Not possible. "Who?"

Zoe slipped the memory stick into a hidden pocket buried in the flowing fabric. "And in case you haven't noticed, the locals are straight shooters. I doubt they will cotton to a neighbor who doesn't fight fair. And that's why nobody will come to your little fundraiser."

"You can't blackmail me with a lie," Bonnie said in a fierce whisper.

"Who's to say it's a lie?"

"You publish that information and I'll sue you for slander so fast your lawyers will have to clear-cut half the trees in Tyler county to file all the responses."

"Oh, I don't think it will come to that."

Bonnie tossed the end of her shawl over her shoulder like a Continental soldier. "Hide and watch."

"I mean," Zoe said in an exaggerated drawl, "that once the story is out, the damage is done, whether or not you win the lawsuit. And how many doting parents are going to send their innocent daughters to Bonnie's Barrel Racing Bunkhouse to be trained by the disgraced champion?"

If it were possible to focus the heat of your hatred through your eyes, all they would have found when they came looking for Zoe would have been a little pyramid of cinders. Sadly Bonnie was not equipped with such a death-ray stare.

What Bonnie couldn't figure out was why. Why would the prima donna be doing this? "All for a silly little Christmas party that you don't even care about?" Bonnie asked.

But she knew it wasn't about the party. That was just the battlefield, not the war. It was about dominance, social or otherwise—the very reason that Bonnie had concocted this ridiculous idea for a competing fundraiser. But to go from a cat fight to global thermonuclear war—this was crazy.

Zoe stared back without saying a word.

Bonnie spun on her heel and left the evil guru-ette sitting in the lotus position, plotting world domination one blackmail at a time. She stormed into the room and up to the bar where Mitch sat talking to Chip.

"Take me home," she said.

Mitch flinched and turned to her. "Now?"

"Can you do it sooner than now?"

He squinted at her, trying to parse it out. "Not without monkeying with the space-time continuum, which is contraindicated in cases with these symptoms."

"Then it's now." She stood there waiting for his prompt compliance. What good was a doting doctor if you couldn't get a ride when you wanted?

"Sure." Mitch slipped off the stool and placed a hand on the bar to steady himself.

Just what she needed. A drunk doctor. "Are you okay to drive?"

He pulled out the keys. "Are you kidding? I'm Irish."

"And that makes you immune to chemistry?"

"No, just immune to reason." He smiled. "Or you could stay here tonight."

"No, thanks." Bonnie snatched the keys from his hand. "I'll drive."

"What about on the way back?" His smile broadened. "Or I could just stay at your place."

She spun around and headed toward the front door. "You'll be okay. I hear you're Irish."

Out on the road, as Bonnie drove Dr. Payne's monstrous Cadillac toward the gate, Mitch studied her with a lazy smile.

"What's the hurry? It's early."

"Your childhood friend has a funny way of making a girl feel welcome."

"Zoe?"

Furrows lined his forehead, rendering him even cuter than before. She kept her eyes on the road.

"What do you mean?" Mitch asked.

"She has just threatened to ruin my business unless I go along with her stupid Art Deco Christmas." She surged through the automatic gate with only centimeters to spare and whipped the Caddy onto the blacktop. "I mean, ever heard of a sense of proportion, anyone? A party versus my career? Seriously?"

She realized she had gestured with both hands to emphasize the depth of her outrage and grabbed the wheel just in time to save the car from veering into a ravine.

"Whoa!" Mitch said. "Maybe I should drive after all."

"Not necessary." Bonnie took several deep breaths to calm down.

Mitch turned in his seat and leaned against the passenger door, his concerned expression illuminated by the glow of the dash light. "How exactly did she threaten your career?"

"You don't seem surprised."

He sighed, and it seemed like he exhaled a decade of experience. "I love Dr. Payne like a father, but here's what you need to understand about the Paynes. They're old school. Wild West. Winning is what matters, not how you play the game."

"Well, she may be able to hornswoggle those Austin society types, but out here in Bolero, we know a thing or two about the armadillo."

"What did she say?"

"Doping." One hand involuntarily shot out into the space between them. She reeled it back in and latched onto the steering wheel. "She claims to have some blood tests that prove I doped Barnabas to win my trophies." She risked a final gesture. "Like I would ever shoot up Barnabas with drugs."

"Of course not!" Mitch blurted out. "I mean, you, of all people. Who would believe it?"

"You know how people are. They love to watch you rise, but they love even more to watch you fall and then whisper 'I knew it all along' to each other."

"But, I mean, really. Who could look at you and think for one second that you are anything other than the very picture of virtue?"

Bonnie eyed him in the dim light of the front seat. How many drinks had he consumed while she was out in the gazebo? A picture of virtue? That was pushing things a bit far. You didn't live on the rodeo circuit without learning a thing or two about a thing or two.

And there was that one thing, the thing that made her wonder what Zoe really knew. But that wasn't possible. The person she was thinking of would never talk, not even if he was tortured. Or drunk.

What it came down to was that she needed to know the name of the vet who gave her the info. If such a vet even existed. Zoe might have faked the whole thing.

Either way, somehow Bonnie had to find out what was on that memory stick. Difficult, if not impossible. Or maybe not.

She turned to Mitch. "Exactly! She's faked up a bunch of documents on a memory stick. We need to see what's on it."

"We do?"

"Of course we do!"

"Right." Mitch nodded like a bobble-headed doll in the back window of a family sedan.

Bonnie pulled the Caddy up in front of her house. She killed the engine, turned to Mitch, and put her hand on his arm.

"When you go back to the house, make a point of mentioning that I've decided to give up the fish fry."

"But what about the firemen? And all that stuff for the kids?"

"It's just to throw Zoe off her guard. To make her think she's won."

"Ah. Sneaky," Mitch hissed with obvious appreciation for her cunning plan.

"Yes, and then sometime after midnight you'll sneak into Zoe's room and get that memory stick."

"I'll . . . what?" His eyebrows lowered and his eyes flared into an incredulous stare, as if she had suggested he don a tutu and do a pirouette on the breakfast table tomorrow.

Bonnie squeezed his arm and leaned in. "You'd do that for me, wouldn't you, Doctor Flood?"

Mitch looked back with a confused amalgam of expressions. "Uh, sure . . . I mean . . . really? Sneak into her bedroom? They're like family."

It was time for the heavy artillery. She ran her fingers up his arm and into his hair. "You know, from the moment I first saw you, I knew we were soul mates." The thing was, she really had thought that when she saw him. She hated that she had waited until this moment to say it.

"You too?" Mitch breathed. "Do you believe in love at first sight?"

"I do now," Bonnie whispered. And she did.

"Me too."

They kissed, a long, slow kiss that almost made Bonnie forget this whole ridiculous thing about Zoe and the blackmail. Almost. Finally she pulled away and opened the door. Before she got out, she turned back to Mitch.

"After midnight. One or two is better."

CHAPTER FIFTEEN

JL led the boys in a stealthy flanking maneuver around the dark side of the house to the barn, the metal detector in one hand, a flashlight in the other, and the GPS under his arm. He circled the barn, found a door in the back, and pulled it open, wincing when it emitted a long, groaning creak.

One of the boys let out a sputtering raspberry laugh.

"Hold it down," JL whispered fiercely. "This isn't a school field trip."

He held the door open as the boys filed in, then followed. JL played the light across the walls of the barn, looking for a likely spot to stow the gear. It flashed across a large rectangle of glass, and JL brought the beam back to investigate.

If he was seeing right, someone had stored a large rope, like the kind they use on big boats, in a glass case. Strange. He leaned forward for a better look and suddenly found himself staring into the hypnotic eyes of a gigantic snake. Its tongue flickered out.

"Jiminy Christmas!" JL dropped the flashlight and lurched back, knocking the boys over as the room plunged into darkness.

But they weren't in the dark for long. A click echoed in the room and halogen lights bathed them in a harsh glare.

An inside door slammed against the wall and a wiry geezer stormed into the room, a shotgun swinging in their direction. "I got your ticket to hell right here, boys. All I need is a reason to punch it."

JL froze. The boys scrambled behind him, no longer laughing. The old guy looked a lot like some of the janitors JL worked with, like a broom handle topped with a bristle brush.

The geezer squinted at them. "Now this can go easy or it can go hard, although I'm kinda partial to letting one loose, so I'm hoping you try something." He shrugged. "Up to you, mister, but I'd drop that thing you got pointed at me if I was you."

JL looked down at the metal detector in his hand and dropped it like it was a snake.

The old man held the gun pointed in their direction with one hand while he reached into a back pocket, pulled out a flask, took a hit from it, and slid it back into the pocket. "Now supposing you tell me what you think you're doing in my barn."

JL held up his hands. "Just storing some gear for the boys' hike tomorrow."

The old man eyed them. "You with the doings up at the house?"

"Sure. I'm JL Martinez and these are my boys. And you are?"

The barrel of the gun eased down toward the floor. "Henderson."

"Well, Henderson." JL stood, careful not to make any sudden moves. "Can you help us find a spot for this gear?"

Henderson hesitated. JL reached for his back pocket and the gun swung back up.

"Whoa!" JL said. "Just getting this." He held up his wallet, slipped out a twenty, and held it out.

Henderson frowned at the money. JL pulled out two more bills and folded them with the first. Henderson's face twitched. Then he lowered the gun, stepped forward, and reached for the money like a cobra striking.

JL put his wallet away. "So, Henderson, where can we put this stuff so that nobody will bother with it?"

After a minute of studying on it, Henderson opened a cabinet door, turned around, and left the way he came, flicking off the light as he closed the door.

Using his phone for light, JL found the flashlight and directed the boys to carry the gear to the cabinet. He grabbed a backpack and unzipped it, showing the contents to the boys. "MREs and water."

He checked to make sure they were paying attention. They nodded.

"Remember to stay hydrated. This isn't one of your video games where you can just start over or some movie where the actors get a second take. This is the real thing. A real desert, a real buried treasure. And out there, even in November, the sun can suck you dry before you know it."

JL held up the GPS. "The coordinates for the possible sites of Pancho Villa's treasure are already programmed in, along with the most efficient path to each of them."

After he showed them how to work the GPS, he stashed it in the cabinet and led the boys to the front of the barn. "You circle around and go in the front door like you're coming from the car. I'll come in through the back by the pool."

He waited until they disappeared around the side of the house and then scoped out the situation. Everyone appeared to be congregated in a room that looked like some kind of library, only with a full bar. As he strode up the levels of the patio, he saw Yvonne playing pool with Mr. Trust Fund who was here to film some western movie.

The guy seemed like a middle-aged loser with more regrets than dreams, but he had flown his own private jet down from Austin, so he must have more on the ball than was apparent to the naked eye.

On the other hand, the man was ignoring the hot cougar he had come up here with and was making a move on Yvonne, so how smart could he be?

JL smiled as he reached for the handle of the French doors. Maybe he should teach them both a lesson and have a go with the cougar.

CHAPTER SIXTEEN

Yvonne aimed for the six ball but hit in the fourteen by mistake and scratched to boot. Not that she was surprised. Her brothers had tried to teach her to play pool back in Louisiana, but it was all about angles and she was never good at geography.

She was just glad JL wasn't here to see it or she never would have heard the end of it. Not like Billy, who gave her a reassuring pat on the shoulder and congratulated her for trying such a tough shot.

The French doors to the pool opened and Zoe stepped through them, all wrapped up in white like a movie star in one of those silent films. It set off her tan and her jet black hair. She was so pretty you just couldn't help but love her, even if she did ignore you for the whole evening, and her the hostess and all.

How in heaven's name did she get her hair to stay so perfect without a hint of hairspray or gel? And that outfit. If Yvonne was to wear that to dinner, she'd look like a baboon in a potato sack, but Zoe looked like one of those vestal virgins she'd heard a preacher talk about back to home. Or at least what she had always pictured when she thought of that sermon.

Zoe flowed across the room to the bar and demanded a drink from Chip, who threw it together without even looking at her and then made a martini for himself. Zoe didn't say boo to anyone else in the room, just took the drink and sat down on the couch by Summer without so much as a thank you to Chip, but why should she thank him when he treated her like that is what Yvonne wanted to know. It was like he didn't even realize what he had. What he could lose if he wasn't careful.

Chip looked up at her like he had heard her thoughts, then took his martini and threw himself into an over-stuffed leather chair and grabbed a magazine.

"Your turn," Billy said.

"That quick?" Yvonne glanced at the table. She wasn't sure, but it looked like half the balls had been knocked in, most of them hers. She turned a fake pout on him, the one that used to work on JL back before the boys came along. "Have you been naughty?"

Billy gave her a "Who, me?" look of innocence.

Yvonne rolled her eyes and leaned across the table to try to sink the five. Her stick hit the cue ball low and it bounced over the three and right into the pocket.

Billy pulled the cue ball out and placed it on the dot. "Try that again. You didn't take enough time to set it up."

That was what Yvonne was talking about. How many men really cared enough to make a girl feel special?

"What happened to JL?" Billy asked.

Yvonne took her time to line up the shot. She connected with the cue ball this time, but missed the five completely. Embarrassed, she turned away from the table as the ball bounced off the sides. Then she looked around the room, surprised that she hadn't even given JL a single thought since they came in here.

"Who knows? Probably out gawking at that bull."

"Why on earth would he do that?" Billy chalked his cue stick.

Yvonne shrugged. "He wants to breed beef cows."

Billy set the chalk down and blew the dust off the tip of his cue. "From what I hear, he's come to the right place. According to Dr. Payne, that bull is as randy as a billy goat."

Yvonne laughed. "Maybe JL should take notes." She clapped her hand over her mouth. Who was being naughty now?

Billy laughed.

Yvonne laughed with him and glanced around the room.

Zoe and Summer looked up from a giant coffee-table book, but only for a second. As they looked back down, the French doors opened and JL walked in like he had just been announced at some fancy party with butlers and footmen standing around.

Yvonne turned her back to him but watched his reflection in the window. He walked behind the bar like he owned it, pulled down a bottle of scotch from the top shelf, and poured half of what was left into a glass like it was iced tea. She knew what that meant.

A head of crazy red hair poked in the hallway door. It was Mitch, that doctor who looked so cute with that cowgirl, Bonnie. "Night, y'all."

"Mañana," Billy said and took a shot.

Zoe and Summer said goodnight.

JL said, "See you in the morning, bright-eyed and bushy-tailed."

Chip just sat in his chair, staring at his magazine.

Yvonne stole a look at JL, but he was focused on something else. She followed his stare to the couch where Zoe and Summer sat with the coffee table book spread across their laps. Which one was he looking at? Probably Zoe. She was the prettiest one in the room. Although Summer looked pretty good for someone who was probably on the wrong side of forty.

She looked back at JL. He must have sensed it, because he glanced over as if he had been caught and then flashed a big smile. He walked up to the table and mussed her hair with the hand that wasn't holding the drink.

"Hey, darling. I've been ignoring you. Let me make it up to you."

He held out his arm. She looked from it to Billy. He offered a sympathetic smile and held out his hand for the cue. She forced a smile, passed the stick to him, and walked out of the room on JL's arm.

CHAPTER SEVENTEEN

Summer sat alone on the leather couch with her feet tucked under and the Art Deco book on her lap. Dinner had been a tiresome affair. Old man Payne carrying on about beef and dove hunts. Zoe tweaking Chip for some unnamed offense. And now Billy at the pool table mooning over JL's trailer-park wife. It was almost bad enough to make her ask Chip for a cocktail. Almost.

Finally the door swung open and Zoe came in. She got a drink from Chip and dropped down on the couch next to Summer.

"Where have you been?"

"Taking care of a minor problem." Zoe took a long drink and let out a satisfied sigh. "Problem solved."

Summer opened the book. "They might be a hundred years old, but some of these designs are very forward thinking."

"Exactly," Zoe said. She turned to a page. "Look at those lines."

Summer flipped to the next page. "They were all about angles. The bold statement."

Laughter from the pool table interrupted their discussion. Summer glanced up. Billy and JL's wife laughing self-consciously over some inside joke.

Zoe nudged her. "Thrown over for a geriatric Cajun?"

"Don't you worry your pretty little head about it." Summer eyed Billy as he lined up a shot. "He thinks he's teaching me a lesson. Like yours." She nodded at Chip, who was guzzling a martini like it was lemonade, flipping through a magazine. From here it looked like it was upside down.

Zoe dismissed Chip with the flip of a page in the coffee table book. "Well, if he thinks he can teach me anything, he'd better think again."

The patio door flew open and JL stepped inside like Doc Savage returning to the Fortress of Solitude after clubbing a baby seal. He walked behind the bar like he owned it, pulled down a bottle of scotch from the top shelf, and dashed it into a glass like Hemingway might have done.

Mitch poked his head into the door. "Night, y'all."

"Mañana," Billy said.

"Night," Summer said along with Zoe.

JL said something macho, but Summer wasn't listening. A thought had arrested her attention. Billy, bless his bumbling heart, was over at the pool table playing some kind of game, but two could play at that game. And compared to Billy, Summer was sitting on an arsenal. He'd come crawling back, admitting defeat, before it was over.

JL walked over to the pool table and tousled his wife's hair. "Hey, darling. I've been ignoring you. Let me make it up to you."

Her smile almost broke Summer's heart. So full of resignation and lost hope. She was a bottle-blonde cheaply manicured cautionary tale. She handed her pool cue to Billy and followed JL to bed. Billy racked the cues and left the room without a backward glance.

"I am woman. Hear me roar," Summer said.

"Well, at least he didn't club her and drag her out by her hair," Zoe said.

"Oh, didn't he?"

Zoe elbowed her and nodded at Chip, who was now snoring in an armchair, the magazine over his face.

"I see he's taking it well." Summer checked her watch. Give Billy ten minutes and he would be snoring like Chip. Not a problem. She always packed earplugs. And if she was any judge of the future, tomorrow would hold a few lessons for Billy the No-Longer-a-kid.

CHAPTER EIGHTEEN

Berf turned Jake's car north toward Bolero and the ranch. They had run the gauntlet of Uvalde nightlife and then had stopped off for a few drinks at the Horseshoe Road Inn on the way north.

Buzz, the imposing bartender, had topped off their rations as required with the minimum of chatter, and the locals, the usual small-town collection of hipsters, goat ropers, and jocks forced to share the only available road-house, had the good sense to give these two road-hardened strangers a wide berth. Just the kind of down-home common sense found in the burgs and villages of Texas.

Berf looked over at Jake, who was slumped against the window, pretending to be asleep. Hank the Jack Russell sat between them on the console, watching Berf drive like his life depended on it. Or maybe like Berf might toss him another bite of Slim Jim.

Berf cleared his throat. He should probably warn Jake of what they were headed for. "It's unfortunate, really, how these things happen. It's like two forces of nature, old man Payne and me. I know what you're thinking, Jake. Really, but it's not like that."

Hank yawned. Jake snorted. Or maybe snored. It was hard to tell the difference with Jake.

"No, now let me say my piece. When strong personalities cross, sometimes sparks fly. You can't fix it by backing down. You lose respect and make things worse. You have to set your sights and ride it out."

A pickup running with fog lights glaring raced up behind. Probably a bunch of high school kids out on a Friday night, trying to get to a convenience store before midnight to buy a six-pack with a fake ID. Berf held his hand up to block the headlights from the rearview. The truck whipped around and the taillights disappeared over the next hill. When Berf topped it, nothing but the moon-silvered road met his eyes.

"You remember when Orrin Sackett and Tom Sunday got crossways on that cattle drive? No amount of plain talk could uncross them. But Orrin couldn't abandon his principles and kowtow to old man Pritts, even if he was sweet on Laura. That's how it is with Payne and me. But in this case, Payne is Sunday and Pritts rolled into one."

Berf pulled another Slim Jim from the inner pocket of his sports coat and ripped it open with his teeth. He bit off a chunk and tossed it to Hank, who snuffled it up like bacon. He held it out to Jake, but he was still pretending to be asleep.

"Not that I'm saying Payne is an unprincipled land grabber like Pritts or a drunken, murdering gunslinger like Sunday, or anything like that. He'd give you the right arm off his back. We just don't see straight on some things."

He bit off a judicious portion of Slim Jim.

"I'm an independent type, kind of a loner, like Tell Sackett. Payne thought I was trifling with the affections of his daughter. I explained about the Code of the West. That I was a man of honor, that I would rather die than break my word once given. The problem is, I don't think Payne's read a single Sackett novel. He didn't even watch the movie. Not that I blame him. It was a turkey."

Berf slowed and turned off the blacktop. He punched in the code and waited for the gate to open. "Here we are."

This was going to be a ticklish operation, getting the ring to Chip without anyone seeing him. He glanced over at Jake, who barely stirred.

"I'll sneak in, slip Chip the ring, and before you can say 'Amelia Barker,' we'll be back in the saddle and on our way to Mazatlan, where the gentle waves caress your body and the umbrella drinks caress your brain."

Chapter Nineteen

Mitch shot up in bed like he'd been electrocuted and wondered why. He glanced at the nightstand. His phone glowed like a Christmas tree, an alarm reading "Memory Stick."

It all came back. The memory stick. Bonnie. Zoe. Had he dreamed it, or had he really agreed to sneak into Zoe's bedroom and steal a thumb drive? Fresh from a dead sleep it sounded crazy. Heck, it *was* crazy, and the more he thought about it, the more he thought he hadn't really said anything one way or the other. Maybe he would just roll over and work it out in the morning.

But then he thought about Bonnie, and that was no dream. That was the real thing.

He threw off the covers and swung his legs over the bed, suddenly aware that he was still fully dressed. He recollected lying down in his clothes for a catnap like he did at the clinic when doing a double shift, always ready for action. But this was no double shift. More like a double cross.

The room captured the hazy light of a full moon a few degrees off high midnight. Mitch pushed aside the gauze curtains, stepped out the sliding door that opened onto the patio, and paused in the shadow of a balcony to get his bearings.

Out past the patio and the pool, the landscape glowed a fuzzy grey like some forsaken fairyland in a dystopian western fantasy, like something out of a Cormac McCarthy novel, maybe. It was just like he remembered it from his summers here as a kid.

Mitch considered again the project under consideration. Could he really sneak into the bedroom of his adopted sister, the daughter of the man who had taken him in as the son he had never had, the man who had guided him truer than his own father had done? And then betray their trust and steal their property for the sake of the woman he loved?

It gave a man pause when considered in this light, however murky it might be. But then he considered how Zoe had threatened Bonnie with that information. And for what? For her little games. No one knew those little games better than he did. And here she was, a full grown woman, still playing those games, but against grownups, for grownup stakes.

That didn't sit well with Mitch. Not when it was Bonnie that was in Zoe's sights. The image of his true love shimmered before him in the moonlight. He realized how it must look to everyone else, like he had gone plumb crazy, like he'd never had a girlfriend, but he didn't care.

He'd dated plenty of girls, pretty ones, but there was something about Bonnie that made a guy forget. Forget other girls, forget what he was thinking. Forget his own name, even. He had it bad. He realized that. But if this was having it bad, then bring it on, is what he thought. For the first time, he had met someone he couldn't imagine living without.

The moment had come to choose, and Mitch made his choice. To set aside his past, no matter the cost, and embrace the future. He took in the view, the ranch, the house, and realized this might be his last night here. When what he was about to do became known, he wouldn't be welcome anymore.

He stood in the shadow, steeling himself for the deed. Zoe's room was directly above his. He stepped out into the half-daylight of the full moon and looked up. The room was dark and silent. The sliding door was open, the gauze curtains undulating in the night breeze.

"Now's the time. The time is now," he whispered to himself.

Mitch slipped down the levels of the patio like a ninja and approached the barn on silent feet. He extracted an extension ladder without disturbing Henderson, stole back up to the house, and nestled it against Zoe's balcony rail as gently as brushing away a mosquito from a sleeping baby.

He was on the second rail when he heard a noise from the side of the house. He leapt down as softly as a cat and disappeared into the shadow of the gazebo.

A figure emerged from the dark side of the house, stopped in the ghost light of the moon on the patio, and looked around. The form looked familiar, but Mitch couldn't place it. It fixed on the ladder and moved to it with a deliberate purpose.

When the mysterious stranger started up the ladder, Mitch stepped from the shadows and stepped toward it. As he arrived at the base, the figure vaulted over the rail and slipped into the room.

Mitch was halfway up the ladder when he heard a crash. He was at the top, about to jump onto the balcony, when a light flared on and he heard Zoe's voice.

"Berf! What are you doing here?"

CHAPTER TWENTY

Berf crept around the corner of the mansion, the ring case in his left hand. Chip had said to come to his room facing the pool but had failed to provide trail markings to guide him to his destination, such as a stack of three smooth stones or a bundle of three blades of grass pointing the way. He paused on the patio to reconnoiter and cut for sign, and he spied the ladder. Simple. He repented of doubting his old frat buddy.

He proceeded to the ladder and scrambled up it like a mountain-bred pony up a washout. He flipped the curtain aside, stepped in, and promptly walked into an obstacle. Something crashed to the floor. He knelt, felt around, and grabbed whatever had fallen. Then light flooded the room.

Shielding his eyes, Berf looked up to see Zoe standing by a canopy bed, her hand on the light switch. She wore a long, white nightgown. Probably to keep warm in the fresh night air from the open door. Sensible woman. Chip was a lucky man, no question there.

But even such a humble garment as a flannel nightgown was unable to disguise the fact that, though she was a slight creature, she was doing her share where it counted. It surprised no one, least of all Berf, that she never had trouble filling her dance card. In fact, for a brief second, memories of their college days and the three engagements played before his eyes like a magic lantern show, but Zoe's question dispelled the nostalgia.

"Berf! What are you doing here?"

It was a good question, a marker of her good breeding and common sense, considering the circumstances. Of course she couldn't know why he was here, that he had come to the aid of a brother in dire need. But it was also a difficult question to answer without laying out a considerable amount of groundwork beforehand. And spoiling the surprise.

"I . . . Zoe? I . . . Where's Chip?"

He could tell from her reaction that he had said the wrong thing. A feller had to play the hand he was dealt, but it was always hit or miss when you were working without a script.

Zoe drew in a sharp breath and expanded to her full height, which wasn't much, but she knew how to make five foot two look like ten foot twelve.

"What do you want with Chip?" she demanded.

Berf took a moment to ponder on his answer. It was as tight a spot as an old trail hand could find himself in, and it demanded a proper amount of consideration. For a moment, he tried to tease out what Tell Sackett would say in such a circumstance, but the full canon of L'Amour's life work didn't offer a similar situation. He could not conjure up a scenario in which Tell would find himself in this position, not even in pursuit of Ange Kelly. He would have to play it as it lay, but that was not a challenge for the king of wing.

He took inventory of the situation. Here he was, on one knee, a small velvet-covered jewelry case in his left hand, a bouquet of flowers in his right, a vase on the floor next to an overturned table. That complicated things, no question, but he'd been in tighter spots and had turned them to stripes.

"Just a little matter Chip and I need to discuss. Won't take more than a New York minute."

Zoe's eyes narrowed. "What's so urgent that you have to talk to Chip at midnight?"

"Well . . . there's this . . . thing that has come up, and . . . it must be settled tonight." Berf focused his most serious expression on her. "It's a matter of honor."

Zoe's expression changed in a split second and Berf sensed that his first go at it came short of the brass ring. It was a familiar, wistful, pitying look that reminded Berf far too much of the past. A past he had thought was safely distant.

"Oh, Berf! You silly bear," she said.

He bought himself some time with a simple, "Yes?" But considering the situation, he didn't cotton to the informality of "silly bear." He was about to offer a gentle but firm rebuke for this lapse of decorum when she blurted out something even worse.

"Forever the hopeless romantic."

Berf didn't necessarily object to being considered a romantic. Occasionally, anyway, but not right here and right now. This was the time and place for restraint, not for the taking of liberties and forgetting the boundaries of decent society. He cast about for a trick to throw her off the scent.

"Would you call it that? I've always considered myself more of a pragmatic idealist, actually. Kinda like Tell Sackett—"

"First our song. Now flowers and a ring."

"Our song? A ring?" Berf glanced down at the box in his left hand. "Oh. No! Not a ring." He whipped the ring behind his back.

"Yes! Last night at the gala when you sang to me, I knew. You still love me."

"That old song? It's just . . ." What did she say? "I still love you?"

"There! I knew it. Up my balcony like Romeo, on one knee with flowers and a ring. Let me see it."

"See what?" Berf blurted.

"The ring."

"Oh . . . ah," he said as forcefully as he could, but he had landed smack in the middle of it. He could retreat down the ladder and light a shuck for Mexico, but he had come a long way on short rations, and he would stay long enough to get the ring to Chip. He hesitated, and then opened the little box.

"Oh, Berf," Zoe breathed, her hands to her throat. "Yes!" She snatched the ring from the case, slipped it on her finger, and admired it. "Yes, yes, yes!"

"Yes? Yes, what?"

"Yes, I will marry you!"

This last statement hit Berf like a shot from a buffalo gun. He was as sociable as the next hombre, but on the list of things to do before the end of the year, getting married was dead last. And marrying Zoe came after that. In fact, the whole point of this trip was to not get married.

Not that he was opposed to marriage qua marriage. And Zoe was a fine prospect, no question, but Berf had always suspected that she was not a strong believer in The Code. Too much like her father in that respect. Plus she was about to be engaged to Chip.

"You'll marry me?" he said, hoping he had misheard.

"Yes! Yes!"

Berf leapt to his feet, suddenly certain that the only option left to him was an immediate retreat to Mexico, which surely had no extradition treaty when it came to breech of promise suits, when he was arrested by the sudden report of the bedroom door slamming open and the appearance of Dr. Payne in heliotrope pajamas, a teal silk bathrobe, and slippers, bearing a shotgun.

Berf didn't know which was more shocking, the wardrobe or the gun.

"No! No!" Payne said.

"Daddy!"

"Dr. Payne!" Berf said a few octaves higher than he had intended.

"What in blazes is going on?" Payne demanded, altogether too free with the shotgun for Berf's peace of mind.

The old man was badger tough and coon smart, Berf would give him that, but he always felt somewhat uneasy when they were in the same room, even without the shotgun.

"Oh, Daddy!" Zoe said. "Berf proposed!"

"In a pig's eye!"

Zoe held out her hand. "See?"

To Berf's relief, the barrel of the shotgun dropped toward the floor. "What happened to Chip?" Payne asked.

"Oh, don't even mention his name," Zoe said. "I never want to see him again."

"Sure you do!" Berf insisted. What was she thinking?

"No, I don't!"

Dr. Payne gave her a hard look and turned a harder look on Berf. "I refuse to believe that you are as stupid as you look. Tell me you didn't sneak up here in the middle of the night to propose to your best friend's girlfriend."

While Berf could not endorse the full statement without a little editing, at least Dr. Payne was talking sense. "Of course not!"

The doctor looked relieved, but Zoe bristled like a pine cone with a toothache.

"Then why are you here?"

Berf took the question under advisement. It wasn't a simple question to answer, not like "How many fingers am I holding up?" or "What's the square root of two?" and his hesitation left a lull in the conversation into which Zoe leapt.

"Because when a guy climbs into a girl's bedroom after midnight, that girl has to question a guy's intentions. Whether they're strictly honorable."

Dr. Payne let out a deep breath, checked his watch, and cut his eyes toward Zoe.

"You know Berf," Berf said. "As straight as a chorus girl's stocking seam. You couldn't find a more honorable intention if you ordered it from the U.S. Mint with expedited shipping."

"That's what I'm saying," Zoe said. "You're not the type to sneak into a woman's bedroom to take advantage of her when she is vulnerable and unprotected."

This was more along the right lines in Berf's view. "Exactly."

"You live by a code."

"By The Code," Berf said, just to make sure she understood the capitals were not optional.

"You always do the right thing."

"Right."

"And treat a woman with deference and respect."

"As would any gentleman worthy of the name."

"And there's only one reason such a man would be in a woman's bedroom in the middle of the night, uninvited."

"Precise—"

"To ask for her hand in marriage."

"Yes. I mean . . . I can think of a few alternate scenarios."

"Such as?"

Berf surveyed the horizon for a few hypotheticals that would fit the bill, but sometimes the truth is the best option, particularly when working under a deadline. "The thing is . . . did I ever tell you how fate is a funny thing? I mean, think about it. Here I was, packing for Aruba, when the phone rang and it was Chip asking me—"

Electricity crackled around Zoe. "Oh, Chip. Don't talk to me of Chip."

Berf was beginning to get the impression that the bloom was off the rose. A mere fifteen hours ago Chip had been bursting with bonhomie and joy. Then five hours ago he was giving Berf instructions for a clandestine drop. Something had transpired during the intervening ten hours, something that could have disastrous consequences for all involved. Especially, reading from left to right, one Berford Oswald Wiggins.

"But you see," Berf said. "He is madly in love—"

"With himself. I know. Believe me, the scales have fallen from my eyes and I'm just grateful that it happened before it was too late." Zoe tossed Chip aside with a wave of her hand. "Let's forget Chip. Let's talk about why you're really here."

"I was just getting to that—"

"You've always been the strong, silent type, unable to put your true feelings into words, and reluctant to admit them even when it became obvious. The song. The flowers. The ring. Sneaking up the balcony like Romeo."

"But—"

Zoe placed a single finger on his lips. "Hush, my love. You doth protest too much, but we both know better."

"But—"

"Sh. I will say the things you can't. Yes, I will marry you."

Berf looked at her, then at Dr. Payne, who yawned, and back to Zoe. The way he saw it, he had three options. One, pretend that he had indeed sneaked into her bedroom for dishonorable purposes. Well, that wasn't going to happen, so really there were only two options. One, wear her down until she would listen to the truth, or two, go along with the engagement thing until he could get the full story from Chip.

"Good. I'm glad that's settled," Berf muttered

"Oh, Berf!" Zoe gave him a glancing kiss and turned around. "Daddy! I'm engaged!"

Dr. Payne shook his head and turned his gaze upon his future son-in-law with less enthusiasm than usually desired. "Come on, nitwit. I guess you need a room."

Berf deflated like a pup tent erected by a tenderfoot. "I guess I do." He tossed a longing glance at the top of the ladder peeking above the rail of the balcony. "Oh, and one for Jake, also."

"Who's Jake?" Dr. Payne demanded.

"Ex-brother-in-law."

Dr. Payne turned, muttering under his breath, and walked away.

Berf followed, but before he cleared the door, Zoe rushed him and planted a passionate kiss on his mouth. Berf pulled away, giving it his best effort to be supportive without offering encouragement. He thought it went well.

As he slipped through the door, he glanced back. Zoe picked up a picture frame that lay face down on her nightstand. A picture of Chip. She smiled, but it was not a smile designed to give Berf comfort.

If fact, it filled him with dread.

Half an hour later, Berf sat in the corner of a guest room with two single beds and threw back a shot of Bulleit for the pain. Then for good measure, he uncorked the bottle, poured another healthy, but entirely inadequate considering the circumstances, portion of bourbon, and set the bottle aside.

Across the room, Jake unpacked his suitcase in stoic silence. Hank the Jack Russell sat on the far bed, absorbing the tension with rigid attention.

"You see, Jake, Regal Sackett was right. Sometimes womenfolk have powerful imaginations and can read things into a man he never knew were there, and like as not, they aren't."

He took a gulp of the bourbon. He was not a man given to overindulgence as a rule, especially when on the trail, where at any moment an unexpected threat could spring from the darkness and blindside you. But once you were blindsided good and proper, a certain level of anesthesia was called for, and he was sure the good doctor would back him on this one.

In fact, Berf expected that Dr. Payne was himself applying this specific remedy at this very moment, if of a different vintage as suited his taste.

And, while Berf appreciated the subtlety of Bulleit's nuanced sweetness when taken as a libation, he recognized the affront to civilized society of gulping it down in medicinal quantities.

The thought of Cancún and Rita teased the edge of his mind, but he thrust it away. After all, he only had one bottle of bourbon and there wasn't a liquor store for miles.

Then another thought gamboled across the pasture of his consciousness like a newborn colt. "And I guess I'll have to reimburse Chip for the ring."

Jake arranged a shirt on a hanger with a measurable level of restrained violence. "Why can't you just tell her it was a mistake?"

Berf almost choked on his drink. He sometimes wondered if he and Jake were even of the same species. "Weren't you listening in the car? A Sackett does not trifle with a woman's affections. He does the honorable thing."

"You're not a Sackett," Jake snapped. "A sap, maybe, but not a Sackett."

Berf reminded himself that Jake wasn't from Texas and thus had to be given a little more bridle rope. He was from San Francisco, where they didn't understand matters of honor.

"It's The Code of the West. A man of honor keeps his word, even to his hurt."

"Well, this one, it's going to hurt. Big time."

Berf took a shamefully thoughtless plug of Bulleit and mentally apologized to the ghost of Elijah Craig. "That's why you have to find us a way out of it."

Jake dropped the slacks he was fussing over. "I already told you—"

"A way that won't violate The Code." It gave a feller pause, really, how often the man had to be reminded.

Jake picked up the hanger and resumed his finessing. "Oh, well, sure. That should be easy." He reached over, grabbed Berf's glass, and took an gulp of the bourbon. Then he restored it to its former position in Berf's hand.

"You realize how serious this is," Berf said. "If I marry Zoe, that means she moves in."

"Of course," Jake said as he placed the hanger in the closet.

"Into our house. With us," Berf said.

Jake turned from the closet and stared at Berf as if he had suggested that they catch the early-bird special for a LuAnn platter at Luby's.

"Forget Aruba," Berf said. "Keep that deposit. You're going to need it to find another place."

Jake didn't say a word. He just grabbed the bottle from the nightstand next to Berf, jerked out the cork, and took a big slug with no regard for the finely crafted flavor profile.

Berf nodded. Jake finally understood the gravity of the situation.

Chapter Twenty-One

Saturday morning the sun rose on the southwest corner of the Texas Hill Country, casting long, spectral shadows across the scrubby plains to the west, plains dotted with buttes and mesas, crisscrossed with gullies and arroyos. Desert birds—grebes and coots and wigeons—made sure everyone else knew about it. A few early-bird reptiles peeked out from under their rocks, testing the air for warmth.

After a night of revels and stratagems, the rambling hacienda on a sixty-thousand-acre ranch showed very few signs of life beyond the sonorous snores emanating from selected rooms, the occasional creak of box springs as a sleeper sought a more satisfactory position, or the groan of an afflicted dreamer.

Despite the fact that he barely had his driver's license, Zachary, the elder of the Martinez boys, was floating twenty feet above the River Walk in San Antonio like a drone, dropping cow skulls on tourists with a satisfied smile, when something suddenly jolted him, and he plummeted into the disgusting sludge that some people called the San Antonio River.

The water slowed him somewhat, but not enough to keep him from hitting the bottom, which was slime-coated concrete. He pushed away, shuddering at the thought of the horrific infectious diseases he had just acquired, and clawed to the surface.

He broke through, took in a deep gulp of air, and shrank away from the face looming over him.

"Get up, boys," JL said. "It's a beautiful day, the sun is shining, and there's gold in them there arroyos."

"Are you kidding me?" Zachary rolled over and pulled the pillow over his head. A flying dream didn't come very often. If he could get back to sleep, he might be able to pick up where he left off.

The pillow was ripped away.

"Perfect weather. Highs in the upper sixties, not a cloud in the sky."

"Come on, Dad." Zachary groped for the pillow, but JL had thrown it at Josiah on the other bed.

"You boys don't appreciate the opportunity I've dropped in your hands."

JL jerked the covers off Josiah, who was rolled up like a doodlebug, same as always. "Do you realize that out of the seven billion people on this entire planet, only three are in possession of this information, and they're all in this room on this ranch at this time?"

Josiah stayed curled up with his eyes closed and kept breathing deeply. He figured JL would give up like he usually did. But he was mistaken. Instead, two strong hands grabbed his hands and feet and stretched him out like a bungee cord.

"How many kids out there have a map to two million dollars in gold?"

Zachary groaned, swung his legs around, and sat up. Once JL started one of his rants, he didn't give up until he had harassed everyone in the room into agreement. It was best to capitulate immediately. "Just us lucky two." He squinted at the figure in the other bed. "Right, Jo?"

Josiah scrambled for the covers. "I don't care." The gold had been there for hundreds of years, right? It could wait until the afternoon, at least. He had the blanket halfway to his chin when JL grabbed the other end. Josiah lost the short tug-of-war and fell back on the bed like a wounded warrior.

"Don't forget about the swimming pool."

Josiah shot up. The swimming pool! They had come in too late last night to have a swim. He jumped to his suitcase and pulled out his trunks. "Come on, Zack. They have a pool."

"You can set out on the trail right after breakfast." JL left.

They grabbed a couple of towels and dashed down the hall, but Yvonne came out of her room.

"Where do you think you're going? It's way too cold to go swimming. The water will be freezing."

Josiah stopped. "But Dad said—"

"And you think he will lift a hand to nurse you back to health after you die of pneumonia?"

Zachary didn't even slow down. Yvonne could argue the ears off a brass billy goat, but she had no defense against wordless determination.

"Zack, I said it's too cold."

Josiah saw his chance and followed Zack down the hall. In a few seconds they were around the corner, out of earshot of Yvonne's complaints. He pushed past Zack to the door, ran down the levels to the pool, tossed the towel aside, and did a running watermelon into the pool.

The shock knocked the breath out of him and time stood still. He felt the bubbles ripple past his forehead as he tumbled in slow-motion toward the bottom, felt his frigid limbs deploy into a spread-eagle, waited until his momentum faded, and then stroked his way to the surface, where he pulled in a long, ragged lungful of air. This was nothing like the Gulf, where the water might be as brown as the River Walk, but at least it was warm. He considered getting out immediately, but two things stopped him. First, admitting that Yvonne was right, and second, the sight of Zack standing on the edge watching.

"How's the water?"

Josiah forced a grin onto his face as he treaded water. "It's great!" He clamped his jaws shut to keep his teeth from chattering and took a few strokes to the shallow end, more to keep warm than to get anywhere.

Zachary dropped his towel onto a chair and dove in. He had two thoughts in rapid succession. First, his underwater scream could probably be heard in Japan, and second, Jo must die. Soon, slowly, and excruciatingly. He clawed his way to the surface, caught his breath and his bearings, and churned a path toward his lying brother standing in the shallow end.

With a shout of triumph, Josiah dove to the bottom, swam under Zack to the deep end, and grabbed the edge.

Zack might be two years older, but he was also two years dumber, and Josiah could swim circles around him.

The battle for revenge occupied the next few minutes, and by then the water felt fine and they stayed in the pool until Yvonne called them in for breakfast, griping the whole way to the rooms about how if they died of pneumonia they shouldn't come crying to her.

Breakfast was boring, and then they got the gear from the barn, got a heading from the GPS, and set out to find the gold.

CHAPTER TWENTY-TWO

Berf awoke to the sounds of the Old West. The odd cluck, whinny, and moo filtered through the fog that drifted through his brain. He took a deep breath of clean country air, sighed the sigh of the contented, and rolled over.

He was awakened some time later by a shotgun blast. He raised an inquiring eyebrow, but didn't get churned up about it. Out here in the rugged West, a body came to expect the sound of firearms being discharged. Probably ranch hands up to some kind of horseplay.

Although it felt uncommon early, he chanced the opening of one eye and then another. The universe had pulled its braces up over its shoulders and grabbed ahold of another day. He took inventory of his room from his position twisted in a blanket in the single bed. A chest of drawers crafted from rough-hewn wood graced one wall, a matching wardrobe on the opposite wall. A wag-on-wheel chandelier hung on iron chains from the plank ceiling. The matching bed was empty, the covers made with military corners.

These Paynes, they knew how to do a feller right.

An urgent message from his stomach interrupted Berf's morning reflections. An inquiry as to whether his throat had been cut. Berf slid from between the covers, draped some suitably rustic duds over his slender frame, and wandered the halls in search of breakfast.

He passed a doorway through which he caught a glimpse of Dr. Payne sitting at a desk, papers spread out, laboring with an expression of dogged concentration.

Berf poked his head in the door. "Morning, Doctor. Working hard or hardly working?" He chuckled at the old chestnut, but the doctor was a tough nut to crack and just stared at him the way Berf's third-grade teacher used to. Like he was a tomcat who had just deposited an inferior mouse on the ottoman for inspection.

Berf cleared his throat. "Well, then, could you point me in the direction of the chuck wagon where I could snag a waffle or breakfast taco or other form of nourishment?"

Dr. Payne peered at his watch. "Do you always eat breakfast at eleven?"

"Oh, no, no, no," he assured the doctor. "This is quite unusual, but the influence of this country air, it gets you frisky as a new calf. Otherwise I would have slept in."

Dr. Payne's eyes squinted and he let out a noise that sounded very similar to a duck with a bone caught in its throat. Berf stepped to offer first aid, but the doctor turned away abruptly and began writing furiously on a paper.

Berf shrugged and turned to go just as Summer passed by with a steaming coffee mug.

"Berf," she said. "I just heard the news. Congratulations!"

"For what?"

"Your engagement, of course."

The choking sound echoed and Berf wasn't sure if it had come from the room behind him or from his own throat. He had forgotten about that unfortunate episode.

"Right. Thanks." He leaned forward and peered into her cup. "Is that coffee?"

"Sure. You want some?"

A minute ago Berf would have given half of his kingdom for a strong cup of hot coffee, the kind that grew barbed wire on your chest, but he suddenly felt the need for a more potent remedy for what ailed him. "Got anything stronger?"

"Espresso?"

"You're getting warmer."

Summer frowned. "Bailey's?"

"Warmer."

Summer studied him for a second. "Irish?"

"Now you are speaking my language." He turned back to Dr Payne. "How about you, Doctor? Hair of the dog?"

Payne looked up, confused. "Dog? What dog?"

"Maybe not." Besides, the situation called for clear thinking and quick action. He could self-medicate later. He turned to Summer. "Have you seen Jake?"

"Not since breakfast."

"He couldn't have got far, then. Happy trails."

Berf glanced down the hallway, inspected his back trail for signs of a posse, and turned right. He stepped into the next doorway, which opened onto the library, and came upon Zoe sitting on a couch surrounded by wedding magazines and a laptop. He tried to back out silently, but she looked up.

"Berfie!" She smiled and motioned him over. "What do you think of this cake?"

He scanned the room for cake and turned back to her.

"Here, silly boy." Zoe pointed to the computer screen, the obscenely large diamond prominent on her finger.

Berf leaned over for a look. She had pulled up a wedding blog featuring a monstrous cake sculptured into the likeness of a bride. Life-sized.

"Shucks, ma'am, she looks good enough to eat." He chuckled, but like her father, Zoe failed to see the joke.

"I think Christmas weddings are lovely, don't you?"

If Berf needed a drink before, he needed one in spades now. "Uh, are we in a hurry?"

Zoe's eyes narrowed as she studied him. "You're not having second thoughts?"

"Oh, no, no, no! It's just a lot to get done in such a short time."

She smiled. "Oh, don't you worry your pretty little head about it, Wiggie." She turned back to the computer, clicked through to another photo, and sighed with satisfaction.

Berf didn't wait around to render judgment on her latest discovery. He walked out the patio door, shuddering as he recalled Zoe's penchant for cloying pet names.

Zoe's voice floated from the open door. "Oh, Berfie, I almost forgot. Chip wants to talk to you."

Berf walked away without comment and found an unbelievably blonde woman in a chaise lounge by the pool reading a romance novel.

"Excuse me," he said.

The woman jumped as if she had been poked with a hatpin and emitted a squeak straight from a B-movie.

"Sorry to startle you, but have you seen Jake?"

"I don't know any Jakes."

"Really?" This was a first. "I thought everyone knew Jake. Wiry, about yea high, dark hair. Looks like a fashion model. Male model, of course."

The woman shook her head as if regretful. "Nope. Sorry." She looked closer at Berf. "Do I know you?"

"Sorry." He bowed slightly from the waist. "I'm Berf."

"Oh! So you're Berf. Congratulations!"

It seemed the grapevine had put in some overtime into the wee hours. "Right. Thanks." He took the levels of the patio in long strides.

"Oh," the woman called from the pool. "Chip was just looking for you."

"Great." One thing was clear in Berf's mind. Before Chip found him, he needed to find Jake.

On the south side of the barn, Berf came upon Billy and another guy drinking beer and watching Henderson clean doves. He pulled up to a stop next to them. "Howdy, pardners." He set his hands on his hips and joined them in watching Henderson.

"Hey, Berf," Billy said. "Beer?"

"No, thanks."

"You know JL?"

Berf looked at the Latino guy next to Billy. "Can't say as I've had the honor."

JL nodded at him. Berf nodded back and turned to Billy.

"You seen Jake?"

"No. But Chip was just here. He seemed very interested in talking to you."

Billy gave him a searching gaze, but Berf was as stone. A Wiggins didn't play fast and loose with his secrets.

"Thanks for the warning," he said in an offhand manner. "Well, I guess I'll be moseying along. Take it easy, gents."

"I'll take it any way I can get it," JL said.

"Excellent policy," Berf said over his shoulder.

On the other side of the barn, Berf ran into Mitch, who was working on his short game, putting balls into a soup can. "Emil, is that you?"

Mitch dropped his club, rushed up, and shook his hand. "Berf! Are you down for the weekend? What a wonderful day!"

"Is it?" It was a nice sunny autumn day with a touch of Indian summer to take the edge off the brisk morning air, but Berf stopped short of calling it wonderful. Too many hazards and stratagems lurking about.

"Absolutely!" Mitch gushed, still pumping Berf's hand. "Berf, I've met my future wife. Bonnie Hollingsworth. Do you know her?

Berf wrenched his hand free from Mitch's viselike grip. "Haven't had the pleasure."

"Pleasure is right. You always have the perfect word. Berf, she's like a rodeo angel! Have you ever seen such a creature?"

A shudder rippled through Berf's frame. "Not while sober, thank God." His experiences all pointed to the same conclusion, that women should be approached with a deliberate caution, much like a man attempting to bridle a wild stallion. Let emotion enter into the picture and you could be trampled in the ensuing stampede.

But Mitch wasn't having any. He had the look of a moonstruck calf. "Well, I've seen her, and she's a vision."

"Please, Flood. You're talking to a man with an empty stomach and a pounding head. Rein it in a bit, will you?"

"You have to meet her." Mitch pointed a finger at him. "I'll bring her to lunch."

"Wild horses could not keep me away. Now, I have to tell you something. Have you seen Jake?"

"No, but Chip is looking for you."

"So I hear." Berf scanned the horizon like a nervous cowboy expecting smoke signals bearing bad news.

Mitch returned to his putting practice. Berf proceeded in the other direction. On the far side of the barn he came upon a pasture enclosed in a pristine rail fence. A plaque reading "Tiny" adorned the top rail. Inside, a calf frolicked on landscaped turf.

Outside the fence, Jake knelt on one knee taking photographs with a Polaroid. Hank the Jack Russell watched with unaccustomed patience.

Berf joined them. "I was taught at my mother's knee to live and let well enough alone, but sometimes a man has to step up and stand for what's right, regardless of the consequences." He nodded at the pasture. "Is it fair to name a calf Tiny? All things grow up one day, even calves, and then where's he going to be, a half-ton of steak tartare on the hoof having to answer to the name Tiny? It's enough to put him off his feed. Years of therapy loom in his future."

"Chip is looking for you," Jake said without looking up.

That comment got right in amongst Berf. "That's my point," he said. "Here you are doing your Ansel Adams impression when your own flesh and blood is in danger of matrimony in the first degree."

Jake didn't cease or desist from his artistic pursuits. "Actually, I'm just an in-law. More of an ex-law, actually."

"Jake, I'm shocked at your behavior. It's not like you to abandon a frat brother with his butt in a sling."

"I wouldn't worry too much about it." Jake snapped a picture, waited for the print to eject, and began shaking it.

Berf began to sense that Jake failed to appreciate his own personal stake in this developing crisis. "You don't seem to care that I'm up the tree without a paddle. You disappoint me, Jake. Do I have to remind you that your butt is in the same sling? Right now Zoe is sorting through cranberry swatches for the breakfast nook."

Jake shuddered and faced Berf. "Zoe doesn't want to marry you."

"Then somebody needs to catch her up on the subject. Because last time I checked, she was setting dates and picking cakes."

Jake inspected the photo and slipped it into his bag. "I got the whole story from Chip after breakfast. He had a fight with Zoe yesterday. She's just trying to make him jealous."

"Are you sure she doesn't want to marry me?"

"Get real, Berf. She knows you're emotionally stunted and incapable of sustaining a long-term relationship."

"You're not just saying that to make me feel better?"

"Think about it. If she was going to marry you, she would have done it in college the first two times she was engaged to you."

It was three, but what was the odd engagement among friends? As much as Berf liked the sound of the words, he couldn't deny that his brilliant if naive friend had failed to get a solid grasp on the threat that faced them.

"No, Jake. No. I know you want to think that, maybe you even believe it, but you didn't see how she looked at me when she put on that ring. Like I was money from home." The mere thought melted Berf's bones and he placed a hand against the tree for support.

"At breakfast I saw her give Chip a look that would take the primer coat off a battleship at one hundred yards," Jake said. "She still loves him."

The Texas sun could have effects on a man who stayed out too long, even in November. "Guess again, compadre," Berf said.

"Trust me, buddy. It wasn't the look of a girl who has moved on. She still cares. Deeply. And then there's Chip."

A cry from afar interrupted their discussion. Chip appeared around the barn and dialed his sights in on Berf.

CHAPTER TWENTY-THREE

Berf spun around to face the threat head on.

Jake didn't seem to notice as he continued laying out his theory. "And he wouldn't be so upset if he didn't still love her."

Berf watched Chip approach at an inhuman pace, a gleam of malice in his eye. "Enough of that. Hand me a pitchfork. Or a shotgun. Or a cannon." He dodged behind Jake. "Chip, buddy. I've been looking all over for you."

"Well, now you've found me." He lunged around Jake, upsetting the camera.

"Hey," Jake yelled.

"Chip, the strangest thing happened," Berf said as he slipped from Chip's grasp and danced out of reach to the other side of Jake. "It's funny, really. You'll laugh when you hear it."

"Try me." Chip pushed Jake aside and lunged.

Berf vaulted the fence, with Chip hell-bent for leather behind him. To Berf's disappointment, instead of tackling Chip, Jake followed them, shooting pictures like a sports photographer. Hank brought up the rear, barking.

Berf legged it to the oak in the middle of the pasture. "I delivered the ring to your room, only it turned out to be Zoe's room."

The calf joined the fun, nearly knocking Berf to the ground in its enthusiasm.

"When do we get to the funny part?" Chip asked in a spare breath.

Berf staggered to the tree and leapt for a branch, swinging himself up just as Chip's fingers grazed his heels. "Zoe got the wrong idea," he said from his perch on the branch.

"Oh? Like when you sang 'Kiss to Build a Dream On' to her Thursday night?"

Chip jumped for the branch, but Berf swept his hands aside with his foot. "That's another funny thing. Amelia Bark—"

"Like the thing where I reach down your throat, grab your tail, and jerk you inside out?"

"No, something even funnier."

Chip made another attempt for the branch, but when Berf tried to kick his hands aside, Chip grabbed his ankle and pulled him from his perch. Chip landed on a root and Berf landed on top, knocking the breath from both of them and ringing the bell on round one.

Hank commenced to prance a victory dance on their bodies, simultaneously barking and licking them.

"Jake says Zoe still loves you madly," Berf said.

"She has a funny way of showing it," Chip said between gasping breaths.

Berf rolled off Chip and pushed himself up on one elbow. "As you know, women often talk with forked tongue. It is the way of their people."

He crawled to his feet and dusted himself off. "You can trust Jake. He's as smart as a tack. He understands women right down to the ground. After all, he talks to them all day while running his fingers through their hair. He's got the inside scoop."

Berf offered a hand to Chip, who took it and allowed himself to be pulled up.

"Take Jake to the movies," Berf continued, "and by the time the opening credits are done, he can describe the ending, including what the girl will be wearing and who gets the dog."

Chip faced Berf, his hands on his hips, breathing heavily. "So you're saying you're not secretly in love with Zoe?"

"Oh, no, no, no. Not secretly or otherwise."

"You don't want to marry her?"

Berf held his hand up in the Scout salute. "I'd rather be dragged behind a horse through cactus."

Chip did not take this assurance in the spirit in which it was delivered. He frowned and cocked his head to one side.

"Not that she isn't as cute as a white-tailed poney in her own pumpkin-headed way," Berf assured him. "Any man would be lucky to have her. The point is, I'm not in the market."

"But you proposed—"

"A mere technicality, Chipmeister. Just a technicality. I was in the room, on bended knee from having tripped over a cuspidor." Berf demonstrated. He looked up at Chip. "I was holding a ring intended for you when she turned on the light. She took her cue and directed the scene complete with show girls and a dance number."

"Yeah, she can do that."

Berf stood. "But Jake has a foolproof plan to mend the wagon wheel."

They both turned to Jake, anticipating words of wisdom.

"Actually, I don't," Jake said.

Chip threw up his hands. "Well, that's settled. Thanks!" He dropped to the grass and leaned against the tree, holding his head.

To Berf's relief, Jake stepped up to the plate. "Chip, Zoe's just trying to teach you a lesson. All we have to do is convince her to abandon her plan."

"Right!" Chip said in a sarcasm-saturated syllable. "Why didn't I think of that?"

Jake continued, undeterred. "We need a minor crisis. When she sees you're in danger, she'll forget herself and show her true feelings."

"Brilliant," Chip exclaimed. "I'm surprised they haven't shipped him off to the Middle East to settle that little dust up."

Berf stepped forward. It was time to read him from the Book. "Chip, just tell Zoe it was all a misunderstanding and you won't let it ruin a good thing."

Chip stood and dusted off his pants. "Not on your life, buckaroo. She can't expect me to come crawling every time she gets herself engaged to any passing idiot with an engagement ring who can't find the right room with a compass, a treasure map, and a blinking neon X marking the spot."

Berf stiffened. "Hey. I'm standing right here."

"Sorry, Berf," Chip said, waiving away his objections. "But it's time I taught her a lesson."

"Mistake," Jake said.

"No, no, no, my fine feathered friend," Berf hastened to add. "That's her strategy, not yours. It's time for a bit of relational judo. When she pushes, you don't resist, you give way, and she'll topple right into your arms."

"Did Kennedy back down from Khrushchev? Did Reagan back down from Gorbachev? Did Bush back down from Saddam? It's time to stay the course and resist the evildoers."

Berf shook his head. Chip was frequently a reasonable man, but when his Italian side kicked in, he could buck like a sidewinder on a fire ant hill. "Alrighty, then. In that case, what's your favorite crisis?"

The sound of an old bunk house triangle cut off Chip's reply, which was just as well, because it was probably of the more profane variety, and Berf couldn't abide cussing.

CHAPTER TWENTY-FOUR

Immediately after lunch, Mitch slipped out behind the barn to wait for Bonnie. He took a putter and a few balls to practice while he waited, but the longer he putted, the more apprehensive he became about this rendezvous. It had been twelve hours since he had seen Bonnie, and he didn't know if he could wait much longer, but he dreaded disappointing her with the news of his failure of the previous night.

He was lining up a ball when a hand fell on his shoulder and he spun around with his club raised. Henderson flinched back a few steps like a skittish dog.

Mitch lowered the club and tried to lower his heart rate. "Whoa! You should give a man some warning before you pop out like that."

Henderson approached with his grizzled, lopsided grin. "Guilty conscience, lil' Doc?"

"Got a lot on my mind is all." Mitch started to resume his putt, but realized it would be rude. "And how are you finding yourself, Henderson?"

"Can't complain, lil' Doc, can't complain."

"That's good," Mitch said, thinking that from the way he said it, Henderson wanted very much to complain.

Henderson scanned the area and then caught Mitch's eye. "I just wanted to ask you a question."

"Fire away."

"You being a doctor and all, maybe you could help me with a little problem. I got a . . . a friend who needs some help in the old romance department."

"Take a number," Mitch said. "But I'm just a pediatrician. If you need help with romantic problems, you should talk to Berf."

"It's not for me," Henderson said quickly. "It's just that my friend . . . he seems to be having a problem when it comes down to brass tacks." He gave the area another good reconnaissance before proceeding. "You wouldn't have something in that little black bag of yours that could get a bull to step up to the plate and do the needful, would you?"

"Come again?"

"You know, lift his spirits, put a little lead in his pencil, snap the soldier to attention, raise the old flag."

"Ah." Mitch finally understood the old man's meaning. He placed an understanding hand on his bony shoulder. "No need to be embarrassed, Henderson. It's very common for men of a certain age to have—"

Henderson brushed his hand away with a scowl. "No, it's not for me. It's for the bull."

"The bull?" It was strange the euphemisms some people employed.

"The bull." Henderson gestured back at the barn. "Tiny."

Mitch looked over at the barn and back to Henderson. "The bull? An actual bull?"

"If we don't get Tiny up to operating speed today, we won't close this deal."

"I'm not sure I—"

Henderson glanced over Mitch's shoulder. "Oh, never mind." He turned and walked off, muttering.

Mitch spun on his heel. As he watched Bonnie ride up to the barn on Barnabas, his heart did things in his chest that he could not explain medically. She wore a white hat and white jeans, and a turquoise western shirt with white stitching and pearl-inlay buttons, her strawberry-blonde hair pulled back in a ponytail. In a word, she was as cute as a cub coon in a hollow tree.

She dismounted in a smooth motion and greeted Mitch with a kiss that made him forget whatever it was that he was going to talk to her about.

"I've been waiting all day for that," she breathed into his ear.

"It was worth the wait," he whispered back.

Then she pulled away, grabbed the reins, and walked Barnabas to the barn. "Did you get it?"

Mitch retrieved his golf ball, tucked it into his pocket, and caught up. "Get what?"

"The memory stick."

"Oh." He suddenly remembered what he was going to talk to her about. "Well, there was a . . . an incident."

Bonnie stopped dead in her tracks. Barnabas stood patiently alongside. "What kind of incident?"

"It was tricky. I was halfway up the ladder when I heard a noise and had to abort the mission."

"You heard a noise?"

Despite her being a rodeo angel and the sweetest thing this side of the Czech Stop in West, there was something about her tone that Mitch found slightly off-putting. "Yes, a noise. So I slipped into the shadows, and a good thing it was too."

"Because?"

"Because Berf came around the corner of the house and climbed the ladder into Zoe's room. If I had gone in, he would have found me there and then what?"

"What's a Berf?"

"An old frat buddy. Zoe's fiancé before Chip came along."

"And he sneaked into Zoe's bedroom?"

Mitch could practically hear the gears turning under her cowboy hat. "And this morning at breakfast, Zoe announced that she's engaged to Berf. You should've seen Chip's face. It had a passing resemblance to cirrhosis of the liver."

"Interesting," Bonnie drawled as she stared into the cloudless sky. Then she snapped back. "But we still need the memory stick."

Mitch had hoped that the zeal for the memory stick might have faded, but no, Bonnie was still fixated on it. "Why, exactly?"

"I told you. We have to know Zoe's source."

"But if she made it up, she doesn't have a source."

The silence that followed made Mitch uneasy. Had Bonnie doped Barnabas after all? Maybe she wasn't what she seemed.

Bonnie cast what seemed to be a calculating glance at him, and he prepared himself for the worst.

"Mitch, I'm going to tell you something that you can't ever tell anyone else. Have you heard of a horse shaman?"

"Uh, no."

"He's a spiritual healer. He opens the pathways to reveal the underlying blockage that prevents humans and animals from truly connecting."

Mitch considered these words and decided they didn't mean anything, but he kept an open mind. She might eventually converge on something he could latch onto.

"I know it sounds crazy," Bonnie admitted. "But it works. I've got six trophies to show for it."

Mitch shrugged a concession. When it came down to it, the bottom line was results, regardless of the explanation.

"It was all natural herbal supplements. No chemicals, no injections. I would never do that."

"Of course not."

"So there's nothing for Zoe to find out."

"But?"

"But if she somehow found out about Zaqar, well, it might raise some questions among the more . . . traditional people in the rodeo community."

"Maybe you could take the wind out of her sails. Go public with the Zaqar connection, spin it as a human interest story. Get the press on your side."

The expression that flitted across Bonnie's face held a wealth of information that Mitch didn't have time to decipher.

"How much do you know about the rodeo community?" she asked.

"Almost enough to drown a gnat."

"That story would play well in Austin, but I could count the number of barrel racers that came out of Austin in the last five years on one hand and still have five fingers to pick my nose with."

Mitch was impressed with Bonnie's grasp of her market. "So you're saying . . ."

"I'm saying we have to know if she somehow got to Zaqar. I've done nothing wrong, no banned substances, but that doesn't matter if she can spin me as some kind of new-age crystal-gazing weirdo."

Bonnie placed a hand on Barnabas and stopped. She turned to Mitch and transferred the hand to his shoulder. "You told Zoe that I was off the fireman fundraiser?"

He nodded.

"We have to get that memory stick while her guard is down."

Mitch found no comfort in these words. He dreaded what might come next.

"Where's everyone now?"

Mitch considered the question. "Probably in the library."

"Good. I'll keep her busy in the library while you get the memory stick from her room."

"But it's the middle of the day."

"Which makes it easier than while she's sleeping in there."

Mitch couldn't argue with that, although he wanted to.

"Meet me in the library when you have it."

Bonnie led Barnabas away to the barn. Mitch watched her leave, then set his shoulders and trudged toward the house. Inside he leaned the putter against the wall at the base of the stairs and tiptoed to the second floor. He stole to the back of the house to the last door and slipped inside, easing the door closed.

Then he turned and surveyed the room. A king-sized bed, a dresser, a vanity, couch, and armchair around a coffee table, and a writing desk. With a laptop. He went directly to the desk and scanned the space. Then he searched the drawers.

He found the memory stick in a jewelry box at the back of a bottom drawer. Such a small thing to cause such a large problem. He slipped it in his pocket and turned to leave when he heard a noise and saw the doorknob turn.

With a suppressed cry of alarm, he glanced about wildly, ran to the walk-in closet, thought better of it, and dashed through the curtains to the balcony. He looked over the edge, but decided against it. He would wait out whoever it was and then escape the way he had come.

Just as he had settled against the railing on the balcony, the curtains in front of the French doors jerked aside. A cleaning lady locked eyes with him and screamed. Mitch screamed but managed to compose himself.

The lady backed away slowly, her hands up, speaking incoherent Spanish.

Mitch held his hands out and responded in Spanish. "Have you seen my ball? I was practicing my chip shot and it landed up here."

He turned, crouched down on the balcony as if to search, and pulled the golf ball from his pocket, dropping it on the balcony.

"Ah! Here it is." He snatched up the ball and showed it to her.

She continued to back away and grabbed a broom, which she held out in front of her like a lance.

"Thanks," he said and fled the room. Now all he had to do was find a way to get Bonnie alone for the handoff.

CHAPTER TWENTY-FIVE

The scene at lunch ate Berf's lunch. For a strong-natured man, a man with the bark on, but also a man gifted with a finely tuned social antenna, the backhanded parry and thrust of double entendre and subtext was exhausting.

Chip sulked his way through the meal, and Zoe littered the table with so many bless-his-hearts that Berf lost count. And the guests did their best to keep an oar in. Summer and Billy seemed to be involved in some kind of domestic third-world skirmish and the newcomers, JL and Yvonne, offered a demonstration of their own special brand of conversational mud wrestling.

When the bell rang and the contestants rose from the table to retreat to their respective corners, Dr. Payne made an announcement.

"Quail hunt in a few hours. Meet at the barn."

Due to his father's indoctrination program, Berf could shoot the eye out of a mosquito at fifty yards, but the prospect of walking through the brush all tensed to draw and fire whenever a dog flushed a covey filled him with the urge to club himself to death with a cocktail shaker. He had a strong desire to lie down with a cold cloth on his forehead. Best to give the whole pageant a miss. "Proceed on, fellow travelers, but I have to see a man about a dog."

Zoe elbowed him discretely. "Oh, Berfie, bless your heart, everyone goes quail hunting. It's a tradition."

"Oh. Right. I love quail hunting. Never miss it if I can."

Zoe smiled approvingly, slid her arm in his, and guided him toward the library.

JL turned to Dr. Payne. "In the meantime, let's get a look at that bull."

"Just what I was thinking," Dr. Payne said.

To Berf's surprise, Jake said, "I'd like to see him too."

They exited stage left and Zoe led the rest of the gang into the library.

Chip pushed past them to the pool table. The poolside door opened and a small, strawberry-blonde woman in a white straw cowboy hat, turquoise western shirt, white jeans, and alligator boots entered.

To Berf's eye, she was the very image of Ange Kerry, the woman Tell Sackett rescued from the frozen Colorado mountain valley while in search of gold. If, that is, Ange Kerry had been a twenty-first-century rodeo star instead of a nineteenth-century granddaughter of an Irish gold hunter. No wonder Mitch was wandering around like a man suffering from sunstroke, for this could be no other than Bonnie Hollingsworth, Mitch's rodeo angel.

He was about to step forward and greet her as a welcome breath of wholesomeness in this nest of vipers when Zoe's grip tightened on his arm like a lockdown on cell block number nine.

As Chip stepped up to do the needful, Bonnie turned to Zoe, saw Berf at her side, and glanced briefly back at Chip before stepping forward. "Z, who is your friend?"

Zoe's grip on Berf's arm escalated to the tourniquet level. "This is my fiancé, Berf Wiggins."

Bonnie repeated her double-take. "Not Chip?"

"Absolutely not. Yesterday I saw the real Chip and it wasn't a pleasant sight. Thank God I saw it before it was too late."

A barking laugh from the pool table registered Chip's views on the subject.

Bonnie took a long, appraising look at Chip, then turned to Berf and held out a hand. "Congratulations, Berf. You must be a fast worker."

Berf tried to shake hands, but Zoe had command of his right arm and he could do no more than offer a slight T-Rex wave.

"Bless his heart," Zoe said. "Berf has been smitten with me for years. The poor thing." She patted his arm.

Berf opened his mouth to set the record straight, but anything he could say would just be kicking a hornet's nest. He chose the manly response of stoic silence.

Bonnie returned his smile. "Z, let's take a look at that book of yours."

Zoe released Berf's arm, restoring circulation to his right hand, and led Bonnie to the couch.

Berf watched them settle on the couch, Zoe flipping open a coffee-table book, Bonnie leaning in, and sensed an undercurrent in the air, like the faintest whiff of campfire smoke when you thought you were safely alone in Indian country. Something he couldn't quite pinpoint.

But he would wager his leather-bound, signed L'Amour collection that the eggs had gone off in Denmark.

Summer and Billy entered. "I'll go join the girls," Summer said.

Billy selected a pool cue. ""Haven't you caused enough trouble between those two?"

"Oh," Summer said archly. "You think I should find something else to amuse myself?"

"Everyone thinks so. Give it a rest."

Mitch wandered through the hallway door, scanning the room. He saw Bonnie and Zoe consulting on the couch and stopped like a calf staring at a new gate.

Summer walked over to Mitch. "Mitch, honey. You ever had a palm reading?"

Mitch barely registered her presence. "Uh, no."

Summer snagged his arm and led him to a love seat, pulling him down next to her. She rolled his fingers open and sensuously traced his palm. "This is your love line. Mmm, I can see you're going to be very busy."

Berf gaped. He couldn't say for certain, but he had a strong impression that the wheels had come off the chuck wagon.

Billy watched them for a second and then joined Yvonne, who sat at a Scrabble board piecing together words. "Shall we?"

Yvonne flinched, glanced up at Billy, and offered a tentative smile. "Oh. Okay."

Billy flipped over the tiles and shuffled them.

Berf strode straight to the pool table and froze Chip with a glare. "I'm going to give it to you straight, Chip. You have fallen on evil ways and must return to the narrow path. Just do it. Go over there, tell her you're sorry, and take it like a man. It's the honorable thing."

Chip made a combination shot without even lining it up. "I have a better idea. I stay here, you shut up, and I don't introduce your head to your nether regions. That's as honorable as I get."

"Somebody has to stop the madness." Berf pointed to the room.

Summer had progressed from palm reading to aura reading or maybe phrenology. She ran her hands over Mitch's head. He sat as if in a trance, staring across the room. Berf followed his gaze.

Zoe pointed to a page in the picture book, but Bonnie was staring at Summer and Mitch. With a visible shudder she returned her attention to the book.

Two voices laughing drew Berf's attention back to the Scrabble game. Yvonne's hand touched Billy's as they drew tiles. She drew it back, and then let it rest on his for a second before setting her tiles on the rack.

Berf turned back to Chip. "Look. It's not just you and Zoe. It's like the ranch is cursed."

Chip shook his head slowly, like a bison shaking off flies. "Zoe has to learn her lesson. Even if that means marrying a buffoon like you."

"For all our sakes, there must be some other way." Berf collapsed on a stool and dropped his head into his hands.

Yvonne's laugh cut through the room. "Okay, Billy, I'm fixing to challenge you. Epy-tome ain't a word."

"It's epitome."

"Oh."

Berf couldn't bear to look over to see the expression on Yvonne's face. Billy's response was barely audible.

"It's an unusual word. I only know it because I was a regional spelling bee champion back when they taught obscure words. Way before your time, I'm sure."

Considering all the ways the room had gone crossways, it seemed to Berf that nothing short of a Russian invasion could reunite the inmates in a common goal and restore them to sanity.

"Just shoot me now," he moaned. And then it hit him. He rose up in a eureka pose. "I've got it!"

All conversation stopped as everyone turned to look at him—Yvonne and Billy at the Scrabble board, Mitch and Summer on the love seat, Bonnie and Zoe on the couch, and even Chip, who was racking up the balls.

"The winning lottery number! I'll shoot right down to the 7-11 and get a ticket!" Everyone turned back to their pursuits dismissively. Berf turned to Chip and spoke in a hoarse whisper. "Here's what we do. I'll shoot you on the quail hunt."

"You already got Zoe. No need to shoot me." He drove the cue ball into the triangle of balls with vicious force. "Although you might as well," he added.

"I won't really shoot you, I'll just pretend to shoot you. I'll take the pellets out of the shells first."

"I'm sure it makes perfect sense on your planet. You pretend to shoot me and . . ."

"And Zoe rushes to your side, apologizing and showering you with kisses and saying that she never stopped loving you and can you ever forgive her."

Chip stared at him like a dog being shown a card trick. Then it seemed as if the words began to seep through the haze. "You think it could work?"

"And, what's more, she learns her lesson."

"It might work."

"Of course it'll work. You're catching Berf at his best, early in the day, just after lunch."

"Except for one thing," Chip said. "I take the pellets out of the shells."

Chapter Twenty-Six

Henderson sat on a bale of hay, smoking a cigarette and reading the latest issue of *Herpetologist Monthly*. He skimmed the scholarly articles on toads and nematodes and the like, adverts for mail-order-nymph-crickets and such, and then flipped to the back where they posted the jobs.

Mainly teaching positions and zoo jobs, as usual. He didn't have the degrees for the first, nor the sex appeal for the second. Zoos liked young, photogenic herpetologists who could give tours of the reptile house and deliver fun facts about creepy-crawlies without creeping out the kids. Not likely for a face carved out of the native stone through the timeless geological processes of field work and rough living. They wanted a Donny Osmond but he was more of a superannuated Iggy Pop with a buzz cut and three days' growth on his jaw line.

He looked over the top of the magazine at Lolita, a bulge clearly visible about a third of the way down her eight-foot length. She was good for two weeks, when the new moon came out. Or didn't, as it were.

Henderson was thus engaged in contemplation of such weighty matters when Payne stuck his hairless head into the inner sanctum.

"You're on deck. Martinez wants to see Tiny in action."

It was the moment Henderson had been dreading for the last twenty-four hours. The way he saw it, if a two-thousand pound bull didn't want to do a thing, it was tampering with the natural order of things to try to argue with him about it. The Beatles had it right when they said, "Let it be." That was wisdom, right there.

But Payne had a different view on the subject. To him, Tiny wasn't a force of nature, like a black hole, that one should give wide berth, affording it the respect it deserved. No, Tiny was an underperforming asset, a bad investment to be shoveled off on some poor unsuspecting sucker. And Henderson was the shovel.

Henderson peeked out the back door of the barn. The fates had cut him a little slack. Tiny was already in the corral. He moseyed out to the pasture to recover the heifer, who was a more reasonable half-ton and moderately compliant if you moved real slow and didn't propose anything complicated.

Being careful not to turn his back on anything that weighed more than a Harley-Davidson Fat Boy, Henderson opened the connecting gate, circled around behind the heifer, whom he had come to think of as Jezebel, and issued encouraging grunts until she started moving. After a few minutes, she was in the corral with Tiny.

Henderson closed the gate and leaned against the back fence, watching the three men on the other side of the corral.

Payne had one foot on the bottom rail, leaning his forearms on the top rail with expectation, as if he was under the delusion that Henderson had somehow come up with the secret sauce overnight.

Martinez stood next to him, his hands on his hips, a Peterbilt cap shading his eyes from the afternoon sun, his face unreadable, but Henderson could read it well enough. *Show me the money*, was what it said.

A third guy stood on the other side of Martinez. Thin guy in a black felt cowboy hat with silver concho hatband, black long-sleeved shirt with red stitching, bolo tie with an armadillo carved from bone, black jeans, and black boots, his arms crossed. Henderson half expected to see pearl-handled revolvers hanging from a gun belt.

All of them watched Tiny as if he might explode with testosterone any second now, but as usual, Tiny did his strong, silent type impression, nosing at a bull nettle that had poked a branch over the bottom rail.

Jezebel eased up next to Tiny as if she might blow in his ear, but he continued his inspection of the nettle as if he had found a new species and was hoping to get a doctorate on the strength of the discovery. Jezebel snorted loudly and drifted in Henderson's direction toward the back of the corral.

Payne cleared his throat. "You saw the pedigree. His record speaks for itself."

"Too bad you weren't here yesterday," Henderson said. "He was ringing her bell like a fire alarm."

Jezebel shook her head, ringing the bell on her neck, and Henderson flinched back from the fence.

"Now that's exactly what I'm looking for," Martinez said. "If the barn is rocking, don't bother knocking, right?"

He elbowed the man in black, who moved a step or two back, and asked, "So will we see round two today?"

"Naw," Henderson said. "One round with Tiny is enough."

"Not typically," the man in black said.

Martinez looked over at the man in black as if hearing a new and compelling theory. "What are you saying, Jake?"

"What he means to say," Payne interjected before Jake could answer, "is that we've found it's best to space the sessions out."

Henderson spit into the corral and nodded. "Let the poor heifer settle a bit before he has another go at her."

Martinez nodded. "Good idea."

"Why exactly?" Jake asked. "It's not customary."

Henderson was developing a deep enmity for this Jake feller. "Well, you can see for yourself, Tiny's not your usual and customary bull. He's so enthusiastic, the old girl needs a few days to recover."

Tiny chose that moment to turn toward Henderson and snort. In a matter of half a second, Henderson put a three-foot buffer between him and the fence.

"You have the progeny report here?" Jake asked.

"Report?" Martinez turned from Jake to Payne. "You got a report?"

Payne regarded Jake with undisguised hostility and then looked at his watch. "We should be getting ready for the quail hunt. I'll track that report down for you later."

He spun on the heel of his boot and strode back to the house. Probably going to his office to create a progeny report, if Henderson read the cards right. Although that could come back to bite him on the butt.

CHAPTER TWENTY-SEVEN

With nary a cloud in sight, the afternoon Texas sun was relentless, no matter that it was only sixty-eight degrees. Various and sundry snakes sunned themselves on the rocks of their choice, the lizards choosing their sunning locations more discretely.

It was not a place where the casual observer often found a human, much less two of them climbing in and out of gullies, consulting a map, shading the display of a GPS unit from the sun to get a reading.

Zachary looked up from the map and pointed south. Josiah looked up from the GPS and pointed west. They stared each other down for several seconds, each holding his arm out in his chosen direction. Then Zachary grabbed the binoculars and scanned the landscape, despite the fact that they were still looped around Josiah's neck.

"Dang it, Zack." Josiah peeled the strap over his head and shoved Zack and the binoculars away from him.

Thus freed, Zachary searched the southern horizon for the butte that the topographical map said was a mile out there somewhere. All he saw were more gullies.

Josiah jerked the map from his hands and held it up, facing west. He consulted his GPS and rotated the map ninety degrees to the right. "It's right over there."

Zachary glanced over at him. "You got it sideways, you maroon."

"That way is north." Josiah held up the GPS for proof.

Dropping the binoculars to the ground, Zachary snatched the GPS out of Josiah's hands. Jo tackled him, and they both rolled back down to the bottom of the gully.

CHAPTER TWENTY-EIGHT

Out in the fresh afternoon air in the shade of the barn, Berf felt like he had finally taken ahold of the handle on this situation and turned it around. Chip had warmed to the plan like a Gila monster on the rimrock at noon. Chip and Zoe would be reunited before the dinner bell rang. He grabbed the pith helmet that he had found in the tack room and settled it on his head.

"No," Jake said.

"No?" Berf said in disbelief. "What do you mean, no?"

Jake slipped shotgun shells into the loops on a khaki hunting vest. "No, as in nein, nyet, non, negatori. It won't work."

"The plan is flawless." Berf emptied all the shells out of his shotgun. "You're just jealous that you didn't think of it first."

"And when she doesn't see a wound?"

Berf waved away the objection. Evidently Jake was not as attuned to the feminine mind as previously advertised. "By then the words will already be out of her mouth and they will be reunited. She will be even more relieved when she realizes he's not in danger."

Jake looked up from his preparations. "Chip bought into this?"

"Bought into what?" Chip walked up, his hand held out. "Here's the shells."

Berf took the five emasculated shells Chip offered and shoved them into the slot. Jake shook his head, picked up his shotgun, and walked away.

Chip watched him go and then turned to Berf. "What?"

"Don't pay him any mind." Berf racked a shell into the chamber and followed Jake to the ATVs in front of the barn.

Dr. Payne took the lead vehicle with JL, Billy, and the dogs. Chip, Berf, and Jake took the second ATV. Mitch got behind the wheel of the third ATV, but before Bonnie could grab shotgun, Summer plopped down in the seat, her hand on her large sun hat. Bonnie stared at Summer for a long second and then got in the back seat with Zoe.

The caravan followed a rough cattle trail a few miles to where a small pavilion had been set up with three tables, a dozen chairs, and some coolers. The hunting party debarked and refreshed themselves with lemonade. Then Dr. Payne cut the dogs loose and the hunters spread out in a ragged line, walking forward slowly.

Berf held back until the others were a dozen yards ahead and then inched forward to the left of Chip, who flinched and jerked around with the snap of every twig. Berf had not considered the risk of making a tenderfoot the centerpiece of his plan. There was nothing for it now but to press forward and hope the dogs flushed a covey pronto.

Jake ranged further to the left, evidently lacking confidence in either Berf's aim or Chip's ability to strip all the pellets from the shells.

To the right, Summer hung on Mitch's elbow, chatting incessantly. The poor guy would never get a shot off like that. Behind them, Zoe walked with her shotgun tucked under her arm and dangling over her forearm like a pro while she talked to Bonnie, who wasn't giving Zoe or the hunt much of her attention. She kept her eyes on the couple in front.

Berf allowed himself a grim smile. The next few minutes would be tricky, but it would be worth it to see the glow on the faces of lovers reunited and to taste the sweet air of freedom.

At the bustle of wings, he realized he had allowed his laser-like attention to stray from the task at hand. He heard the report of guns from his right and saw two birds go down. Could be Jake or Zoe or both. Mitch couldn't have gotten off a shot that fast with Summer latched onto him like a Leon River leech.

Fumbling to get a shot off before the birds scattered, Berf swung up his gun, pulling the trigger when it veered in Chip's general direction, but taking care to aim wide in case Chip was better at picking out stocks than pellets.

And despite Berf's doubts, the greenhorn did his part. Chip wheeled around, dropped his gun, and clutched his chest. "Agh!" He staggered a few steps and collapsed. Errol Flynn couldn't have done better.

"Chipper!" Zoe raced to his side and knelt. "Chipper, are you okay?"

She reached to pull Chip's hands away, but he moaned and rolled to break her line of sight to the wound.

Berf ran to the couple and knelt on one knee. "Chip! You walked right into my line of fire!" He turned to Zoe. "He ran right into my line of fire!" He placed a hand on Chip's arm. "Hold on, buckaroo. Can you hear me? Stay with us. If you see a bright light, stay away from it."

Mitch appeared on the other side of Chip. "Chip, let me see it."

Summer and Bonnie arrived and stood by like a Greek chorus ready to provide commentary or interpretation should the need arise.

Zoe pulled on Chip's arm. "Chip. How bad is it?"

"Zoe?" Chip said in a faraway voice. "Is that you?"

"Talk to him," Berf said. "Keep him with us."

Mitch tried to pull Chip's hands away from his chest, but Chip turned away, which put him facing Zoe again.

"Chip, you have to let me help you. Where were you hit?" She pushed aside his hands, then again with greater force as Chip covered his chest. Finally she grasped a wrist and jerked his hand aside. All that lay beneath it was a wrinkled shirt.

"You weren't hit."

Chip didn't open his eyes. "I wasn't?"

Zoe smoothed out the wrinkles. "There's not even a hole in your shirt."

"Are you sure?" Chip opened one eye and inspected his chest tentatively as if expecting to see a gaping wound.

Zoe stood, looked down at him, and then kicked him. "Now I can add coward and wimp to the list of your reprehensible qualities."

She whirled around and stormed off in the direction of the pavilion and the ATVs. Summer followed.

Mitch looked down at Chip with a frown. "What in the world is going on?"

"I could have sworn I shot him," Berf said.

Chip sat up, glaring at Zoe's departing back, then turned to Berf. "Any more bright ideas, Einstein?"

Jake walked up. "So how did it go?"

Just then, a covey of quail burst out of the brush in a cacophony of wings. Berf whirled and got three shots off right in amongst them before he remembered he was shooting blanks.

Mitch stepped over Chip and grabbed Berf's gun. He held it up to a bush and pulled the trigger. It didn't even blow the leaves off. He handed the gun back to Berf. "Nice trick, but you forgot the special effects."

"You're going about this all wrong," Bonnie said.

Berf had forgotten she was there. She studied Chip for a few moments, glanced at Mitch, and walked off in the direction of the pavilion. "Let's go."

Chip climbed to his feet and dusted off his pants. "What did that mean?"

"I'm afraid to find out," Mitch said.

"Take a number," Berf said.

Chapter Twenty-Nine

JL squinted into the late afternoon sun from the back seat as Payne pulled the ATV up to a ridge with a nice view west. He ducked behind Billy Trent's straw hat to block the sun and wondered how many more shots Trent had on his list.

He didn't give a flying burrito about movie locations, only possible locations of buried treasure, but the trip gave him an excuse to get the lay of the land. Too bad he couldn't pull out the map and the GPS and get a fix on the more likely spots.

The way he saw it, he and this Trent guy were on parallel tracks, both looking for the big payoff. They were just approaching it from different directions. Trent needed investors to pony up tens of millions of dollars, and then he had to endure weeks of sunup to sundown filming under brutal conditions, all for the slim chance that everyone would make their money back plus some.

JL, on the other hand, just had to do research in the comfort of his Alamo Heights home, spend a few hundred dollars on gear, and set his kids loose. And if you calculated the odds of a payoff, JL would probably come out ahead of Trent. He shaded his eyes and scanned the desert floor, which was crisscrossed by arroyos.

Trent looked up from his clipboard and nodded. "It has potential."

Payne leaned his arm on the steering wheel. "Now, you see, what you got here is access. Highway comes within a mile of the entrance. Dirt roads carved all through here for hunting. Get your gear to any place you want."

JL pulled out his smartphone and brought up maps with the satellite view. He had the top five coordinates set up as favorites. One of the dots appeared on the grid, a mesa just a few clicks north.

Trent pointed north. "That way looks interesting. Let's check that out."

The problem with that suggestion was they could run into Zachary and Josiah. JL swiveled to the left. "I was thinking you'd want to follow the wash south a bit. Looks like it opens up into a tank, there in that grove of cottonwoods."

Trent shook his head. "No, I like the looks of that mesa over there."

"North it is," Payne said.

JL put his phone away. It was getting late. With any luck, the boys had already checked the site and were on their way home.

CHAPTER THIRTY

On the ride back to the house, Bonnie did some figuring. From what she could see, there was more drama to be had at the Payne ranch than on daytime TV. More than on the rodeo circuit, and that was saying something.

For some reason, Zoe threw over Chip for Berf, who, if not exactly a Rhodes scholar, seemed nice enough. And in an obvious move to annoy Billy, Summer vamped on Mitch, who, bless his heart, looked like a hog stunned with a hammer.

Then Billy retaliated by lurking around Yvonne like Dracula at a blood bank.

And then Chip cooked up this crazy scheme with the shotgun to jolt Zoe to her senses. From what Bonnie could see, Chip had brought a knife to a gun fight.

Anyone could see that Zoe's domestic policy was simple: it's my way or it's global thermonuclear war.

There was only one way to deal with a bully. Chip had not yet committed to the nuclear option, but Bonnie was about to drag him into the atomic age.

She jumped off the ATV, distanced herself from the guys, and strode up from the barn to the pool. Zoe and

Summer were already settled at an umbrella table near the cabana. Yvonne reclined on a chaise lounge by the pool, reading a romance novel.

Bonnie stepped behind the bar and poured herself a cranberry juice and seltzer. She would need her wits about her for the coming storm, much of which she would precipitate herself.

Chip pushed in behind her and took inventory. "I'll have to restock from the kitchen," he announced.

Zoe looked up from her position on the patio but pointedly not in his direction.

"I'll help," Bonnie said. He had played right into her hand.

As Bonnie followed Chip up the levels, Summer intercepted Mitch with a handful of star charts and dragged him to another table. Berf dropped into a chair at a third table, looking like he'd been rode hard and put up wet, mumbling something about needing a drink.

Bonnie wished him luck. If the dominoes fell right, it might be a while before drinks were available.

Chip moved around the kitchen like a pro, collecting bottles, cans, lemons, limes, olives, maraschino cherries, and ice and loading them onto a stainless steel cart.

Bonnie drifted through the lavishly provisioned kitchen. "I hear you're a venture capital guy."

"I get around." He was obviously in a mood.

Bonnie drew a small jar of maraschino cherries from the cart, pulled one out, and twirled it in her lips. "How about a proposition?"

Chip stopped, a stalk of celery in his hand "Shoot."

Bonnie hit him with everything an investor would want to hear. "I got the land, I got the horses, I got the championships."

Chip pulled a few bottles from the cart and commenced to mixing a drink on the spot.

She smiled and continued with her laundry list. "I got a blog with two hundred thousand hits a month and an e-commerce link selling DVDs, books, supplies, everything. I got the newsletter mailing list of nine thousand girls who think they are the next Bonnie Hollingsworth and who also think I can get them there."

Chip handed her a drink. "Sounds like you got it all."

"Nope," Bonnie said, closing in for the kill. "I don't have bunkhouses, a kitchen, a clinic, a riding ring, a barn, a corral . . ."

She paused, trolling for the signs that she had hooked his venture capitalism heart. His escalated breath told her all she needed to know.

"But once I do, I'll sell out the schedule every year. And every time one of my girls wins a local race, ten more will sign up. When one wins a championship, and she will, we open a second ranch in East Texas and double the business in a year."

She moved in close to Chip, put her arm on his shoulder, and ran her fingers in his hair just like she had done with Mitch, only this time it was business, not pleasure.

"All I need is a partner." She kissed him. "With cash. Plenty of cash. And a desire to make more. Lots more."

If the world were such a place as she wished it were, she would not be driven to such extremes. But the world was what it was, and she was what she was, and she had to find out what was on that memory stick.

Chapter Thirty-One

The shadows stretched across the desert, ominously long, as the sun inched down to the horizon. On the south face of a mesa, two small figures struggled up the scree of caliche and limestone. They paused, milked the last few drops from their water bottles, and stumbled to the top.

Josiah cast a nervous glance at the proximity of the sun to the horizon and consulted the GPS for the location of the final site. But before he could get a fix on it he heard a whoop.

Up on the mesa, Zachary ran the last fifty yards to the ruins of a villa. It had been a full day, digging around in caves eroded out of the walls of arroyos by flash floods, and in disappointing cracks in ridges and what not, raking the metal detector in every direction until they had sucked the last drop of juice from the batteries, finding nothing more than the occasional rusted beer can.

But now they had hit the jackpot. If this old building didn't have a two million dollar treasure buried it in, he would eat his Timberland boots. And Jo's too.

The original limestone arch of the front door was still intact and fragments of the wall led off in both directions. He rushed in and inspected all the nooks and crannies of the ruined rooms, giving wide berth to the gushing clumps of prickly pear cactus that populated the space like sadistic furniture. He was already picturing the 1966 Cadillac Coupe deVille he would buy with his share, the one they used in *Reservoir Dogs*.

"Over here," Josiah called as he came upon a set of rotting cellar doors. He kicked a few planks aside and started down the stairs, pulling the flashlight out of his pack.

Zach arrived, blocking out the sunlight, and Josiah flipped on the flashlight. He played the beam across the room like he was in *Tomb Raider*. The beam fell on pyramids of cannon balls, teepees of rifles, belts of bullets, and crates of dynamite, but no chests brimming with gold.

They browsed through the various containers, but the only thing that glinted was the light in their eyes. Then the noise of an internal combustion engine drew them out of the ground like a sunrise enticing a worm.

Josiah shaded his eyes to squint at an ATV cresting the western slope. He walked to the edge and looked down. This was much easier to climb than the southern face. Leave it to Zach to ignore insignificant details like the spacing of the lines on the topographical map.

As the vehicle skidded to a stop in front of the villa, JL called from the back seat. "Hey, boys. How's the leaf collection coming along?"

Zachary frowned and said, "Huh?" Then Jo elbowed him. He shoved Jo away before remembering the cover story. "Yeah, right."

"It's been okay," Josiah said. "But we didn't find the *golden*-leaf loblolly."

JL shook his head, his eyes rolling up to the left, like he did sometimes. A lot of the times, actually. Josiah shook his head back at him. The whole leaf-hunting code was his idea, so why the drama?

"The what?" Payne said.

From what Josiah could see, the old man wasn't fooled by the code names. He knew something was up, but no way could he know the truth.

"Those are hard to find," JL said.

Billy jumped out of the front seat and raced up to the ruins. They were beautiful beyond his wildest dreams. "This is beautiful beyond my wildest dreams," he said.

"Think you can use it?" Payne asked.

"It's perfect for the scene where Tell Sackett and Dorset Binny bed down in the ruins after rescuing the kids from the Apaches." He held up his hands to frame the picture. "We can CGI in the stream and cliff walls in post production."

He stopped abruptly and looked at the mesa with new eyes. "Or the opening scene. Tell Sackett holed up with a slug in his leg, a Bowie knife, a Sharps rifle, and two bullets."

He stepped to the edge of the mesa and pointed toward the sunset.

"Five Comanche warriors approach on horseback, backlit by the setting sun."

He pulled out his camera to document this incredible find.

The whine of a motor caused the entire party to turn around. A four-wheeler topped the edge of the mesa and skidded to a stop next to the four-seat ATV.

Jake sprang from the seat, took in the view that Billy was pointing out, then turned and eyed the ruins. "Unexpected, wouldn't you say?" He walked under the arch and looked around.

JL didn't like the glint in Jake's eyes as he examined the ruins. Like he was looking for something, and not just a backdrop for an opening shot. Something else. Something valuable. He climbed out of the ATV. "You boys want a ride back?"

Zachary shrugged.

"Sure," Josiah said, relieved that they wouldn't be walking back in the dark. But when he dropped the metal detector in the back, Payne's eyes narrowed.

"We should be heading out," JL said loudly for Jake's benefit. "Don't want to lose the light before we get back."

But Jake didn't respond. Pretending not to hear was JL's take on it.

"Doc, I'd like to get another look at that bull," JL said. "What do you think, Jake?"

Jake looked up from his explorations. "Sure."

But when Payne drove the ATV over the edge, Jake was still back there, snooping around.

When they pulled up to the barn a half hour later, Jake was already there, walking into the barn with a drink and Berf at his side. That didn't scan in JL's mind and he didn't like it, but it would look funny if he followed them in.

Instead he glanced beyond the ridge where the sun touched the horizon. They had a few more minutes of light to check out the bull.

Henderson was out in the corral, hovering in the same zip code as Tiny, the heifer pacing back and forth desperately.

JL walked up to the rail fence. "She ready?"

"Not quite."

Hank the Jack Russell danced around the bull, barking. Tiny turned and studied him with one eye.

"He's more interested in the dog," JL said.

"Well, fact is, he's very territorial," Henderson said.

"You ever actually seen him do it?" JL asked.

Chapter Thirty-Two

Berf hadn't seen a train wreck like this since who flung the chunk. His best laid plans had *gang aft agley*. He was now reduced to sitting at a table alone without a drink, facing the prospect of life with Zoe. Yes, she was a fine girl, a flower of the old west, but a bride worthy of Orrin Sackett, which was a qualified approbation any way you looked at it.

Not that he had anything bad to say about Zoe. Out loud, anyway. But he wasn't looking to settle down right at this particular moment. Not this week. Not next week either. Or even the week after next.

He realized that this might sound strange coming from a man who had been engaged more times than he could remember, but it had never been on purpose. Even though he had been present on every occasion, he had never been sure how it had actually happened. One moment he was being his normal charming self, pleasant to one and all, the next the woman beside him was flipping through a bridal magazine.

Fortunately, in the past, the bloom had come off the rose long before a date was set, and the fixture was scratched, usually by the initiating party, or sometimes through avoidance and attrition.

Now Chip, he was the kind of guy who was ready to settle down with a girl at the drop of a hat, even two hats if you could get up a quorum.

But even if Berf had a mind to change his position on the when, there was still the who. You had to find the right one, and once you found her, nothing could stop you from going for it. Not bullets nor desperadoes nor hired killers. But she had to be the right one or it was all for nothing. And Zoe was not the right one. Not for him. He had seen that long ago.

Zoe, while easy on the eye, was hard on the psyche. There was a certain ruthlessness in her that harrowed the soul. She was an opportunist. When it came to The Code, she could talk a good game, but she would toss it aside like a soiled hanky if it ceased to serve her purpose.

Much like Chip, whose success in the world of high finance was due not only to his charming personality but also to a certain moral flexibility that Berf could never sanction. And that was why Zoe and Chip were the obvious couple, if only someone could talk sense into one of them.

The noise of a door slamming startled him from his ruminations. Chip pushed a cart from the kitchen. Bonnie had draped herself over him like a cheerleader hanging on the football captain at the homecoming dance. Chip steered the cart down the circuitous route mandated by the Americans with Disabilities Act of 2008 for public accommodations, although the Payne ranch was far from a public accommodation, and he took his time doing it.

It was as plain as pudding that Chip had come up with a scheme on his own to turn the tables on Zoe, and any fool could see it would be a disaster. This is why you left these things to the professionals.

Berf took the temperature of the couple at the next table. Mitch looked up from his horoscope session with Summer and frowned at the sight of the unwelcome conjunction of Chip and Bonnie. Berf knew just how he felt. A Chip-Bonnie alliance, while interesting for viewers of *Survivor*, was just another example of just how *agley* his plans had *gang aft*.

He glanced at Zoe, and her expression did not melt his heart. More like froze it. In fact, when you studied on it a bit, you could see how it tended much more closely to the Sherman scorched-earth policy than Berf felt appropriate for a fiancée.

Berf rushed to her table to distract her, speaking softly so as not to attract attention. "Zoe, it's time for me to speak plainly."

She was still riveted to the image of Bonnie clinging to Chip like a bull rider trying to squeeze out a measly eight seconds against the odds.

"Zoe," Berf repeated like a man who'd come to read her from the Book.

Zoe dragged her stare away from Chip. "You were saying?"

"Zoe," Berf breathed with the whole of his heart, plus some. "It's time for the painful truth. It's about Chip."

Her gaze returned to her former boyfriend. "You mean that yellow-bellied sap sucker with a head like a watermelon? That Chip?" Zoe said at a sound pressure far above Berf's comfort level.

"Yes. I mean, no. I mean . . . Zoe, I can see you still love him."

Zoe turned a dispassionate gaze on him. "You have me confused with someone else."

Berf steeled himself to the task that lay before him. It wasn't a pleasant job he had to do, but there was no one else to do it, and at times like these, a man buckled on his spurs, the California-style, deep-rowel variety, and put his back into it. "You're putting up a brave face, but I see through your heartbroken masquerade."

"Berf, don't be ridiculous."

"And what's more, Chip still loves you. In the worst way."

"That's the only way he knows."

She looked like she was ready to fight at the drop of a hat, and she'd even drop it herself, but Berf refused to turn to the left or to the right. He surged forward. "Can't you see his heart is breaking over this silly lover's quarrel?"

Berf followed Zoe's gaze to where Bonnie sat on a barstool, feeding Chip olives across the bar as he leaned on his elbows, and he nearly lost hope. Here he was bailing out the boat and there Chip was blasting new holes in the keel with a Henry rifle.

"Oh, yes," Zoe said. "I can see how devastated Chip is by this whole thing."

"Don't be fooled," Berf exclaimed. "That's just a man who has lost his only love and has nothing left to live for. Inside he is a hollow shell, wasting away." And if Chip wasn't a hollow shell yet, he would be when Berf got him alone. In fact, Berf would hollow him out personally. With a spoon.

"A girl could get the idea you don't want to marry her." Zoe turned her basilisk stare from Chip to Berf. "Are you breaking your vow uttered in the presence of witnesses?"

A lesser man might have taken this opportunity to suggest that they reset the odometer to just before midnight and replay the events with a little more knowledge of the location of Chip's room, but a lesser man wouldn't have been in this fix in the first place. When a Wiggins said it, it remained said and would not be unsaid, no matter what anyone else said.

"Oh, no, no, no. Berf's your man, stalwart and true. But I can't let my own selfish desire stand in the way of the happiness of my closest and dearest friends."

"You know what would make me happy, Berfie? If you had a little better aim with a shotgun. Now, let's talk tuxes. I'm thinking cutaway tails."

Berf couldn't think of a more desperate circumstance, not even when Tell Sackett found himself deep in Indian territory in the Sierra Madres trying to rescue Orry, who didn't even exist as it turned out, but of course he didn't know it at the time, and good thing he didn't or he never would have rescued Henry Brook and the Creed boys.

At the sound of an ATV roaring out of the heart of the sunset, Berf set aside thoughts of Tell and Orry and Henry. It was Jake on a single-seat four-wheeler.

A lot of good he was turning out to be, joy-riding across the desert while the wheels were coming off on the home front. On the other hand, when it came down to it, a man had to face a man's problems a man's way. Berf may have mistakenly charged into Zoe's room intent on delivering the ring that would forever join in holy matrimony his frat brother and his former fiancée, but once he had, however inadvertently, pledged to love, honor, and cherish her, and if he couldn't gently lead her to reason, then he could do no other than keep that vow, even to his hurt. And it did hurt.

Berf glanced at the neighboring table where, despite her best efforts, Summer had failed to keep Mitch's attention on the fully qualified horoscope she was laying out.

At that moment, fate intervened. Or at lease she tried to throw her hand in. Mitch's love for golf provided the rest.

With a roar like a mountain lion with a hangover, Mitch wrestled himself from the horoscope and took a step toward Chip and Bonnie. He pulled something from his pocket, and the next thing anyone knew he began teetering like the watchtower on *F Troop*. A golf ball skittered from under his feet and he went down in a windmilling crash of glory.

Summer left the horoscope behind and rushed to his aid, but instead of helping him, she snatched up something that had fallen from his pocket.

"What's this?"

The warm light of the late afternoon glowed on something about the size of a Bic lighter.

Bonnie was the first to react. She launched off the barstool like a bronco blasting out of the gate, and in much less than eight seconds had snatched the object from Summer's hand.

Zoe was halfway to the locus of contention before Berf realized she was no longer seated next to him. "That's mine, is what it is," she said, reaching for the object.

Bonnie jerked her hand back and slid the thing into the pocket of her jeans, which were so tight that Berf was surprised it went in without ripping the seams. "I need this one. I'll buy you a new one."

Zoe's expression was not what a guy likes to see on the face of his fiancée, or even an ex-fiancée. It had much too much of Jack Nicholson in that movie right before he yelled, "Truth? You can't handle the truth!"

The three women stood in a circle on the middle level of the patio, halfway between the house and the pool, glaring at each other with such intensity that Berf began to suspect that the gewgaw in Bonnie's pocket was not a cigarette lighter.

Chip, Mitch, and Berf remained motionless. The air seemed to thicken with the surge of emotion swirling out from the vortex of the three women, like a spell pulsing out from the three weird sisters in Macbeth.

In this miasma of fury, everything seemed to slow down to the pace of a dream. Zoe reached out toward Bonnie, whether to attack or recover the mysterious object, Berf couldn't tell, but he was certain it wouldn't end well. He tried to intervene, but it was like running underwater.

Then a sound shattered the silence. The sound of someone clearing his throat. Jake strolled from the barn toward the women.

"You know, I've been giving the matter of the Christmas gala some thought."

This bit of conversational judo threw everyone off balance. Zoe froze, her hand hanging halfway between her and Bonnie.

Jake closed the distance. "I understand that settling on a theme has posed some difficulty. You simply must catch the current exhibit at the Browning Museum. Caspar Blaine."

Jake stepped into the circle of the women. "Blaine has synthesized Art Deco and Western styles. Kind of Deskey meets Remington. He calls it West Deco." He took Zoe's outstretched hand. "Vera Cliff is working on a fashion spinoff. Very trendy. Bleeding edge, you might say."

Zoe's head tilted to one side like the Victrola dog. "Vera? Really?"

"She told me about it when I was doing her hair Thursday. Strictly confidential. You girls can keep a secret?"

"Oh, of course," Zoe said. She turned to Summer, who nodded.

"Built for size four, no doubt," Bonnie said.

Jake shook his head. "She's keeping it flexible to accommodate what you might call the expanding American demographic." He turned back to Zoe. "Vera's looking for a trial venue, something off the radar before she has the Dallas debut in March."

"Berfie, honey, fetch me the laptop," Zoe said, not breaking eye contact with Jake.

The spell broken, Berf dashed into the library and grabbed the laptop. When he returned, the three women were seated at a table, the astrological charts pushed aside. He delivered the laptop and Zoe dismissed him with the wave of a hand.

Jake held up a glass. "Chip. How about a Manhattan?"

The guys convened at the cabana bar.

Berf dropped onto a stool and leaned across the bar where Chip marshaled his resources. "Chip, what do you think you're doing with Bonnie?"

"It's all part of my plan," Chip said as he flung a cocktail shaker around with abandon. "Give Zoe a taste of her own medicine."

Mitch leaned across the bar in a more menacing manner. "It's a good thing for you that I'm a doctor, 'cause you're going to need one once I'm through with you."

Berf took the first drink that came up, not caring what it was as long as it was strong. "Jake, I don't know what just happened, but good work out there. Now you have to step up to the plate and find something to bring Zoe and Chip to their respective senses, such as they may be."

He slammed the empty glass on the bar. "I can't keep this up much longer. My nerves are shot. It's enough to make the pope lose his religion."

Chapter Thirty-Three

Before the echo of Berf's words died out, Jake dragged him off the stool and out toward the barn. As they approached it, another ATV pulled up. Dr. Payne was at the wheel, Billy riding shotgun. JL was crammed in back with his two boys.

Berf didn't care for the way JL peered at them, but before he could register his objection, JL jumped out and went to a pen where Henderson was annoying a gigantic bull. His boys wrestled something that looked like a mutant hockey stick out of the back of the ATV.

There was something distinctly not right about that family, but out in the West you let other folks do as they saw fit as long as it didn't spook the horses.

Instead Berf addressed the situation foremost in his mind. "Jake, in these here parts it's considered bad manners to separate a man from his drink."

"This way." Jake slipped into the barn. He led Berf past the stalls and over the threshold into what was evidently Henderson's sanctum sanctorum.

They came to rest in front of a cage filled with rats. To the right, a casket-sized terrarium contained the most obscenely large python Berf had ever seen.

"This is the answer," Jake said.

Berf had a sinking feeling. After years of operating at peak speed, the finely tuned machine of Jake's mind had finally thrown a rod. "The snake? Or the rats?"

"The wingless bats that will ultimately reunite Chip and Zoe."

As Berf had learned from years on the trail he liked to call life, the best policy was to face these things head on. It was no mercy to pussyfoot around the bush. He set a warm hand on Jake's shoulder.

"Mi amigo, there comes a time when a man has to pull up his socks and face the facts as they lay. I'm not going to put lipstick on the lily. I'm just going to lay out the unvarnished truth.

"The stress of the divorce has unhinged your legendary skills. You have gone off the rails and are grasping at straws. It might not be too early to solicit recommendations for reputable rest homes with tenderhearted orderlies. Even Doc Holliday had to submit to the nurses at the end. But fear not. In this and every other regard, I am still your huckleberry."

"Are you through?" Jake asked with more than trace amounts of snip.

"I could go on, but I think you have the gist of it. You were but a brief blazing light in the night sky, a shooting star that has burnt out, a mere shadow of the former giant, a—"

"So you're through."

"I'm through."

"You remember how Chip and Zoe met."

"Of course. Congress Avenue bridge. The Bat Festival."

To Berf's increased alarm, Jake broke out singing. "'I don't like spiders and snakes. And that ain't what it takes to love me.'"

Then the scales fell from Berf's eyes. For the first time in nearly twenty-four hours, he saw the hint of a sliver of sunshine breaking through the ominous cloud bank that had followed him like he was Joe Btsplk for the past twenty-four hours.

"You hide in that pile of hay near the door with the rat cage on a hair trigger," Jake said. "I tell Chip you want to speak with him in the barn. Once he's gone, I tell Zoe the same thing. They meet here, as if by chance. At the psychological moment, you release the rats."

Berf almost busted loose and cut a rug right there on the spot. "And they work their voodoo that they do so well. Returned psychologically to the moment of their first love, Zoe freaks and jumps into Chip's arms. And as he is wont to do, Chip does the manly thing."

"And Chip, reunited with Zoe, spurns Bonnie like a rabid dog, leaving her free to return to Mitch."

"And, more importantly, leaving Berf free to return to the drifter's life."

Berf flexed his flanges, infused with the confidence that came upon a man when he had a well-ordered scheme by the short ones, and turned to the rats. However, something about the way their eyes gleamed redly with a subcutaneous malice set him off his feed. He took stock of the alternatives. Every man has his strong suit, and Berf saw himself as more suited to the role of Mercury in this scenario.

"And so how about you hide with the rats and I deliver the messages?"

Jake shook his head. "Talk sense. When you tell Zoe I want to see her in the barn, she is skeptical. What possible need would I have of a word with Zoe in a barn? On the other hand, she is used to illogical requests from you and won't question it."

Berf shook his head sadly. "Point taken. Under protest, for the record."

"Duly noted. For the record." Jake left Berf to tackle the rats.

Approaching the cage obliquely to avoid their eyes, Berf wrenched it from its location. It was heavier than he expected and he staggered back, slamming against the terrarium. He gave the snake a quick glance, but it didn't seem to resent the intrusion. He bowed a quick apology to the creature, crossed to the hay bales, and burrowed deep within them, the cage at his side.

He experienced a brief twinge of guilt for doubting Jake's powers but quickly shook it off. The man had been through a rough divorce and a few subsequent hair-raising experiences, showdowns that would have turned a mere mortal's brain to mush. That his hair hadn't turned snow white was in itself a minor miracle.

Something touched his ear and he flinched, emitting a squeak like a chew toy. He glanced around to make sure no one had detected his presence and then looked over his shoulder. A bit of straw sticking out from a bale had tickled him. He pulled it out, stuck it in his mouth, and resumed his vigil, keeping the door in view through a crack between two bales.

The rats rustled around in the cage, agitated and frisky. The sound of their little claws scratching on the newspaper on the bottom of the cage made him squirm behind the bale. Ever since hearing about the bubonic plague in elementary school, he'd had a fear of rats. A healthy fear, in his opinion. They were, after all, a major vector of epidemics.

If he had his way, he would just up and pour the whole mess of them into the python cage right now and let them look to their own concerns, but he had to sit tight and stick with the plan, like Tell Sackett waiting for Bigelow and his boys to make their move for the gold when the thing he wanted most was to get Ange Kelly off that mountain before the blizzard hit.

Berf released a sigh, one of the large economy size, and poked his head up to make sure nobody had come in without him noticing. Surely Chip or Zoe should be here by now. Or, depending on the order of their summons, Zoe or Chip. One of them at any rate. Or both. What was Jake doing, stopping off for a round with the guys?

Berf pulled his phone out to check the time. Just coming on seven. They'd be ringing the dinner bell any second. He slid the phone back in his pocket when it chimed to signal a text message and he pulled it back out. First he put it on vibrate. No good it going off in the middle of the festivities.

The text was from Jake. It contained one word: *Incoming.*

Berf pocketed the phone and crouched in readiness, his hand poised above the latch of the rat cage door like a gunslinger's hand hovering over his pearl-handled revolver.

The first to enter was Hank the Jack Russell. If Berf was a cussing man, he would have said a few choice ones right then. The way Berf saw it, the barn had at least one too many Hanks, and somebody need to toss a loop around the hound and bunch him up with the rest of the roundup. Somewhere far from here. He held his breath, hoping Hank would find something to investigate in the next county.

Then suddenly Chip loomed in the doorway and Berf flinched, hitting the cage door. He glanced down to make sure it was still closed. A premature rat-ulation would be a disaster. It must be at the psychological moment or not at all. He glanced up between the bales.

The first thing he saw was Hank the Jack Russell standing pert and alert, focused on Berf's bales. Another time when a cuss word would come in handy, but Berf had no time to build his vocabulary. He leaned over to see the door.

Chip stepped inside and scanned the apparently empty room. "Berf? You there?"

Berf tracked him through the gap between the bales with a slow lean to the left as Chip walked deeper into the room.

A voice from the door froze Chip in his tracks and caused Berf to ratchet back to the right to fix his sites on the door again.

Zoe stood in the doorway, staring at Chip like he was a gray hair that needed plucking. "Oh. What are you doing here?"

"Me? Why are you here?"

Berf veered to the left to catch sight of Chip, who frowned at Zoe. At least at first, but as a silence fell between them, his frown faded, replaced with an expression that could almost be called tenderness. Berf angled back to the right like a praying mantis to see how Zoe took this.

She seemed to be on the verge of saying something but instead started fiddling with the obscenely large diamond Berf had delivered the night before, sliding it on and off her finger.

"Well," Chip said at the same time that Zoe said, "Umm."

They both stopped and waited for the other to finish. But someone else beat them to it. In all the excitement of the two young lovers on the brink of reuniting without the benefit of providential intervention, Berf had lost track of Hank the Jack Russell. He learned the error of his ways when the dog jumped up on the bales and began barking at Berf.

Berf rocked back, knocking over the cage. The door sprang open and the vermin scurried out like water from an overturned bucket. Berf scuttered back, attempting to shush the dog when something tickled his ear. He reached back to brush aside the straw, but it was no straw.

Instead, something long and cold and slick eased past his head, giving his cheek a passing lick as it homed in on Hank the Jack Russell. The python!

Chapter Thirty-Four

Berf exploded out of the pyramid of hay like he'd been sitting on a crate of dynamite in a gold mine, screeching like the whistle on a steam express train passing through a ghost town. The python hugged his shoulders like a boa on a dancehall girl. The rats bubbled through the breach.

Zoe's scream joined Berf's, and she dropped the ring. Hank the Jack Russell promptly snatched it up and followed Berf and the rats out of the barn.

But no matter how hard Berf ran, he couldn't escape the snake, which had begun to coil around his upper body. He was brought up short by running into a rail fence, and then his instincts took over. The convulsive, undulating dance finally disentangled the snake from his twitching body.

Berf had never been the squeamish type. Spiders and snakes didn't overly concern him as a rule. He was content to admire them from afar and give them space to live life as their natures demanded. But when they decided to wind their way up his body like he was some kind of reptilian barber pole, well, let's just say that there were some things up with which he would not put. Specifically, in order from left to right, overly friendly snakes.

He smoothed out the remaining spasms from his frame as he watched the snake slither away, its scales glistening in the light of the rising full moon.

Zoe raced up and pointed past the fence into the pasture. "The ring! Hank has the ring!"

Chip arrived next. "What was that?"

"The ring!" Zoe danced around impatiently and pointed at Hank the Jack Russell, who was running around the large oak in the middle of the pasture.

"Right," Berf said. When it came down to brass tacks, a man did whatever it took to get the coon. He vaulted over the fence.

"Hey," Chip yelled. "That's Tiny's pasture."

Berf wasn't worried about a gamboling calf. That ring cost a hundred grand if it cost a quarter. He was halfway to the oak when Chip tackled him and tried to drag him back to the fence.

It seemed that the stress had finally unhinged Chip and he was chasing anything that moved. Berf shoved a foot between Chip's ankles and he went down. Berf rolled to his knees and climbed to his feet, but before he could take a step, Chip was up and on him like a junkyard dog.

Chip grabbed Berf's shoulders and Berf grabbed Chip's arms, each trying to force the other in the opposite direction in a weird slow-motion dance.

Then Zoe yelled, "Look out!"

Berf looked over his shoulder. Zoe pointed to the opposite corner of the pasture. Berf turned and looked over Chip's shoulder. A large blob of darkness separated from the shadow of the oak, moving like a runaway locomotive.

The details were hard to work out in the black-on-black scene, but in the next second the noise reached him. The thundering of hooves. By then the steamrolling shadow resolved into two-thousand homicidal pounds of underdone steak.

Berf's jaw bounced off his chest and Chip turned to see what he was staring at. Then they pushed apart from each other, diving north and south as the enraged bull passed between them with only centimeters to spare.

But the creature wasn't content to provide the two of them with ample fodder for decades of nightmares. When it got to the fence, it whirled around, tearing great divots out of the turf, and assayed to correct the slight error of failing to impale either of them on the first go around.

From the corner of his eye, Berf noticed Zoe standing just outside the fence, her fingers over her eyes. Then she peeked between them, saw Tiny peel out toward them, and ran toward the house screaming for help.

That was all Berf had time to take in before he was once again in the spotlight, swerving and cavorting like a matador at the Saint Vitus ball. If he could have scared up an audience, they would be throwing roses and awarding him both ears and the tail.

After what had to have been a few years of such acrobatics, Berf found himself a dozen yards from the oak with the bull once again charging. He sprinted to the tree and ran halfway up the trunk to the first branch, which he caught with both hands, and swung up on it.

Chip was right behind him. He got one hand on the branch. Berf grabbed the other hand and hauled him up into the tree. They settled on two different branches, leaning against the trunk and breathing like a blacksmith's bellows.

Below, Tiny stood twenty feet away and snorted and pawed the ground. Hank the Jack Russell ran frantic figure eights between his legs.

Chip caught his breath first. "I guess that was your bright idea."

Berf didn't have the breath to set him right. He cut to the nub of the thing. "Desperate times call for desperate measures. You left us no choice."

"What if Zoe doesn't come to her senses?"

"When you gave her a tender look instead of a frown, she came within a frog's hair of caving. You're just one short apology away from marital bliss."

"And setting myself up for a lifetime of taking the blame for everything. No, thanks."

Berf shrugged. "Then it's ninety-nine to life for Berf."

"But you don't love her."

"I do, but like a sister. Not like a wife."

"Then tell her, and she'll give up this ridiculous game!" Chip's exasperated gestures almost cost him his balance. He grabbed the branch for support and settled back against the trunk.

"I will not trifle with a woman's affection." Berf turned a few degrees toward Chip to hammer home his point. "It's The Code."

"You and your stupid code."

"It's not *my* code. It's *The* Code."

"Come on, Berf. Haven't you outgrown that ridiculous romantic drivel?"

Berf was horrified to hear his friend speak such words unbecoming a gentleman. He turned the rest of the way, hanging both legs off the branch so he could face Chip. "Outgrow honor?"

"Welcome to the twenty-first century."

That was the problem with this generation. No grounding, no bottom to them. Just a hollow shell all the way down. "Stocks may rise and fall. Skirts may rise and fall. The globe may warm or cool. But The Code remains. And Berford Oswald Wiggins will always do the Right Thing."

"No matter how stupid it might be?"

"As a great philosopher once said, 'Stupid is as stupid does.'"

"Exactly," Chip said.

Berf opened his mouth to reply when he was arrested by a strange sight. Jake on horseback leading a heifer by a halter.

"Permission to come aboard," he called from the gate.

"You'll have to ask Tiny," Berf said.

Jake leaned down, opened the gate, and led the heifer in. He proceeded to the tree and handed up a metal detector. "You should be able to find the ring with this."

Then he led the heifer between Tiny and the tree. The bull quit shaking his horns at the interlopers in the branches and turned a wondering eye at the heifer. With a snort he changed direction and followed Jake, who directed the horse away from the tree and toward the barn.

Berf looked beyond Jake to the house, where the entire party spilled out of the door, racing down to the pasture to rescue Berf and Chip. Chip jumped down from his branch. Berf handed him the metal detector and joined him.

They wandered through the pasture and wanded the grass until the detector beeped.

Berf knelt down. Something glinted in the dark. "Hey, you're in my light."

Chip stepped aside, pulled out his phone, and brought up the flashlight app. Right at his feet the diamond ring rested atop a large cow pie. "Thank you, Hank."

With great care, Berf plucked the ring from its ignoble setting. He stood, cleaned it off as best he could with his shirttail, and handed it to Chip. "Here you go."

Chip turned it over, watching the facets glisten in the moonlight, and then held it out to Berf. "It's not mine anymore."

Berf reluctantly took it back. He had braved a plague of rats, a demonic serpent, and a minotaur, only to end up exactly where he had started.

They walked in silence to the crowd by the gate, but if they had expected a hero's welcome, they would have to learn to live with disappointment. Instead the entire group watched, with a mixture of expressions and emotions, the unlikely, raucous, and somewhat unsightly paring of Tiny and the heifer.

Berf stepped through the gate, feeling invisible as conversations erupted around him.

JL slapped Dr. Payne on the back. "Now that's what I'm talking about, Payne."

Yvonne leaned over to Billy, but Berf caught her not-so-subtle whisper. "Talking. It's what he's best at."

Payne walked over to Henderson, who stood back from the crowd. "What did you do to him?"

"Nothing," Henderson said.

"Okay," JL said, turning to Payne, but discovered he was talking to air. He searched the crowd until he located Payne. "Okay, you got yourself a deal."

Payne watched Tiny and the heifer for a while, although Berf didn't know how he could stand it. He'd turned his back on the whole indelicate business as soon as he'd stepped through the gate.

"You can sleep on it if you like," Payne said without taking his eyes off the phenomenon.

"Oh, no, Payne. We had a deal. A gentleman's agreement. I expect you to honor it."

Berf threaded through the crowd until he found Zoe. He held the ring out to her.

"Oh, Berfie! You were so brave!" She slipped it on her finger. Then, before he could stop her, Zoe wrapped her arms around his neck and kissed him square on the mouth.

Berf looked past Zoe's hair to see Chip standing a few feet away, watching. Then Bonnie slipped up next to Chip and slid her arm around his neck. "Hey, partner, let's go find a dark corner and talk about mergers."

Chip pointedly removed her arm and dropped it. "I don't mix business and pleasure. Call my office next week and make an appointment."

He stalked off toward the house. Bonnie watched him for a few seconds, then went off after him.

Berf realized Zoe was still kissing him. He pulled back a little, and she transitioned into a tight hug, the kind that threatens circulation to vital extremities.

A few feet away, Summer stood talking intently to Mitch, but Mitch's eyes were on Bonnie as she followed Chip into the house. He turned and walked off without a word to Summer.

Berf tried to extricate himself from Zoe's embrace, but she grabbed his shoulders, leaned back, and studied him. "Maybe I was wrong about you all along."

"Oh, no, no, no. You weren't."

Berf was not a man given to melancholic reflection. He took life as it came, with the bark on, and set to. But Zoe's expression broke up his stoic resolve like quartz under a miner's sledgehammer and sent despair leaking down through the cracks into his core.

It wasn't the ardent, determined expression she usually directed toward him, like a wrangler approaching a wild mustang. It wasn't the flouncy, flippant expression she used to railroad him into whatever she had decided was best for him.

It was an expression both unexpected and terrifying. The look of a young girl who has just been handed a puppy of her own. A look of sincere affection and joy. He hadn't seen that expression since back in college, the first time they got engaged. It was as certain as the dawn and as final as a firing squad. No scheme could save him now.

Then she twirled around as if she hadn't just driven a stake through his soul, rushed over to Summer, and began chattering like a schoolgirl.

A horse shuffled to a stop in front of Berf, blocking the view of his fiancée. Jake dismounted.

Berf accosted him. "You have a lot of explaining to do."

"About?"

"Pretty much everything."

"My folks didn't get along too well. I spent the summers on my uncle's ranch in Montana. I picked up a lot."

"I'll say."

Jake took the reins, and they walked the horse back to the barn. Henderson scrambled up to them as Jake pulled off the saddle.

"Lolita! Have you seen Lolita?"

"Who?" Berf said.

"Lolita. My python."

Berf looked at Jake. "Lolita?"

Jake shrugged and turned to Henderson. "If she gets ahold of any of those rats, she's probably not going to get far. I'd start looking in tight, confined spaces around and near the barn."

CHAPTER THIRTY-FIVE

Like tinhorn outlaws who heard that the marshal is coming to town, the inmates of the Payne ranch quickly gathered their effects and slipped away into the sea of the night.

Bonnie was the first one out of the gate. She had nothing to pack, and in a dash she had Barnabas saddled and headed down the road. In the dark, it was best to stick to the roads, or at least to the right-of-way along the road.

She wasn't sure of how she'd left it with Chip. Was he in or out? One thing was for sure, they wouldn't be dating and that suited her right down to the ground. Maybe he would back her, or maybe he wouldn't, but the top priority was finding out what was on that memory stick.

Mitch took perhaps thirty seconds to stuff his clothes in his backpack and fire up the Triumph. About a mile south of the gate he passed Bonnie riding her horse on the side of the road in a slow walk. He didn't acknowledge her existence, other than to throttle up the bike and disappear over the hill.

He couldn't figure it out. He had felt something, something real, and he was pretty sure she had felt it too. And then Zoe plays her little Cold War games and Bonnie goes and moves her missiles into Cuba and escalates things to the brink of open war.

He had recovered the memory stick to defuse the standoff. And he had thought that when Bonnie had it in her hand, she would abandon the whole charade with Chip. After all, it was just a part of the game, right? Okay, so instead of thanking him, she had joined Zoe and Summer in planning the party. He got that. He hadn't made it to where he was by being impatient. He could bide his time. And everybody got sidetracked with the whole bull thing. But after, instead of cozying up to Mitch, she had flung herself all over Chip like it was for real.

Well, okay. Fine, if that's the way she wanted it. It's not like Mitch came to the ranch looking for a soul mate. It was supposed to be nothing more than a relaxing weekend, and the way things stood now, he'd be a lot more relaxed three hundred miles south.

Meanwhile, back at the ranch, Summer packed their stuff while Billy went to prep the plane. It had been a strange weekend, not at all what she had expected, but that was to be expected around Zoe.

As she dragged the suitcases across the patio, she thought about the last twenty-four hours and she wasn't particularly proud. Sure, Billy needed to be taken down a notch, and the cowgirl too, but she hadn't really thought through the collateral damage. Mitch was a good kid and he didn't deserve to be treated like a pawn in their little power struggle. She looked around, hoping for a chance to apologize, but didn't see him.

At the hangar, she handed the bags over to Billy. He stowed them, went through the pre-flight check, and took off without a word. It was going to be a long flight.

Out by the barn, Yvonne couldn't believe how long it was taking to get that stupid bull into the trailer. She sat in the car, ready to get out of this crazy ranch and back to her house in San Antonio, but of course they couldn't do that, could they? They would have to take the bull to their ranch in Bulverde and get him settled into the barn. And by then it would be midnight, if they were lucky. Probably more like two in the morning, and they'd have to sleep at the ranch. Wonderful.

She turned around in the seat. "So, boys, how'd your day go?"

Zach looked at Jo, Jo looked at Zach, and they both shrugged.

"Come on, now, don't be like that. You spent the whole day out in the wilderness, got a sunburn and everything. What did you see?"

They did the looking thing again and then spilled it. The whole story. Pancho Villa's treasure, the map, the GPS, the ruins, the munitions, Zach describing everything like it was a movie he was filming, Jo like he was playing some video game.

And the more they said, the madder she got.

When JL finally got in the SUV, she let him have it with both barrels before they were even off the property.

"What kind of father are you, roping my innocent children into your scheme to swindle that poor old man?"

JL stared at her for so long, she thought he would run off the road. "Right. What about you playing the wayward woman straight out of Proverbs with that movie guy?"

"Lord help them," Yvonne declared. "Their poor mother disgraced by the shame of extramarital Scrabble."

Out on Ranch Road 337, Berf looked out the passenger window of the Volvo and into the night. Could it have been a mere twenty-four hours ago that he had stared out this same window at the lights of Uvalde, wondering what strange chance event awaited to change his future?

Well, now he knew.

The problem with that whole frying pan versus fire scenario was that when you were in the frying pan, you didn't get full disclosure about the alligators in the river below the cliff. You had to call it like you saw it, but you never could see the other it, could you? The it you were jumping into.

It wasn't like Berf was opposed to the idea of marriage. In principle, at least. Heck, he'd been engaged a dozen times. Maybe more. But when the ideal came down to the actual, it was often less than ideal. And he wasn't the only one to think so. The engagements had been broken off for him, sometimes even before the new had worn off and the trail had begun to beckon.

He thought about that expression, the look Zoe had bestowed upon him after the bout with the bull. What was it she had said?

Maybe I was wrong about you all along.

It had freeze-dried his soul at the moment, but now he wondered if maybe he had failed to keep an open mind about the whole thing. Perhaps in his case, four times was a charm. Could it be that a relationship that had followed the trajectory of the yoyo over the last ten years had somehow matured into the real thing? Some kind of *When Harry Met Sally* thing sans the Katz deli scene? Perhaps Zoe thought he had changed because in reality she had changed, and he just hadn't bothered to look closely enough to detect it.

Berf turned to Jake, whose face was illuminated by the dash lights like a B horror flick. "You think Logan Sackett might have been right after all?"

He responded with a flicker of the eyebrow, which was plenty for Jake.

"You remember what he said about Em Talon when he was riding from the MT ranch to Brown's Hole."

Jake didn't respond, but Hank the Jack Russell nuzzled Berf's hand. Berf scratched him behind the ears and quoted Logan.

"There's nothing better than two, a man and a woman, who walk together. When they walk right together, there's no way too long, no night too dark."

Jake gave a grudging, but qualified, nod. It was uncommon what Jake could say without opening his mouth.

"You think Zoe could be that woman?" Berf asked.

Jake's silence said twice as much as the nod had. But Berf knew what he was thinking. There was a time when Jake had found that woman, had sailed off into the sunset with her. But something had *gang agley* even then. A year later, he had showed up in Austin, sunburned and emaciated.

Berf hadn't asked any questions. He had just gone out on the deck, fired up the chimenea, cracked open a bottle of reserva tequila, and broke out the Cubans.

Before the night was over, Berf had offered to set Jake up in a high-end hair salon as a silent partner. It was the least Berf could do, considering that the whole debacle had been his fault, from soup to nuts. With the best intentions, of course. Another case of lack of full disclosure about the fire part of the equation.

Even now Berf had no idea what had happened with Jake off in the south seas. It could be something as random as the thing with Tell Sackett and Ange Kerry up on the Mogollon Rim. He never asked, and Jake never volunteered the information.

Berf understood that. On that same trip, he had found the one, the woman Logan had talked about. And he had never spoken about that to anyone either. There were some things that just couldn't stand up under the weight of a conversation.

Thinking back on that time, that woman, Berf realized Jake was right. Zoe couldn't be that woman for him any more than China could have been that woman for Jake.

He should call Zoe right now and call it off, but he couldn't push the image out of his mind. The look on her face when he gave her the ring he had recovered from the cow patty.

In that moment, she had taken a step. Something in her had changed, had moved beyond the spiteful game to teach Chip a lesson. And Berf could not, would not, dash her dreams to save himself.

After all, he had a Code.

CHAPTER THIRTY-SIX

Bonnie watched Mitch's taillight disappear over the hill with the throaty rumble of his bike, taking her heart with it. Life wasn't fair, but she knew better than to expect it might be. You didn't win six trophies by waiting for life to hand them to you. You decided what you wanted and you went for it.

Surely Mitch could see that. He was a doctor, after all, a man of science and ambition. But something told her that he wouldn't see it that way.

For the first time, she wondered if maybe she had made the wrong choice when she followed Chip into the kitchen. Up to now in her career, the choices had been easy. The rodeo circuit was cut and dried. Everybody was there to push that career, take it to the next level, hit the sweet spot that would secure the endorsement deals and set them up to ride the wave as far as they could take it. Some, like Bonnie, had a vision for a sustainable end game. The rest were just cannon fodder.

But Mitch was a gift horse of a different color. There was a career, and then there was a life. The cowboys she had encountered on the circuit were all about the former but had no clue about the latter. Mitch was all about the latter.

Bonnie had spent her life focused on her career and that was what she had to focus on now, right? There would be time enough for a personal life once she had her franchise established.

As she rode into the barn and dismounted, she realized with a shock that, when it came down to it, she was like the rodeo cowboys, focused on the brass ring. Mitch deserved better, someone who would take the time to appreciate him instead of always thinking of the angle. But if not now, then when? Would she ever be satisfied? Ever call time and settle down?

She shoved those troublesome thoughts aside, rubbed Barnabas down, and went straight to her laptop.

The memory stick had six PDF files on it, various forms and reports and affidavits. It took her an hour to read through them all carefully, but the name Zaqar didn't appear anywhere, just some veterinarian named Dr. Peter Stirling. She did a word search on every document, but Zaqar was blissfully absent.

Then she googled Peter Stirling and discovered he was the companion of Francis the talking mule in the movies from the Fifties. Bonnie pulled the memory stick out and tossed it aside. It was about as threatening as a Labrador puppy.

Zoe evidently had farmed out the creation of the documents to some geek with a sense of humor and hadn't bothered to check them herself. Once the name of her authority was connected to the movies, she would be laughed out of court.

Bonnie chuckled quietly to herself as she closed the laptop, but it was the hollow croak of a general who has won a battle but lost the war. To extinguish this threat she had used Mitch like a pawn, moving him around the board at will and sacrificing him when he had lost his usefulness.

She wandered through the house toward the kitchen, poured herself a French pinot noir, and headed back to the bedroom. As she passed the laundry room, a splash of salmon cloth in the hamper caught her eye. She pulled it out. "Property of Santa Anita Children's Clinic" was stenciled across the front. She pressed it to her face and inhaled.

It was like picking out the nuances in the flavor profile of a fine pinot noir. First the musky man-smell of working a twelve hour shift and then riding a bike in the sun for five hours, second the citrusy notes from the spilled cocktails. But underneath she picked up hints of hospital antiseptics and maybe a trace of cigar.

And because of her actions in the last twenty-four hours, with special focus on the last few, she was reduced to sniffing his dirty laundry and chasing it with a glass of wine when right now she could be melting into the embrace of those beefy arms that looked more like they belonged to a dock worker than a pediatrician.

She tried to tell herself she had no choice, that the threat to her career justified the means, but right now in this cold, dark, empty ranch house, it sounded false, even to her.

Perhaps Zoe had won after all. But anybody who knew Bonnie knew she wouldn't go down without a fight.

CHAPTER THIRTY-SEVEN

Monday morning Berf came down to breakfast at the crack of noon. Two brisket tacos and a steaming vat of coffee awaited him on the breakfast nook table.

Of course Jake was to blame for this happy discovery, and it occurred to him that a woman wouldn't see things the same way somehow. In the new regime, there would be an expectation of charming conversation over eggs, toast, bacon, and coffee at some ungodly hour, or worse yet, oatmeal and prunes.

Then, with a quiver, Berf realized that a bristly, mis-shapen troll sat opposite him at the table. The smell of stale cigarettes mingled with the aroma of the tacos. He glanced in alarm at Jake, who stood with his back to them, laboring over the butcher-block island at some kind of baking project.

Berf looked back to the troll and the features suddenly resolved into a familiar face. "Tom, nice of you to join us for breakfast."

The cabbie finished off his coffee and stood. "Already had mine. Just bringing back your ride, mate."

He snatched a set of keys from his shirt pocket and held them out to Berf.

"Right." Berf took the keys and glanced out the bay window. His silver 1966 Jaguar XKE sat in the driveway, shining like a freshly caught trout. Had it been only three days since he'd sent Tom off in search of it?

A cab sat at the curb, a skinny guy with blonde dreads, leaning against the front fender smoking a cigarette. "Any trouble tracking it down?"

"Nah." Tom leaned in, the delicate bouquet of stale tobacco and halitosis drifting across the table. "Trade secret. You're looking for a car left behind in the wee hours, go trolling the car parks of nightspots just after sunrise. Won't be but two or three cars in the lot and Robert's your father's brother."

"I'll file that between *How to Start a Campfire in the Rain* and *Removing Bloodstains from a Tuxedo*."

"Found it at Justine's."

"Of course," Berf said.

He waited. Tom waited. Jake continued to ignore them as he labored away.

"Sure you don't want a taco?" Berf asked.

"No, mate, I'll just be taking my pay and getting on my way."

"Ah," Berf cried, the light suddenly coming on. "I'll just fetch the needful."

He dashed upstairs, extracted a Benjamin from his wallet, and returned. Tom took the bill, tipped an imaginary hat, and departed.

Berf took a seat, stuffed a napkin in the collar of his pajamas, and set to like an infantryman. The cilantro and jalapeño cut through the smoky brisket and jack cheese, and the grilled onions formed the perfect fifth leg of this culinary stool. Life was good, and so was the coffee.

"Cracking tacos, Gromit," Berf said when he came up for air to refill his coffee.

"Torchy's," Jake said over his shoulder as he beat a thick crust into submission.

"What gives with the Martha Stewart impression?"

Jake wiped his forehead with the back of his hand, leaving a streak of flour behind. "Major Grey's mango chutney cobbler."

"Derivation?"

"Dreams induced by leftover Indian takeout."

"That would do it." Berf reached for the second taco. "Aren't you supposed to be at the shop?"

"Had a break between appointments." Jake gestured with a rolling pin at a magazine on the table. "Zoe left that for you."

Berf pulled it closer. *Southern Weddings*. Perfect. "When?"

"Couple of hours ago. Said she'd be by later to pick you up."

Berf shot to his feet, the taco dropping from his trembling fingers. He swiveled around and peered out the bay window. "Here? Today?"

He darted toward the swinging door.

"She's your fiancée," Jake said. "You can't run and hide every time she shows up."

Berf stopped with his hand on the door. "I don't see why not. It worked last time."

"You're getting married in a month. Might as well get used to it. Sit down and finish your breakfast."

In the silent kitchen, the seconds ticked like a sledge-hammer slamming a spike into his coffin. Berf let the door swing back into place and returned slowly to the table. He took a bite, but it might as well have been an assembly-line Taco Bell abomination for all he noticed.

Zoe would no doubt want to talk over breakfast. Not to mention she'd probably want to have it at some ungodly hour when there was no oxygen in the universe, like six a.m. He poured more coffee and took a gulp, barely noticing as it scalded its way down the first stages of his alimentary canal and sloshed around with the untasted taco.

He flipped open the magazine to a page marked with a sticky note reading, "Berfie, honey, this tux is so you!" He flicked the note away and looked at the smiling model in a cutaway tux with tails. It would be perfect if it were black, not turquoise.

If he was going to have a wedding, surely he would get to pick his own tux. Right? He opened his mouth to pose the question when the doorbell rang. He jerked around and looked out the bay window but didn't recognize the Accord in the drive. He turned to Jake with a pleading shrug. Jake held up his flour-covered hands.

Berf peered back out the window. One thing was for certain. It wasn't Zoe and it wasn't Dad. How bad could it be?

He walked down the hall and pulled open the door.

Amelia Barker stood on the porch, dressed like she had just come from church. "Hey, Berf!"

Berf's pulse shot up to the woodpecker setting. He checked his initial impulse to slam the door, retreat to his bedroom, and disappear under the aptly named comforter.

"Amelia, what a surprise," he said instead. "A pleasant surprise," he rushed to add.

Amelia didn't respond. Instead, her eyes raked over his outfit, and he realized he was still wearing electric-blue silk pajamas, fuzzy slippers, and a cotton Japanese yukata in a gold and black dragon-tiger print.

"Well, come on in and make yourself to home." Berf held the door open.

Amelia walked past him cautiously, as if he might abduct her and pop her into a cage in the basement.

He showed her to the living room and gestured to the couch.

She took a seat. "I came back Friday night for dinner, but no one was here. Or Saturday, either."

Berf sat down at the opposite end of the couch. "I was called away unexpectedly. Family emergency."

"Oh, is everything okay?"

Berf shook his head. "Not by a long shot." Then he realized what he had said and added, "I mean, we worked it out."

Amelia seemed confused, but then she looked in his lap. "Oh! You're already planning the wedding?"

That was when Berf realized he was still holding the wedding magazine. And also when he realized what Amelia was now assuming. "I'm afraid so."

Amelia took the magazine from him and opened it to the sticky note. "You're not serious." She looked at him with undisguised horror. "Turquoise?"

She shook her head slowly with the expression she would use when telling her firstborn that he couldn't keep the puppy that followed him home. "I hate to break it to you, puppet, but this is not going to happen."

Berf sighed. It was heartbreaking, really, what he was about to do. Just as he opened his mouth, a thought weaseled into his brain.

Amelia could be his ticket out of the engagement with Zoe. Kind of an "I'm sorry, punkin, but Friday I forgot to mention I was already engaged" kind of thing.

Of course that still left him with the original problem that had prompted his flight from the bosom of his home. He had no desire to marry Amelia either.

But then, again, if one was forced to choose, Amelia was preferable to Zoe, despite her equine aspect and excessive maternal instincts. Or was she? Would he rather be ruled with an iron fist or smothered with good intentions? It wasn't really a fair contest, was it? Kind of like saying would you rather be tied out on an ant bed or drowned in a vat of beer?

Neither was the only sane answer.

He took a deep breath, but Amelia cut him off at the pass.

She pulled the sticky note from the page. "Berfie?" She frowned. "Honey? Who wrote this note?"

Berf was saved by the sound of the front door opening and closing, and then a familiar voice asking, "Berfie! Are you ready?"

Perhaps saved was the wrong word. What was worse than having a fiancée? Having two? And worse still? Having them both in the same room.

Amelia cocked her head like a horse eyeing a questionable apple. "Berfie? Was that—?"

Zoe walked through the door and stopped like a poleaxed mule, staring at Amelia sitting on the couch with Berf in his pajamas.

Berf sprang to his feet and opened his mouth, but nothing came out.

Zoe turned to Amelia. "Out raising donations for the Friends of the Library? I didn't know you made house calls."

Amelia's smile didn't fool anyone, and Berf doubted that it was meant to. "Oh, hello, Zoe. Come on in and make yourself at home." She pulled Berf down next to her and patted the couch on the other side.

If Amelia's smile had seemed Velcroed on, Zoe's smile looked as authentic as clown makeup. She turned to Berf.

"Berfie, honey, why aren't you dressed? We have to pick out the flowers."

In his three decades on this blue-green whirling ball of confusion he liked to call the Earth, Berf had on occasion been up against it with a vengeance and twice on Sunday.

There was the scuba trip miles from shore where he found himself surrounded by a dozen sharks.

There was the skydiving trip where his chute failed to open.

There was the time he was locked in a hotel bedroom with the bed on fire.

There was the time a paid assassin held him hostage in a bathroom.

But being trapped in his own living room waiting for the moment when each of his fiancées realized he was also engaged to the other woman in the room beat them all.

Okay, maybe not the time his chute didn't open, but the others, definitely. His nerves were so tightly wound that if the assassin had materialized at this moment to finish him off, the bullet would have bounced off him like a tennis ball off a trampoline.

Suddenly Berf realized that this could be the miracle he had been praying for. He could lay the facts out, and with any luck, in a few minutes he would be free of all fiancées. He stood, turning so that he could keep both of them in sight. "Did I ever tell you how engagement is a funny—"

Zoe turned to Amelia, ignoring Berf's question. "Sorry, dear. You'll have to collect for charity some other time. We have a day."

Amelia's smile froze and shattered. "Flowers? I can pick out my own flowers, thank you very much."

"I'm sure you can, dear," Zoe said curtly.

Berf cleared his throat and tried a different tack. "As a great philosopher told me back in the day, 'Once you eliminate the impossible, whatever remains, no matter how improbable—'"

Zoe reached for Berf with her left hand, flashing her ring blatantly in Amelia's general direction.

Amelia stared at it like a priest finding a bagel on the communion plate and sprang to her feet. "And we don't need your suggestions about a tux." She reached for Berf's other arm.

"Berf, you go and get dressed," Zoe said. "I can't be late for my hair appointment."

"First, I should mention that—" Berf began.

But Zoe seemed to finally register the operative word from Amelia's pronouncement. She turned slowly. "We?"

"We. Berf and I. We can make our own wedding arrangements without your help, if you want to call it that. I mean, seriously, a turquoise tux?" Amelia pulled Berf toward her.

Zoe pulled back. "You must have spent too much time with the library paste, bless your heart, but in case you haven't noticed, Berf is engaged to me." She flashed the diamond ring again.

"Well, now that you bring that up," Berf began, but was once again cut off.

"But Friday morning, right there in the breakfast nook—"

"You must have misunderstood," Zoe said.

Berf tried again. "Speaking of misunderstanding—"

"What about Chip?" Amelia's eyes narrowed.

"Chip?" Zoe barked out a laugh that could have flash-frozen a side of beef if one had been handy. "He's available, if you're in the market."

Amelia squeezed Berf's arm like she was kneading bread. "Berf? What's going on?"

"Did I mention?" was all he got out.

"Friday night," Zoe said. "Berf knelt before me with a bouquet and this ring and proposed. It goes without saying that I accepted."

"But Friday morning—" Amelia said again.

"Do you have a ring?" Zoe asked.

Amelia ignored her. "Berf, is this true, what she's saying?"

Berf reviewed Zoe's statement. "Pretty much, but—"

"But at breakfast Friday—"

"That's all settled then," Zoe said. "We're running late." She gave Berf a push toward the stairs. "Clothes."

Berf turned to Amelia. "It's a funny thing, if you think about it, how—"

"Hilarious," Amelia said.

"It's not like I—"

"No, of course not."

"Berf, honey. Clothes."

Berf retreated up the stairs, defeated by the barrage of artillery from a superior force.

He felt that if he could have put forth his case, in the end they both would have realized that the whole thing was little more than a comedy of errors and they all could have had a good laugh and then retired to their respective beds with hot cocoa and a little light reading.

But a nuanced story such as the one he had to tell could not be communicated in sound bites and bumper sticker slogans, and it was clear that present company would not permit him more than five words in any given half hour.

He felt bad about Amelia, but it wasn't her first rodeo, and she would land on her feet.

Most of all, he felt bad about the fact that despite the perfect storm, he had emerged still engaged to Zoe. It was enough to make a feller rethink his faith in a just universe and the ultimate triumph of the righteous.

But, as another great philosopher once said, it wasn't over yet.

Chapter Thirty-Eight

Yvonne paused in her story to admire Jake's work in the mirror. She wouldn't normally go to the beauty shop two weeks running, but it was really JL's fault. If he couldn't figure out what rolling down the windows at seventy miles per hour would do to her hair, then he could just pay for another do.

And once she heard that Jake owned a salon, well, he was so nice, and he obviously knew about style. Plus the drive up to Austin would get her away from JL and his non-stop rants about Dr. Payne cheating him on that dang bull.

She just hoped that the boys finished college before JL's get-rich-quick schemes bankrupted them. At this rate, they'd be spending their retirement in a cardboard box under a railroad trestle eating expired SpaghettiOs.

The first half hour went like a dream. They sat down in a little lounge area with hot tea while Jake asked her all these questions about what she wanted to do with her hair. Then he sent her off to the first girl, who added highlights and wrapped the strands in foil until she looked like a Rastafarian robot. Then to the little room with dim lights, scented candles, and that Enya music, where they had to wake her up when it came time for the shampoo and massage.

And then to this glass cubicle separated from the rest of the stations. Jake came in and started working on her hair without a word. Well, after a minute or two, she started talking, because it just wasn't natural for two people to be in a room and nobody saying anything. And all the weirdness of last weekend kind of gushed out, like gas bubbling up in a swamp.

"You were saying?" Jake asked.

Yvonne pulled her gaze away from Jake's hands to his eyes. "Oh, yeah. So then he sends the boys out on some harebrained scheme to find Pancho Villa's buried treasure. He's been obsessed with that treasure since he was a kid. Pancho Villa this and Pancho Villa that. For our honeymoon he took me to the Pancho Villa museum in Mexico, the place where he was killed. Can you believe that?"

"Did they find it?"

"Find what?"

"The treasure. On the ranch."

"Are you kidding? Like there was any treasure to start with, and if there was, like JL would be the one man on earth who knew where it was." If anything, JL would be the last man on earth to find something like that. "All they found was a dilapidated shack with a bunch of cannon balls in the cellar."

Jake looked up from his work and caught Yvonne's eyes in the mirror. "How disappointing."

"Oh, that's not the worst of it. That didn't cost us anything besides a GPS and a metal detector, but he already had all that. Next thing he dips into the boys' college fund to buy that stupid bull, who wouldn't know a cow from a couch if it took out an ad in the Chronicle."

"You mean it's not . . ."

"Not even! He got a cow up to the ranch in Bulverde yesterday, and that dumb bull didn't pay it any more mind than an elephant would a flea. Just stood at the fence and stared at the emus."

Jake returned to his work. "So now what?"

"JL's scanning that contract with a magnifying glass is what, trying to get an annulment or something. He says Dr. Payne knew Tiny wasn't worth a tinker's dam the whole time."

Jake set down the scissors and fluffed Yvonne's hair. "I have an idea. Why don't you buy Tiny?"

Yvonne snorted. "One over-sexed, under-performing ox is enough."

"Yes, but what if you could turn him into an over-performing ox?"

Yvonne eyed him in the mirror skeptically. "Which ox are we talking about?"

"Tiny."

Yvonne squinted at him. Jake seemed sane enough, but things weren't always what they seemed. Look at that bull, for instance.

Jake scanned the room outside the glass cubicle, leaned down, and whispered into her ear.

She listened for a moment and then jerked her head around to see if he was serious. "Really? Linseed oil?"

Jake nodded solemnly.

A smile grew on Yvonne's face like the long-awaited dawn after a longer night. It was time José Luis Martinez learned a lesson or two. Long past time.

As Jake dried her hair, she planned how she would deliver the final blow. She went out to the receptionist, paid her tab with a nice tip, and turned to go, but froze in her tracks when Zoe walked in the door.

Zoe walked past her, not even glancing her way, and announced herself at the reception desk. Yvonne stood, feet pointing to the exit, face turned back to Zoe. It wasn't that she had been ignored as much as not seen, right? Should she go back and say hello or just take the hint and leave?

Of course, somebody like Zoe, young, rich, fashionable, beautiful, wouldn't want to be bothered by somebody like Yvonne, a middle-aged bayou rat with teenagers. Even one with a fresh, fashionable do.

Yvonne turned to go, but as her hand touched the door, she thought better of it. Here she was about to drive out to the ranch in Bulverde and intimidate JL into giving up his precious bull, and then rub his face in it. What was some rich, sheltered kid, no matter how pretty, compared to that?

The thought made her laugh and she turned back around to discover all eyes on her. She must have laughed louder than she realized. Yvonne immobilized Zoe with a piercing stare and walked up to her with all the southern Louisiana sass Austin could stand in one location.

"Zoe, I thought that was you. I didn't know you came here too. Imagine seeing you so soon after the weekend in the Hill Country." She placed a limp hand on Zoe's shoulder. "Have you set a date yet?"

Zoe flinched away slightly but recovered nicely, Yvonne thought.

"Oh! Uh, Yvonne, isn't it? Yes, nice to see you again."

Yvonne waved a hand dismissively. "Well, do send me an invitation. I must be going. Have to see a man about a bull."

Then she turned with a Louisiana sashay and walked out, not bothering to look back. In the parking lot she leaned against the door and caught her breath, astounded at her own audacity. She barked out a laugh like a sea lion, and her hand flew to her mouth, but she reconsidered.

When it came down to it, Zoe was nothing more than a hothouse flower who wouldn't survive a minute without her daddy's money to back her up. Yvonne would like to see her take on JL. Then she might have something to be so snooty about.

Yvonne climbed into the Lexus SUV, swapped out her heels for flats, and set her sights on Bulverde. One down, one to go.

Chapter Thirty-Nine

Zoe dropped Berf off at his Tarrytown residence, rushed off for her hair appointment, and considered post-wedding residence requirements. It could be nice to have a place in Tarrytown, especially after late nights at social and charity functions, but the main residence would have to be in Westlake. That was not up for discussion.

She valeted the car and walked into Jake's salon. As she waited for the receptionist to recognize her, a noise like a donkey getting its tail caught in the barn door turned her right around.

A woman stood at the door. No, not a woman. That woman. The one out at the ranch this weekend, the poor creature married to the boor who bought Tiny. What was her name? Oh, no, here she comes!

Zoe muddled through the conversation somehow, rescued by her innate social acumen, until the woman mercifully tottered out the door on her nosebleed heels.

Once ensconced in the Zen room, she let the encounter slough away and gave herself to the ministrations of

Jake's capable staff. In the chair, she bounced her ideas for the wedding off Jake. As she knew he would, Jake offered several nice tweaks to her initial thoughts but then took a tangent into left field, talking about some dilapidated barn he had seen out at the ranch.

"From what Billy says, and I understand he's researched this quite well," Jake said as he set aside the scissors and picked up a razor, "it's not just a disintegrating shack. It was a hideout for Pancho Villa's gang."

Zoe had tired of this side discussion and wanted to get back to wedding planning. "I guess that's good for Daddy. They might pay more to film the movie."

Jake issued the tsking sound for which he was justly famous. "It's more than that. It will be in the National Registry of Historic Sites. UT will probably set up an excavation."

"That's nice. Now about the catering—"

"And it's on your land, which means you have access to it."

"Whyever would I want access to it?" Some archeological dig? As if!

"Well, who wouldn't? I mean, why have your wedding on the society page when you can get it on the front page? A-1."

"Front page?"

"Above the fold. Think about the headline. 'Society Wedding at Historic Site.' You could invite the stars who will be filming there. Maybe a spread in *Texas Monthly*."

Before the words had died out, Zoe had her cell phone in her hand. "Margo, cancel the mission chapel and call Skip at *Texas Monthly*. You're going to love this."

CHAPTER FORTY

When Yvonne pulled up to the ranch house in Bulverde, she saw JL out by the fence, ranting and waving his cowboy hat as if to shoo Tiny toward the cow in the other corner of the pen. She watched him for a few seconds, debating the wisdom of her next move. What if Jake was wrong?

She looked at the bag with the linseed oil she had picked up at Bulverde Feed and Seed. Out at Payne's ranch everyone had seen the results, even her, so it had worked at least once. But would it work for her? Maybe there was a trick to it. If it didn't work, JL would treat her like she was stupid. On the other hand, he already did that, so what did she have to lose?

She checked her makeup in the rearview. If she did this, she would have to go in hard, show no fear, taunt him just enough to make him doubt without him getting his back up and turning stubborn. Or she could just blow it off and go in and start dinner.

Yvonne took a deep breath and crossed the yard to what used to be the emu pen where Tiny was doing his best to ignore the cow.

"Come on, you worthless hunk of hamburger," JL yelled, his back to Yvonne. "You call yourself a stud? Do I have to come in there and show you how it's done?"

Yvonne walked up to the fence. "As if."

JL whipped around, his face disturbingly like an overripe persimmon on the verge of exploding. "What?"

She tipped her new hairdo toward Tiny. "How's Casanova getting along?"

"He's not."

"Lost his nerve?"

JL shoved his hat back on his head. "He's going to lose a lot more than that if he doesn't watch out."

"Not to mention what you're going to lose."

JL jerked his head toward her. "What's that supposed to mean?"

Yvonne shrugged. "You'd save a fortune if you just gave him away. I mean, feeding him will cost more than feeding the boys." Not that he had any idea how much of their grocery budget the boys wolfed down, but she didn't say that. "And when the word gets out, you won't be able to unload him even for free." On the next sucker, but she didn't say that. Just like the emus, but she didn't say that either.

She eased into the proposition. "Tell you what, JL, I got a nice do at Jake's salon and I'm feeling generous today. I'll take him off your hands."

He stared at her as if she had grown a third arm and then slapped him with it. "You'll what?"

"I'll buy him off you. Take over. Do it myself."

"You think you can do better?"

He needed a reality check. Yvonne cast a lazy glance at Tiny, who stood at the back of the pen, studying a nearby emu on the other side of the fence. The cow waited in the other corner, bored.

"I couldn't do any worse."

"You don't know a dang thing about investing. Or breeding cattle."

Yvonne shrugged. "The way I see it, that makes us even."

JL threw up his hands and backed off from the fence. "Fine. Go ahead. Take your best shot, and I'll take over when you crash and burn."

He didn't get it. Yvonne took a stance, facing him head on. "No. If I do it, it's all on my own. Bill of sale, title in my name, all or nothing."

JL studied her for a bit, much like Tiny studying the emu. "I ought to. Just to teach you a lesson."

"Go ahead. Teach me."

"All right, then." JL pulled his hat off, rubbed his hand across his buzz cut, and put it back on. "I'll sell him to you for what I paid, no profit for me."

Now that the hook was set, it was going to be fun. "Nope. Ten percent of what you paid."

"What?"

"If he's so bad, why should I pay full price?"

"Fifty percent."

"Twenty."

"Thirty-five percent."

"Twenty-five."

"Woman, you've gone crazy."

"Twenty."

"You already said twenty-five."

"Fifteen."

"Wait, you can't go backwards."

"I'm the only bidder. I can do what I want. Ten."

"How you going to run a business? You don't even know how negotiation works."

"Last chance."

"God bless America, Yuh-vonne!"

Yvonne shrugged. "Okay. I'll leave you to it."

She turned and walked away. He would stop her. Wouldn't he? After all, if she failed, as he seemed to be certain that she would, then he would be able to taunt her with it forever.

But he didn't stop her. She kept walking, refusing to look back. Then, as her foot hit the bottom step of the porch, he called out.

"Wait."

Yvonne stopped, but didn't turn around.

"Okay. Ten."

She walked back to him and held out her hand.

"Mister, you got yourself a deal."

JL looked at her hand a long time before he reluctantly shook on it.

CHAPTER FORTY-ONE

Seven weeks after that fateful weekend, Berf sat on his bed, an open suitcase beside him, and stared at the turquoise tux with the cutaway tails hanging on the closet door. He saw the tux as though it were rushing toward him through a long tunnel. The walls seemed to close in around him.

This was probably how Tell Sackett felt in that jail cell in Tucson, knowing the lynch mob was just outside the door with the rope. But Berf couldn't fight his way out of this one.

He found Jake in the breakfast nook, drinking organic, single-origin, free-range coffee and finishing off the last of the mango chutney cobbler. The remains of a bacon-wrapped quail and cheese corn fritter lunch sat on the table. Hank the Jack Russell sat in a chair, staring at the quail bones with unequaled intensity.

Jake looked up from a travel brochure featuring Aruba, land of abductions.

Berf dropped into a chair opposite Jake, leaning on the table. "I'm a desperate man, Jake. You can't fail me now."

Jake picked up his cell phone and held it out to Berf. Zoe's number was already keyed in. "Glasshoppah, you will be free when you can snatch the phone from my hand and call it off."

Berf pushed away from the table, slouching in the chair. The guy was a Johnny-one-note. "You know I can't do that."

Jake set the phone aside. "My Uncle Frank had this funny thing. He couldn't walk through a doorway until he saw someone else walk through it first."

"Remind me to ask you about him sometime."

"He missed his wedding because it was a slow day at the convenience store. He stopped to buy gas but couldn't pay for it until somebody went in or out."

"Forget Uncle Frank," Berf said with considerable vehemence. "Uncle Frank is dead to me. In case you missed the headlines, we're in a crisis, the threat level is orange, and I don't give an armadillo's eyelash about Uncle Frank unless he's loaded for bear and leading a pack of Marines."

Jake continued, unperturbed. "If he had brought someone with him, they could have gone through and he would be married today instead of single and alone."

"Well, at least this pointless story had a happy ending. Now, about Zoe . . ."

Jake picked up the phone. "Snatch the pebble from my—"

"I will not trifle with a woman's affections."

Jake dropped the phone and returned his attention to the brochure. "Live by the code. Die by the code."

Berf pushed the chair back from the table and stood. "It is a far, far better thing I do than I have ever done." He started toward the door.

Jake didn't even look up. "By the way, Amelia stopped by the shop today to get her hair fixed for the wedding. She got a room in a B&B in Utopia and will be at the Christmas gala tonight in Bolero. So at least you have a backup in case this thing with Zoe doesn't work out."

In Berf's view, it was cases such as this one that formed the greatest argument against the principle of karma. Nothing he could have done in this life, or any alleged previous lives, would have rendered him as deserving of such a hopeless fate.

He turned a pleading look on Jake, but Jake didn't answer with an expression of compassion. Instead, he turned the page on his brochure with one hand and held out the phone with the other.

Chapter Forty-Two

On a chilly Friday night just across the Bolero county line, cowboys in orange safety vests directed traffic to the pasture next to the Horseshoe Road Inn.

In the shadows out back, two teenaged boys smoked cigarettes from a pack they had stolen from an unattended jacket. A sheriff's deputy rounded the corner and they lit out around the other corner.

Out front, ranchers and mechanics and grocers and bankers and computer technicians escorted their wives, dressed in the latest West Deco fashion, inside where the roadhouse had been transformed into a winter wonderland of clean lines and sweeping strokes.

Intricate snowflakes, bold snowmen, angular reindeer, and wide swaths of shimmering linen hanging in luscious folds rendered the bar unrecognizable to the regulars. The only thing that remained unchanged from a typical Saturday night was Buzz and Kendall standing behind the bar. And even they wore silver cardboard top hats, Buzz's perched on his melon head like a button on an acorn, Kendall's set at a jaunty angle that complemented her piercings and tattoos.

On the bandstand, Dick Gimble's western swing band jazzed the holiday classics as the patrons of the Pharr Children's Clinic cavorted on the dance floor.

Jake sampled the fare at the catering table, discussing recipes with the chef.

Chip stood next to him, mindlessly chewing smoked salmon hors d'oeuvres and watching Zoe work the room, flitting from a couple here to a group of girls there, dragging Berf in the ridiculous outfit Zoe had foisted on him.

He couldn't decide if the suit was purchased from the estate of Porter Wagoner or stolen from the wardrobe of a mariachi band. Either way, he was glad it wasn't him, although, if it had been him, he wouldn't have agreed to wear that abomination.

That whole outfit was a perfect illustration of why Berf was completely, totally, and in every way the wrong guy for Zoe. She needed someone who would stand up to her, who wouldn't cater to her every absurd whim and directive. For her own sake, really, because evidently she didn't realize how ridiculous she looked dragging Berf around in that costume like a trained monkey.

If it was Chip, like it should be, he would be wearing what he was wearing right now, a zoot suit, which was from the Art Deco period, not from a carnival sideshow, and together they would be the couple everyone wished they were a part of.

Out on the edge of the dance floor, Berf couldn't decide which was worse—the suit or the prospect of being cornered by Amelia.

His thoughts were interrupted by a hand thrust toward him. He shook it absently, the hundredth hand in the last hour.

"Sheriff, this is my fiancé, Berf. Berfie, this is Sheriff John Lawson and his girlfriend . . ."

"Elizabeth," the sheriff said.

Berf looked up, literally, into the face of the sheriff, who was over six feet and built like a hatchet. "Good to meet you, Sheriff." He turned to the girlfriend. "Ma'am."

Elizabeth smiled.

The sheriff eyed Berf's costume as if considering whether to arrest him for disturbing the peace. "Y'all got everything settled for tomorrow night?"

"Tomorrow night?" At this point Berf wasn't thinking any further ahead than ten minutes, max.

Zoe jogged his memory with an elbow to the ribs. "Yes, sheriff, and thanks for the off-duty deputies to help with security."

"Oh, the wedding, absolutely," Berf said. "Champing at the bit. Raring to go."

This was his life now, and he might as well get used to it. At some point, life transitioned from endless possibilities to a series of contractions, like the walls closing in on the garbage hold in *Star Wars*, and evidently he had reached that point. And there was no R2-D2 to sneak into the control room and turn off the compactors. Which naturally led his thoughts to Jake.

Berf scanned the room. The two Martinez boys were ranging through the room, finishing off mixed drinks that people had left unattended. Didn't they have parents? Ah, there they were, sitting at the bar, drinking, eyeing the dancers, not talking, as if they were watching television in separate rooms.

With a shudder, he realized he was staring through a time warp into his own future. A married couple who might as well be single, with even less in common than he and Zoe had now, which was not enough to overflow a thimble.

Was this what William Tell Sackett would do? Hard to say. Sure, he was a straight shooter, and perhaps if it had been Tell that night, down on one knee with a spray of flowers in one hand and a five-carat diamond ring in the other, kneeling in the bedroom of a beautiful woman, perhaps he might have said, "Sorry, ma'am, but I can't rightly lay claim to this ring, nor to these flowers, nor to you. You see, deep inside we both know you belong with Chip, and if you don't marry him, you'll regret it. Maybe not today. Maybe not tomorrow, but soon and for the rest of your life."

Somehow that last part didn't sound quite like Tell, and maybe he was mixing his metaphors, but it sounded like The Code, and that was all that mattered. If only he had been quicker off the line with the right phrase back at Halloween, his Christmas might have been different.

But one thing he knew for sure, that having once given his word, he was bounden by The Code to keep it, even if it made them both miserable for the rest of their lives.

Some things were bigger than happiness, even if his friends were too jaded to admit it. A man had to believe, even when it made no sense. No one ever raised a monument to a cynic.

He looked around for Jake, still holding out hope that there was some scheme that could stop this runaway train before it wrecked his life. But the view that obscured all else was JL and Yvonne sitting there like two strangers on a commuter train, each wishing they had picked a different seat.

Then a movement from the door caught his eye and he beheld Amelia Barker entering. She wore a white dress that, unless he was very much mistaken, could easily serve as a wedding dress in a pinch. He turned to Zoe, who was still talking to the sheriff and his girl. "Darling, I'm afraid I can't rest easy until we take a spin around the dance floor. You'll excuse us?"

The sheriff nodded his assent and Berf whisked her away, doing his best to keep her between him and Amelia.

At the bar, Yvonne sipped her strawberry cinnamon daiquiri and, in consideration of the approaching new year, pondered the expanding horizons that now lay before her. With the stud fees from the past six weeks, she had paid off JL and was contemplating how to best use the current and future revenue. Maybe open a nice beauty parlor like Jake's.

It was nice to think that if you just waited long enough, had a little patience and a little faith, one day the possibilities would be endless. Not like when she was a kid in a backwater Louisiana town.

When she met JL at Mardi Gras, she knew she had found her ticket out of her trailer-park prison, but by the time Zachary came along, she realized she had just traded a hick prison for a suburban cage. JL's traditional views weren't that different from her father's, or her mother's, for that matter, and she didn't really know anything else.

But a word from Jake had changed all that. She should buy him a drink. She scanned the room and there was Dr. Payne walking up to the bar. He slapped JL on the back.

"Martinez," he said. "Merry Christmas. How's Tiny working out for you?" He caught Buzz's eye. "Johnny Walker Blue on the rocks."

JL choked back his scowl. Yvonne smiled.

"As fine as frog hair, Payne," JL said with much more enthusiasm than Yvonne expected. "He's a regular Casanova with the cows."

Dr. Payne's expression was worth every cent Yvonne had paid for Tiny, and also every cent it had cost JL. Those two were in the same boat and welcome to it.

"Great!" Payne said. "That's just great. Glad to hear it." He grabbed his drink and walked away.

JL slammed his glass down on the bar. "Another! Make it a double and make it quick."

Yvonne pushed her glass to the bartender. "Put it on my tab, Buzz. I'm celebrating."

"I'll take a chardonnay," a voice said.

Yvonne turned on her stool. It was that cowgirl, the one from the Halloween weekend at the Payne ranch, Bonnie was her name, scanning the room like she was looking for a lost dog.

She still looked as cute as a bug's ear, but there was something missing. She didn't seem as perky as before. Yvonne started to say something but realized they'd never spoken that weekend. She shrank back down with her drink, but then realized that was the old Yvonne talking, Yuh-vonne as her family would say. She wasn't that girl anymore.

"Hey."

Bonnie flinched and glanced over. It took her a second to connect the dots. "Hey."

"You got a ranch, right?" Yvonne said.

"Yeah."

"I just got a stud bull, making a little money, and was wondering what I should do next. You got time to talk, maybe after Christmas?"

Bonnie regarded her with a very different expression. "What do you have in mind?"

"I don't know." Yvonne shrugged and laughed. She felt better than she had in a long time. "I'm new to all this stuff. Guess I want to make sure I got all my bases covered and then figure my options for branching out."

Bonnie considered this for a longish while, enough to make Yvonne think maybe she had made a mistake, and finally said, "Yeah. I think we could come up with some ideas." She pulled a card from the studded pink leather purse on her shoulder. "Give me a call after the holidays."

"Thanks." Yvonne slipped the card into her clutch and started to say something else, but all of a sudden, that red-headed doctor stepped up, and the next thing she knew, him and Bonnie were on the dance floor and the band was playing "Blue Christmas."

Chapter Forty-Three

The parking lot of the Horseshoe Road Inn was packed, and when the DayGlo-orange-vested cowboys in the lot directed him to the pasture, Mitch just gunned the Triumph and parked it out back. He pushed through the door and walked straight to the bar for a stiff drink.

But before he could order, Bonnie was right there. He held out his hand without a word, she took it, and then they were in the cocoon of the dance floor, slow dancing to "Blue Christmas" as if he had requested it.

After the Halloween meltdown at the ranch, Mitch had jumped on his bike and headed back to Pharr, taking US 83 instead of the interstate, a back-road ride that would give him plenty of time to think.

During that fateful Halloween weekend, the whole gala thing had gone nuclear, and he had evidently become a casualty of war. Well, he could do without that kind of nonsense.

He had buried himself in his routine at the clinic for a few weeks before the calls, texts, and emails came flooding in, and he had ignored them all. He didn't play those kind of games. But in the following month of silence, he found that he couldn't forget her. And this last week he had not been able to suppress the mental countdown to the gala.

She would be there, he had no doubt. And despite everything, no matter how much he tried to talk himself out of it, he couldn't stop thinking about riding up and seeing her again. But he wouldn't let her off that easy. A Flood was no one to trifle with. He would show up, stand off to the side, and let her come crawling back to him, which he had no doubt that she would.

But when he saw her standing at the bar, his resolve melted. He walked directly to her and pulled her out on the dance floor, not sure what he should say. Or if he should say anything at all.

Then, during the steel guitar solo, Bonnie leaned up and whispered in his ear.

"I made a mistake."

"I know."

"Can you ever forgive me?"

That was the question. "Let's find out," he said.

When the song ended, Bonnie looked up and he realized they were standing under the mistletoe.

From her seat at the bar, Yvonne watched Bonnie and Mitch kiss. They made a cute couple and she wished she was part of a cute couple like she used to be back before she had kids and JL went off the deep end treasure hunting.

At a table next to the dance floor, she caught sight of Billy and Summer. They were nursing their drinks and watching the dancers, much like she and JL were doing. Maybe she should go over there and ask him for a dance.

After all, Summer had left him high and dry at the ranch, and he had been so nice to Yvonne. Maybe he was looking to change partners.

She slipped off the stool, but as she approached the table, she saw Summer's hand inch over from her drink to Billy's hand. He squeezed it without looking at her. Then their eyes met and the band struck up "This Christmas." They got up to dance.

Yvonne stopped dead in her tracks, suddenly without a goal, one of the loners hanging on the edge of the crowd, one of the losers when you thought about it too long. It seemed lame to slink back to the bar, her tail between her legs.

She glanced back at the bar where JL was sulking over his scotch. It made her mad. The fact that she was standing here like some loser chick who couldn't get a date on a dare was all his fault. She had given him twenty good years so far, and she had a lot more to give.

And, unlike a lot of the other mothers she knew, she hadn't let herself go. Except for when she was pregnant, she'd worked hard to be able to fit in her high school prom dress, and she still could. A waste of time, for all he seemed to notice.

It suddenly came to her that he didn't deserve her, probably never did, but he was stuck with her, and he could do a lot worse when it came to that. And what was more, she was at a Christmas party, she wanted to dance, and he owed her at least that much. A lot more, actually, but it would do for a starter.

Yvonne strode to the bar with a sense of purpose she had never possessed. It felt so good that she grabbed JL's arm and pulled him off the stool.

He stumbled to his feet. "God bless America, Yuhvonne. You trying to kill me?"

"You're just lucky I ain't killed you already, José. Now let's dance."

JL held back. "You know I don't dance."

"Well, you do now. Let's go."

She dragged him out to the dance floor and powered through the rest of the song, dancing like they were still dating. When the band started on "Rocking Around the Christmas Tree," he seemed to realize things had changed, and it wasn't the disaster he had been moping about for the last six weeks.

Yvonne bumped into somebody and turned to apologize. It was Berf, dancing with Zoe. They looked so cute, she just had to give Berf a quick kiss on the cheek before she turned back to JL, who looked at her as if she was the whole Martian invasion all at once.

Berf stumbled back from the gratuitous kiss from a random crazy dancing woman and glanced longingly toward the bar. He started inching that direction when the song ended, but Zoe grabbed his hand and dragged him onto the bandstand.

Zoe stepped up to the mike, edging the lead singer aside. "I'd like to thank everyone for coming out and donating to the Pharr Children's Clinic. Thank you, Vera Cliff, for the designs. And we have Dr. Mitch Flood from the clinic here tonight. Mitch!"

She pointed at him for the duration of the applause and pulled the mike from the stand. "Also don't forget the silent auction ends in ten minutes. Get your final bids in!"

The crowd milled about indifferently, waiting for the band to start back up. Berf sighted Amelia glaring at him from the crowd and backed toward the drummer.

"And," Zoe said. "I'd like to invite everyone here to the wedding tomorrow out on the ranch at the newly discovered villa of Pancho Villa, a registered national historical site!"

Berf kept inching back, his eyes locked with Amelia's. Then his foot hit air and he fell off the back of the stage, taking a crash cymbal with him. He came to rest against the back door and dashed out, slamming it behind him.

He sprinted toward the front of the roadhouse, looking for the traffic guys to help him extract his car from the pasture. He ran into Jake.

"Hey, Amelia just went in," Jake said.

"Thanks for the warning." Berf legged it toward the darkness of the parking lot.

Jake watched him go, then turned and rounded the next corner where he knew he would find the Martinez boys smoking. Sure enough, they dropped their cigarettes and tried to wave the smoke away.

"Forget that," he said. "We're going for fireworks. Uncle Berf is getting married tomorrow, and we're going to send him off in style. Anything you don't spend, I take back."

Jake handed them each a one hundred dollar bill.

The boys whooped and followed Jake to the car.

CHAPTER FORTY-FOUR

Berf tossed the rhinestone-encrusted jacket into a leather armchair and plopped down on the pillow-infested bed. He was back at the scene of the crime, the point where it all started. El Rancho del Bolero. Dr. Payne's carnival fun house and Hill Country resort.

Where a guy could step into an alternate universe while doing an old frat buddy a favor and get stuck in there.

Over by the sliding door to the pool, Jake sat at a rustic escritoire, a highlighter in one hand, flipping through a real estate magazine with the other.

"Riverside condo, ceramic tile upgrades, utilities paid, no pets. What do you think?"

Berf couldn't think about condos right now, or much else. A dense fog had descended over his soul and his future seemed as desolate as the Lake Travis shoreline in a ten-year drought. "I think I'll join the Navy."

"Air Force," Jake said. "Pilots get all the chicks."

"You say that like it's a good thing. What we want at times like this are fewer chicks."

Jake flipped a page. "I'm thinking east side. More space. Eclectic neighborhood."

Berf let him ramble. Sure he had to find a place, and who liked to do that, but no matter where the place was, he could come and go when he wanted, stay up as late or early as he pleased, eat what he wanted when he wanted, and in general have his own life. Things that would end for Berf in twenty-something hours.

"So this is the way the world ends," Berf said.

"Not with a bang but a wedding." Jake highlighted a listing.

Sometimes Jake could be downright heartless.

The door opened. Chip walked in, grabbed the bourbon at Jake's left elbow, poured a generous shot in a glass, and held it up. "To the groom."

Evidently Jake wasn't the only cad.

Jake held up his glass. "The groom."

They drank the toast as Berf watched, unamused. "Some friend you are," he said with a steely glare at Chip. "You could marry the girl of your dreams and save me from my fate if you would just apologize to Zoe."

Chip stepped to the armchair, tossed the jacket aside, and collapsed into the leather. "You're not the only one with a code, you know."

Jake looked up in horror. "Don't even start."

Berf snorted. "What kind of code is that? Never apologize?"

"It's a sign of weakness. John Wayne."

"That's your code? Quotes from John Wayne movies?"

"Never let them see you sweat." Chip propped his feet up on the edge of the bed.

"That's not John Wayne."

"Didn't say it was."

"It's not even a movie. It's a deodorant commercial."

"If you found a diamond ring in a cow pie, would it still be a gem?"

There were some people who shouldn't try to think beyond their pay grade. Chip, he was a great guy and all, and Berf would take a bullet for him, or at least yell, "Watch out!" when he saw the gun, but Chip's strength was high-level finance, not philosophy, and he was only embarrassing himself with his feeble attempt at assembling a personal code out of scraps of cloth.

Berf roused himself to the cause. "I'm saying you can't base a code on sound bites you've picked randomly from pop culture like sweets from the dessert bar at the Golden Corral. A true code is a unified body of knowledge."

"Like Louis L'Amour novels, you mean?"

"He didn't invent it. It goes back much further, back to the homeland, back to Camelot and the Round Table."

Chip dropped his feet to the floor. "Jake, if you ever see me even thinking about bringing up a code again, shoot me." He stepped to the desk and poured himself another shot. As he corked the bottle, he nudged Jake. "Hey, remember your bachelor party? Now that was a party to remember."

"Thanks a lot," Jake said. "I can't even begin to list the extremes to which I have gone in the last year to block it from my mind."

"And who threw that party?" Berf asked.

"Sure," Chip said. "But you can't ride on the coattails of that forever. Here." He held out a glass of bourbon.

"Turn that frown upside down. If you insist on going through with this, at least have the decency to enjoy it."

"And at that party I did my best to save you from that ill-fated union," Berf said to Jake, taking the glass and tossing off the shot in a single gulp. "Successfully, I might add."

Jake set down the highlighter and turned toward Berf. "So you're saying you want me to scare Zoe off by doing half a million dollars of damage at the wedding tomorrow night?"

"Okay, well, yes, my methods may be drastic, perhaps Draconian, and possibly accidental, but at least I took steps to save you from yourself, and now here you are, finally living the dream instead of trying to mold yourself into some kind of pretzel to satisfy The Man and a woman."

Jake stood and picked up his highlighter and real estate magazine. "I think I'll take some steps myself." He walked out the door.

Chip shrugged and sat down in Jake's chair, propping his feet on the desk and cradling the bourbon bottle in his lap. "A bit touchy."

"You can't really blame him. He's going to have to move out. He's even talking about moving to the east side."

"Wow!" Chip sipped his bourbon. "Say, didn't he go off to Borneo or someplace with some woman? That time you guys went down to Mexico?"

Berf nodded. Those were times of which one did not speak lightly.

"Whatever happened to her?"

Berf poured himself another drink and settled down in the leather armchair. It looked like this was it for the bachelor party. "Didn't work out."

"Shame."

You could say that about a lot of things. A lot.

CHAPTER FORTY-FIVE

It was bad enough being ambushed into marriage, but to get married in the center ring of a media circus, in Berf's mind, was just piling on.

And if there was any question about whether this was the Texas wedding of the year, the mixture of glitterati, paparazzi, and infrastructure removed all doubt. Range Rovers ferried guests from the makeshift parking lot in the ten acres fronting the road to the villa atop the remote mesa. Decorators had coated every horizontal surface of the villa with candles, transforming the ruins into a magical fairy castle.

Berf stood at stage left next to the remains of the entrance arch to the villa. Jake stood to his left holding the ring. A preacher waited under the arch with the solemn countenance of an undertaker. Spread out in the moonlight, a few hundred white folding chairs surrounded by tiki torches held the more important guests. The rest had to stand on the periphery.

A string quartet struck up "Canon in D" and Berf looked up. Now that the moment had come, he had fallen into a strange calm, like a charmed soldier in a foxhole in the middle of a barrage of shells. It was as if it was all happening to someone else, to the other guy who lived in his skin, whoever he was.

As his gaze wandered to the crowd, it fell first on Dad and Trixie, who waved, and then passed briefly to Mom, who offered a watery smile. The next row back, Amelia observed the proceedings much like a Nazi doctor might follow the vivisection of some experimental victim.

Farther back, Mitch's red hair defied taming. Bonnie sat next to him. On the fringe of the glow from the candles, Berf noticed JL and Yvonne and wondered where the boys were.

Then a movement at the back and there was Summer walking down the aisle with a measured pace in a turquoise dress that obviously could be repurposed for use at a cocktail party. She eventually arrived at the front and took up her place opposite Jake.

Then a trumpet stepped out of nowhere, stood next to the string quartet, and took up the descant part. The preacher made a gesture and everyone stood and turned toward the back.

Zoe emerged from the tent erected at the back of the crowd for the purpose of hiding her from prying eyes and began her slow approach. Her white dress and veil were anything but traditional, looking like it had been stolen from Audrey Hepburn. The first marriage, not the second one.

The expression Berf had seen the night he had rescued the five-carat diamond from the cow pie glowed on her face.

Berf made note of it in the bemused fashion of a drunk stumbling down the railroad tracks, remarking on the light of an approaching train. He scanned the crowd for Chip, but he was nowhere to be seen. Probably back at the ranch house opening a new bottle of bourbon. And probably for the best, when it came to that.

Suddenly Jake contracted a coughing fit and Berf turned to him for a second, noticing that the Martinez boys had materialized from the darkness beyond the quartet and were vaulting over the half-wall of the villa.

Berf turned his attention back to the point where everyone else was staring, at Zoe inching toward her goal, giving all the photographers ample time to catch a good angle.

But after a few seconds, a different glow illuminated Zoe's face, and her eyes flashed, not with the intoxication of love, but with pique. Berf turned to see what had aroused her ire.

Behind the walls of the villa, the Martinez boys had ignited a variety of fireworks. Roman candles, pinwheels, fountains, and strobes. It appeared they had sparklers wedged in between each of their fingers in both fists and were waving them around in circles and figure eights and other shapes like those Olympic dancers with ribbons and such.

Berf turned back to Zoe, who sent him a wordless but completely unmistakable command with an imperious nod of her head.

Deal with it.

Berf turned to dart through the arch, but the preacher blocked his path. He kept turning, completing a 360-degree turn without coming up with a plan.

Jake leaned over and said, "I'll take care of it. You just stay here and wait for Zoe."

He vaulted the wall, snatched the sparklers from the boys, and tossed them to one side. Berf frowned when, instead of lying on the ground sizzling and sparkling, the sparklers disappeared. But Jake ushered the boys off into the shadows, tossing the remaining fireworks after the sparklers, and everything appeared to be resolved. Berf turned forward and smiled at Zoe. She smiled back. But only for a moment.

Suddenly the sound of automatic gunfire, or perhaps strips of firecrackers, drowned out the quintet. Berf spun around. From the place where Jake had tossed the sparklers, the erratic flash of fireworks illuminated a column of smoke pouring out of the ground. Larger explosions followed from cherry bombs and M80s. The whine of bottle rockets joined the cacophony, a few escaping into the sky above the ruins.

Berf looked back at Zoe. She stood halfway to the altar, her mouth frozen open, horrified and infuriated at what her wedding had become.

She charged forward as a series of larger explosions sent Berf, Summer, and the preacher scrambling away from the arch and into the crowd, which was already streaming between the folding chairs.

Then a serious explosion rocked the surface of the mesa. Berf grabbed a chair to steady himself, but it folded under his weight and he went down. He rolled over and looked back.

Zoe stormed the arch, leaning toward the hole in the ground that spewed sparks and fire and smoke, as if she could extinguish the entire inferno with a well-placed rebuke.

The noise of chairs being tossed aside caught Berf's attention. Before he could turn around, Chip plowed through the chairs to the aisle and ran forward. "Zoe!"

A second explosion knocked Zoe to the ground under the arch, which tottered above her. Chip stumbled forward, snatched Zoe up as if she were nothing more than a stick of firewood, and carried her away.

A third explosion toppled the arch and half the wall and sent Chip and Zoe rolling down the hill. They came to rest a few yards away from Berf, Zoe on the ground, Chip protecting her with his body.

Zoe squinted. "Chipper?"

"Zoe," Chip said.

"Am I married yet?"

"No," Chip answered confidently. "But we can fix that. There's a preacher right over there, hiding behind that guy with the dog."

"Do you still love me, Chipper?"

"Yes. Furiously. I don't know why, but I do."

"Me too." Zoe threw her arms around his neck and they kissed a kiss worthy of Audrey Hepburn at her peak.

Berf crawled to his feet and dusted off his turquoise tux. Apparently fate had intervened when Jake wouldn't. Berf was reconsidering his views on karma when he heard his name called from the periphery by a familiar and dreaded voice.

"Berf? Berf! I'm over here."

Berf turned woodenly, like an automaton in a Disney ride, to see Amelia pushing through the fleeing crowd toward him. He froze like a bird mesmerized by a cobra.

"Berf, I'm right here. I knew you couldn't go through with it."

As Amelia reached the edge of the sea of chairs, a fourth, much larger explosion rocked the mesa, and suddenly the air was filled with gold, glittering in the light of the candles and tiki torches as coins came raining down.

Before Amelia could recover, JL and his boys darted out from the edge of the retreating crowd and began scooping up coins. As others noted this strange behavior, they ventured back into the torch light.

The word spread in a matter of seconds, and suddenly Amelia was engulfed in a crowd of gold diggers. She attempted to push her way through to Berf, but she was no match for the perseverance of collective greed.

Berf felt a hand on his shoulder and spun around. Jake took his arm.

"This way. Quick."

Jake dragged him away from the chaos to where he had a Range Rover idling, Mitch and Bonnie standing guard.

Mitch held the passenger door open.

Berf paused long enough to shake his hand. "May flights of angels sing thee to thy rest, Emil."

"I'd git while the gittin' is good, hombre."

Chapter Forty-Six

As Jake spurred the Jag down US 83, Berf pulled his cell phone from the breast pocket of his turquoise tux jacket and glanced at Jake.

"I'm guessing you had something to do with that back there."

Jake shrugged.

"My faithful friend and companion, I repent of ever having doubted you in a weak moment. I don't know how you engineered the feat, and I'm concerned that you may be visited in the near future by the ATF, the Treasury Department, Homeland Security, and the Daughters of the Republic of Texas, perhaps singly or en masse, but you shall have your just reward."

Berf scrolled through his contacts on his phone. He was forever safe from the depredations of the mercurial Zoe, but there was still the matter of Amelia Barker.

Of course, he could just tell Amelia "No" and let the chips bury their dead, but there was The Code to think of. You didn't disrespect a woman in love except as a last resort, and he could think of other resorts he could employ first. Like Aruba, for example.

His travel agent answered on the fifteenth ring. "Zelda. It's Berf."

He was forced to pull the phone away from his ear, but such things were to be expected. Zelda was an excitable woman.

"Yes, I know it's Saturday night. You're not busy, are you?"

Berf used the next bout of shouting to adjust the climate control on the Jag. It was getting a bit nippy, even for December. Once the brouhaha settled, he put the phone back to his ear.

"Look, that's fine and I'll be happy to try that with my phone later, but right now I need you to book two seats to Aruba immediately."

He pulled the phone away and leaned toward Jake. "You can take 127 here and cut off a few miles to San Antonio."

He returned to the phone. "From the airport closest to Bolero. Yes, that's in Texas. Try San Antonio first, Austin next. Shoot, we'll drive to Hobby or Bush Intercontinental if we have to."

Berf glanced at Jake, who nodded back.

"Zelda, Zelda . . . Zelda! Look. I don't need all the details. Just call me back and tell me which airport to drive to. And book two rooms in Aruba, indefinitely."

After a few more minutes of abuse, Berf cut in. "Yes, okay, well, I'm pretty sure my mother was married when she had me, but I'll check into it. You could be right. Just call me back on the flights."

Berf placed the phone gingerly on the console. "Remind me to have this decontaminated before I use it again."

He adjusted the seat back a few notches, and for the first time in six weeks, he relaxed. "Well, well, Jake. It seems we've dodged the bullet this time. It just goes to show you." He held out a hand toward Jake. "I hope that now even you can admit that if you just stick to The Code, things have a way of working out."

There seemed to be a sparkle in Jake's eye, but he said nothing. He was a hard one to figure sometimes.

Berf reached into his tux jacket. "Slim Jim?"

Jake nodded and took the Slim Jim. He tore open the plastic with his teeth and took a bite. "Merry Christmas."

Berf opened a Slim Jim for himself. "Feliz Navidad, primo. Feliz Navidad."

They toasted by tapping the two Slim Jims like crossing swords and rode into the night toward whatever adventure awaited.

BRAD WHITTINGTON

ENDLESS VACATION

{ A NOVEL }

ENDLESS VACATION

CHAPTER 5: DAVE

The gate opened as Dave approached his house in Lakeway. He whipped the 'vette into the two-car garage, leaving space for Angela to pull in her Lexus. She met him at the utility room door with a small overnight case.

Dave crossed the utility room, turned on the kitchen light, and held the door open. Angela entered and stopped, staring into the kitchen and blocking his path.

"Dave?" She stepped aside and he saw the room.

The kitchen was reduced to chaos, as if a sorcerer's apprentice had been called away suddenly in the midst of a particularly troublesome spell that had gone awry. He pushed past her and scanned the wreckage.

Dave held his finger to his lips and pulled Angela back into the utility room. Why hadn't the alarm system already brought the authorities? He glanced at the keypad by the door. No flashing lights.

As Dave attempted to decipher this new conundrum, a crashing noise came from beyond the kitchen.

"Stay here," he whispered.

Dave pulled the Glock 27 from his ankle holster, crept through the kitchen to the hallway, and peered to the left into the dining room. Nothing. He slipped noise-lessly across the threshold and looked to the right into the den. Nothing.

He stepped to the left, intending to cross through the dining room toward the front entrance, when his feet tripped on something. He went down, sprawling on the floor. The gun clattered across the dining room, pin-balling through chair legs.

He sat up and identified the cause of his fall, an olive-drab duffel bag. Dave got to his feet and inched his head around the corner. From behind the couch, backlit by the light above the wet bar, a head popped up. A large head with shaggy hair jutting out from under a tight-fitting cloth cap. Dave's pulse quickened. He scanned the room for something he could use as a weapon.

Then the head spoke. "Buckaroo! The hour produces the man!"

Only one person called Dave "buckaroo." From a long time ago. But it couldn't possibly be him.

The figure stood. It wore a long, white woolen shirt partially covered by a robe made of vertical strips of coarse brown-and-ochre cloth. The robe was secured with a long sash that trailed from the hip.

The figure held an ice bucket in one hand and a cock-tail shaker in the other. "Fancy a martini?"

Dave approached cautiously, squinting. "Hensley?"

"In the flesh, as usual!"

A wave of relief and confusion coursed through Dave's limbic system. "What are you doing here?"

Hensley nodded. "Right, then, I'll just fetch some fresh ice." He skirted the couch, kicking aside stray ice cubes.

Seeing Hensley here, in his home, nonchalantly reducing it to a federal disaster area, affected Dave like the arrival of a dozen Vaneks. His right hand twitched into a fist. He longed to squeeze the ice bucket onto Hensley's head like a catcher's mask, but through the fading adrenaline rush he remembered Angela was present. "How did you get in?"

"Come on, Davison. Since when has a lock kept me out of anything?"

"The security system?"

Hensley snorted as he disappeared into the kitchen, then popped his head back out. "By the way, dinner's on you. Edamame salad, filet mignon, chicken Diane, lobster, butter sauce, grilled vegetable medley, bananas foster." He popped back into the kitchen. The sounds of ice rattling into the bucket flowed from ground zero.

The pan-European accent Dave remembered from Mom's funeral had intensified. Mainly British with flourishes of other accents tossed in to make it difficult to pinpoint a specific region. And what was with the gourmet chef impersonation? Dave retrieved his gun from under the dining room table and did a quick reconnaissance of the den. Hensley had set up camp. Clothes, dishes, blankets, pillows, TV on mute showing a Knight Rider rerun. He appeared to be here for the duration. But why?

What were the odds that he would agree to track down Hensley and a few hours later find his prodigal brother in his own house? Evidently, Rex had left out a great many things during his cryptic conversation.

Hensley's voice boomed from the kitchen. "Hullo! Fancy a martini, love?"

Angela's voice answered. "Only if you're having one."

Hensley returned with an overflowing ice bucket, sloughing cubes like bread crumbs on the trail to the wicked witch's house. Angela followed him and stopped at the doorway.

As Hensley passed, Dave studied his outfit. The shirt hung past his waist, the robe down to his knees. Underneath he wore loose-fitting woolen pants tucked into high woolen boots decorated in a maroon, red, and green pattern and secured with blue lashings.

"Don't mind the mess," Hensley said. "I'll attend to it directly." He set the bucket on the bar and began pouring ingredients into the cocktail shaker.

Dave converged on Hensley and whispered, "What are you doing here?"

Hensley answered in his usual stentorian voice. "Do I need an excuse to visit my kid brother?" He dropped ice cubes into the shaker.

Dave studied him. Hensley had a face of the high-mileage variety, craggy and weather-beaten. Not quite to Keith Richards levels but a respectable effort. "When was the last time you visited?"

Hensley shook the martini vigorously, his jowls waggling from the effort. He had no trouble talking over the noise. "Mother's funeral."

"Fifteen years ago. And before then?"

"Father's funeral."

"Thirty years ago. And this time?"

Hensley didn't respond. Dave glanced at Angela. She took in Hensley in Sherpa drag whipping the cocktail shaker around and raised an eyebrow.

Hensley set down the shaker, which was rimed with a frosty coating, and rubbed his hands on his robe to warm them. He dumped the ice water from two martini glasses into the sink, dropped a spear of olives into each, and decanted the liquid. It swirled in the glasses, cloudy with air bubbles and ice particles.

"I found myself between engagements and at liberty to explore other pursuits," he said while setting the shaker aside. He sampled the concoction.

"So, what you're saying is, you're broke."

Hensley breathed out a sigh of satisfaction and lowered the martini. "As always, Buckaroo, you apprehend my circumstance precisely." He held the other martini to Angela. "For you, my dear. May you wear it in good health."

He inclined his head toward Dave. "You're off the clock. Dial it down a few notches and join the party. We're well stocked. I can mix another."

Angela grasped the handle of her overnight case with both hands in front of her like a schoolgirl, an image that would stick in Dave's mind for a long time. Especially since he was powerless to stop the inevitable.

She regarded the martini Hensley held out and shook her head. "I should be going. You guys have a lot of catching up to do."

"You have cut me to the quick," Hensley said, "and laid waste my foundations." He bowed deeply without spilling a drop of either drink. Then he held out the martini to Dave. "It's all yours, Buckaroo."

Dave ignored him and followed Angela to the utility room. "Can I come with you?"

Angela laid a hand on his chest. "That's your brother in there."

"But I like you better."

"You haven't seen him for how long?"

"Not long enough."

"He's family. If that doesn't matter to you, it should."

She kissed him, a kiss that held all the things that could have been but now were not to be. From the darkness of the garage, she spoke.

"Don't forget about St. Croix."

Dave turned back to the devastation of the kitchen. He would have that martini to build up his strength. Then he would have Hensley's gizzard on a spit. Then he'd have another martini to celebrate.

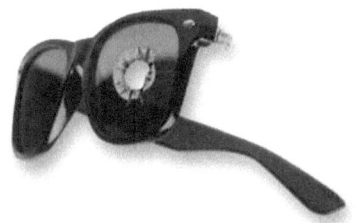

CHAPTER 6: DAVE

Dave returned to the den, claimed the martini, and drank half of it in a gulp.

Hensley pushed buttons on the remote. "Can you get Japanese TV on this?"

Dave turned to the wannabe Sherpa embedded in the recliner like a multicultural meteorite. He yelled over random snippets of surround sound as Hensley bounced through the channels. "Why now?"

Hensley continued to channel-surf. Dave took another healthy sip and snagged an olive. Then he stepped to the entertainment console, grabbed the plug of the power strip, and pulled it free. The entire system died without protest.

Hensley looked up. "Did you say something?"

"Who died?" Dave could think of no other reason for Hensley's presence.

"Two million people die every year. Are you thinking of a particular person?"

Dave regarded Hensley. He did, in fact, have a candidate in mind. He checked his watch. "When are you leaving?"

"No definite plans. I am a creature of whimsy."

"With incredibly bad timing."

Hensley chewed on this.

Dave killed the martini. Perhaps one more before he escalated to fratricide. A pile of foreign coins of various sizes, metals, and countries lay on the granite counter next to the sink. He raked them aside in a burst of anger. They skittered across the hardwood floor like pucks on ice.

Dave had the ingredients in the shaker before Hensley connected the dots.

"Was that an overnight case in that fetching creature's impeccably manicured hands?"

Dave poured the contents of the shaker over the olives and tested the result. Almost as good as The Emerald.

Hensley sprang from the recliner with surprising grace for his build. "I shall take a room in an hotel for the evening. Could I trouble you for cab fare?" He glanced about distractedly and spotted his duffel bag by the kitchen doorway. "And the price of the room, if it's not too inconvenient."

"Too late for that."

Hensley settled back into the recliner. "This is most unfortunate. We must find some way to rectify the situation." He picked up the remote and pressed the power button, stared at it blankly, and set it back down. "Perhaps she would welcome you at her place for the assignation. Don't trouble yourself about me. I can get along on my own for the evening." He picked up the remote again, looked at it, and set it down.

Dave dropped onto the couch, slouched against an overstuffed armrest, and drank his martini. He waved the glass in Hensley's direction. "What's with the costume?"

"I was most recently in Nepal. I proceeded here post haste."

"Because?"

"I felt it was . . . opportune."

He didn't remember Hensley being so evasive, but Dave was only nine when they had their last real conversation. At the clinic in the jungles of Angola. Hensley was sixteen.

Davison plays soccer in the clearing with the locals. Or tries to. More like he runs back and forth, trailing the gang or getting run over when they suddenly reverse field. Then the supply plane arrives and everyone rushes to the dirt airstrip to help unload.

A rock bounces off the crate he's stacking. He looks up, puzzled. From the gloom of the jungle bordering the settlement, Hensley flashes their secret sign, the distress signal they alone know.

Davison runs to the edge of the underbrush. "Hensley, what—"

Hensley shushes him and pulls him farther in, out of sight of the plane. Davison peers back in the direction of the unloading and then at Hensley, confused.

Hensley holds up a finger, drops to one knee, unzips a backpack, and removes a stack of slender red and green albums. His coin collection. He holds them out. Davison hesitates and then slowly reaches for them.

"These are yours now, Buckaroo," Hensley says. "There are still some gaps that need filling."

"But don't you want to—"

"No," Hensley says brusquely. "I travel light."

"But . . ."

Hensley zips the backpack, stands, and slings it on, shrugging his shoulders to settle it. Davison watches, squinting at him at first, head cocked to one side. Then his eyes open wide.

"You're—" No. He couldn't.

"Shh." Hensley puts a hand on his shoulder. "I have to, Davison. But you can't tell anyone."

"But Dad—"

"No one," Hensley whispers fiercely, squeezing Davison's shoulder. "Now you take care of those coins, and one day I'll be back to check on you. But only if you keep this a secret. Otherwise, I'll never come back."

Davison's eyes teem. "Okay."

Hensley tousles Davison's hair and backs away, maintaining eye contact until he turns away with a jerk and runs.

Davison watches Hensley disappear into the brush, his only ally in this foreign land. Then he runs the opposite direction, back to the house, clutching the albums to his chest. He careens through the empty house into their bedroom and stashes the coin albums under Hensley's mattress.

And he keeps the secret, keeps to the code. Every morning he scans the edge of the clearing, hoping to see Hensley emerge from the jungle with a smile on his face. Every evening he watches the sun creep below the trees, wondering if Hensley will sneak in during the night and surprise him.

But Hensley doesn't come back.

———

Hensley smiled at Dave from the recliner. "You still with the CIA?"

Dave didn't bother to correct him.

Hensley studied his surroundings, taking in the flat-screen, the well-stocked bar. "Gone rogue? Soldier of fortune?"

"How did you find me? When you came to Mom's funeral, I was living in Virginia."

"You're not the only one with a vast network of informants."

Uncle Rex. Had to be. But why hadn't Rex mentioned it during dinner instead of telling him to track Hensley down? Dave suddenly felt tired. It had been a strange day. First Rivera pulled a gun on him, then Uncle Rex talked about regret and failure, and now Hensley appears, dressed like a clown and acting the fool. Dave didn't have the strength for this game. Not now.

He took a healthy gulp of the martini and leaned forward with his elbows on his knees. "Tell me you didn't come all the way from Tibet to play twenty questions."

"Actually, it was Nepal—"

"You haven't contacted me once in thirty-two years. Just tell me how much it is you need, I'll tell you no, and you can go back to whatever it is you've been doing."

Hensley's expression was eerily familiar. If Dave hadn't just been thinking of the day Hensley left, he might not have recognized it. Hensley avoided his eye. Dave was suddenly furious. He jumped to his feet, sloshing gin onto the carpet.

"You can go to hell. Who are you to pity me?" He drained the martini and threw the glass at the bar. It bounced off the granite countertop and shattered against the backsplash. He pulled out his wallet, grabbed a handful of bills, and threw them at Hensley. "Take your duffel bag and get out."

Hensley didn't move. He didn't speak.

Dave walked past him, through the demolished kitchen, and out to the 'vette. He paid no mind to his route until he was out of Lakeway. He cast about for a destination and turned toward downtown. He parked on the street, went to the intercom by the front door, and punched in Angela's condo number.

"Dave? What happened to your brother?"

"Jet lag. Right after you left, he dropped like a hog hit with a hammer. But I'm still trying to make up my mind about that St. Croix thing."

The lock buzzed and clicked open. "You've come to the right place. But as I warned you, I can be very persuasive."

Sometime around midnight, Dave and Angela sat curled up together in an oversized deck chair on the balcony, watching the night action in the warehouse district, such as it was. A show at the Austin Music Hall had just finished and the crowd streamed out to bars and cars and whatever trouble they could scare up on a Tuesday night.

Angela ran a fingernail up Dave's arm. "Persuaded?"

"I might need a little more convincing."

She laughed. "You're pretty ambitious for an old man."

Dave smiled. He wasn't even ten years older, but she liked to tease him about robbing the cradle. He recalled his thoughts earlier in the evening and realized she was right. He was ambitious thinking a beautiful career woman like her would want to settle down with a guy looking at retirement in three days, even if it was early retirement. "Not ambitious, just lucky."

"Better to be lucky than good."

"I like to think I'm both."

She laughed louder this time. "And humble, too."

For a while they listened to the sound of shouts and car doors slamming, engines cranking and horns honking as the crowd below dispersed.

"You know, I'm kind of looking forward to this St. Croix trip," Dave said. In the dark, he could almost hear her smile of triumph. "And to spending more time together now that I'm retiring."

"Typical man. Thinks just because his schedule is suddenly open, his woman will drop everything and come running."

"You mean you won't?"

"I didn't say you were wrong, just typical." She settled her head into the crook of his arm. "Although, if you really are a typical man, you're obviously wrong, too."

He gave her a nudge and turned his thoughts to getting enough capital to hold the office space over the weekend. She might be persuasive, but he was definitely determined.

Chapter 7: Hensley

When Hensley heard the garage door open, he sprang from the recliner and peered through the plantation shutters. Davison fled with undue haste in a red Z-51 Corvette. Hensley smiled. A chariot fit for a prince of the realm. And three guesses as to his destination. That left adequate time for reconnaissance and strategic planning.

Despite the impression Hensley intentionally fostered, he was the most efficient person he knew. For example, he would never have saddled himself with this rambling suburban domicile, choosing instead to engineer a way to enjoy its virtues without circumscribing his mobility.

He had developed his personal philosophy—minimum effort, maximum pleasure—through years of direct research among the citizens of the world on every continent and in every social stratum. And he had discovered the key to implementing that philosophy with the three Ps: prioritization, positioning, and personality.

For example, a current assessment of priorities dictated another martini. As Hensley positioned himself at the bar, he noticed the coins scattered across the floor. They would have to be addressed, but not immediately. He assembled the requisite components for a libation adequate to restore the tissues, and then surveyed the room. Davison had achieved a modicum of success but radiated a commensurate lack of depth, a certain bourgeois superficiality.

He'd first noted the signs in the Tarrytown neighborhood where Ellis had said he would find Rex, but the house had been empty. He thought of waiting, but the neighborhood was infested with joggers with strollers and strollers with dogs and a lady inspecting her rose bushes for evidence of malfeasance on the part of her gardener. All paying particular attention to the guy in the Sherpa suit.

So he had moved on to Davison's house in Lakeway where the neighbors returned from work around sunset and drove straight into their three-car garages like Bruce Wayne into the Batcave, entering directly into their ozone-layer-depleting homes without the discomfort of interacting with the great unwashed, assuming one of that clan had the temerity to encroach upon their domain. Where an al-Qaeda cell could go undetected for years as long as they kept their hair and their grass cut, drove the right car, and didn't leave the recycle bin out overnight.

Finding the neighborhood deserted in the late afternoon sun, Hensley compromised the security system at his leisure, used the three Ps to run a quick inventory of the larder, and whipped up dinner.

But the gathering of the clans had not gone as anticipated. First, he had not planned for the presence of a third party, however welcome. And Davison had not been seduced by the well-placed word and the well-mixed cocktail. Hensley found himself nonplussed by the failure of the three Ps. He sat on the coffee table in the lotus position and searched his mind for an explanation.

It came to him almost at once. He lacked information. He had been prioritizing, positioning, and personalityizing, if he could use that word, in an informational vacuum. Or, to put it in the vernacular, he had no idea why he was here. And everyone could agree on the identity of the culpable party.

—

The telegram catches up with him in Nepal in a small village that's little more than a jumping-off place for intrepid thrill seekers on their way to the Everest base camp.

COME AT ONCE. SAY NOTHING TO DAVISON. —R

The contents seem plain enough on the surface, but Hensley takes nothing at face value, especially where family is concerned. He takes the paper and the envelope to the only bar in town. He greets Mingma, the proprietor, and orders a mug of *tungba*, the local liquor made by pouring hot water over fermented millet.

He focuses the insight derived from the first two mugs on searching for the message behind the message, and after a third mug, for the message behind the message behind the message. He studies the telegram like a fortune cookie, trying to decode it, but it fails to yield its secrets. He drags the bamboo mug across the rough wooden table and dips his head to the bamboo straw. The last of the liquor gurgles up the straw with a noise like radio static.

Hensley scans the room for Mingma, catches his eye, and nods. He sets down the paper and picks up the tattered envelope. International Telegram delivered it to the hostel in Amsterdam, but he hasn't lived there for almost two years. The markings on the front of the envelope chronicle its three-week journey through Europe and Asia, with three more addresses crossed out. On multiple occasions he has intended to apprise Ellis of his current address, but other priorities have superseded the thought.

Mingma arrives at the table, holding a kettle with a towel around the handle. "More water for you, Hensley." He pours steaming water into the mug.

"May your house be filled with joy and peace, Mingma."

"May your house be free of sorrow." Mingma bows slightly.

Hensley holds the telegram. "See this? The old man seems to be saying I should leave here immediately. What do you make of that?"

"Yes, sir," Mingma says, smiling.

"Not that it's a problem. I can leave at the drop of a hat." He picks up his Sherpa hat from the table and drops it on the floor. The soft thud is inaudible in the noise of the bar. "In fact, I frequently leave at the drop of a hat. Quicker, even."

"Yes, sir," Mingma echoes.

Hensley returns his attention to the telegram. "And I get the distinct impression that Davison should know nothing of this business. Which is rich because I've only talked to him twice in thirty-seven years." He looks up at Mingma. "Does that strike you as odd?"

"Yes, sir?" Mingma's smile fades slightly.

The thing that most puzzles Hensley is this abrupt summons from the old man. Hensley has been summoned by others, from a magistrate to a dominatrix, and any number of people in between, but never by the aging scion of the Stone tribe who seems content to let slumbering canines snore.

What does it mean?

He is due for a trip to the States. It's been more than ten years. Santa Fe and Chrystal and her kids. They are probably all grown and gone. He smiles, wondering what she is doing now. Perhaps he will do this thing, whatever it is, and then track her down.

After numerous hours of reflection and judicious application of multiple mugs of *tungba* and the three Ps, Hensley makes the journey by a circuitous route, the chief virtue of which lies in the contacts in each locale who owe him favors and can therefore finance the next leg in the trip. He actually comes out ahead.

Hensley came to the end of his martini without achieving enlightenment. Despite Ellis's assurances to the contrary, the one man who could decode the telegram was not in evidence in Austin. Perhaps if Hensley had come an hour or a day earlier, he might have discovered what Rex wanted. He had failed in that regard, but at least he had followed directions. Davison knew nothing about the telegram, just as Rex had intended for reasons that Hensley couldn't guess.

But what to do about Davison and his lack of the spirit of hospitality and cooperation? Should Hensley fold his tents and slip into the night, or stay the course and wear down his opponent through the sheer force of his considerable personality? He needed greater insight into the mind of his subject.

He popped off the table like a man shot from a cannon, gathered the scattered coins from the floor, and considered where to begin his search. In these cases, one must consider the psychology of the individual. Where a person stored an object depended on his attitude toward it.

A treasured memento might be displayed on a shelf or in a case. An object of value might be locked away. The flotsam of souvenirs that followed one about in the move from place to place might be in the garage or the attic or a guest room closet.

It came down to the question of how Davison regarded the object in question. Given his behavior this evening, Hensley doubted it would be on display. But surely Dave would not have tossed it into a box along with childhood diaries, the mortarboard tassel, the World Series ticket stubs.

He found it in the study, locked in a glass-fronted shelf along with an eclectic assortment of first editions—Robert Louis Stevenson, Daniel Defoe, and Ian Fleming. The lock wouldn't keep out the cleaning ladies, much less Hensley. He opened the door, pulled out a slim green album, and opened it to reveal a complete collection of Liberty head dimes from 1892 to 1916. He checked the next, buffalo nickels, and an album of Indian pennies.

Davison had completed the few albums Hensley had left behind as a testament to the unbreakable bond of brothers and had expanded the collection to cover all the

US currency and beyond. Evidently, he was not completely devoid of sentiment when it came to the token of Hensley's promise to return.

He emptied his pocket of the coins he had brought, filled in a few empty slots that matched, and put everything back, leaving the extra coins inside the case before he locked it. Then he returned to the den for a final drink.

The signs were favorable. Hensley would stay. Eventually Rex would surface, and they would discover what this was all about. But just in case, he collected the cash Davison had thrown at him before he exited stage left in a huff and a 'vette.

Enough to get out of town, but not enough to get very far. He needed either a better plan or better financing.

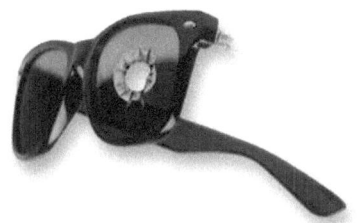

Chapter 8: Dave

Dave drove out to Lakeway with the sun at his back and an open road in front. At six a.m., the eastbound traffic was already starting to pick up. By the time he got a shower and a shave, MoPac would be a parking lot.

Angela was right; she was very persuasive on the matter of St. Croix. But he wouldn't leave town until he had the office space locked down. As he had lain awake, his brain spinning like a hamster wheel, it came to him. The coin collection. Ten years ago it had appraised at seventy-three thousand dollars. It might be over eighty by now. That and his other sources of capital should be enough to get things started, or at least hold the office space until next week, allowing him to take the trip after all.

He pulled into the garage and recalled the circumstances of his departure the night before. Hensley in his Sherpa glory. The last thing he wanted to see in the morning. Dave edged through the utility room into the kitchen and came to a dead stop. It looked like a model home staged for showing. He checked the cabinets and drawers. Everything where it should be, as if the night before had been a hallucination. He started the coffee and watched it drip, trying to remember exactly what had happened.

Knowing it would drive him crazy if he didn't, he searched the house, working his way from the kitchen to the bedrooms and opening every door, even the closets. His search ended in the third guest bedroom.

Hensley sprawled nude on the bed like a murder victim, twisted in the sheets. With a sudden snort, he turned over, entangling himself further. His pasty-white body was hairy and solid, not flabby as Dave had assumed. His duffel bag sat on the dresser, packed and zipped up like he was ready to go. The cash Dave had thrown at him lay on top in a neat stack.

Dave resisted the urge to drag Hensley out of bed and throw him out. Because he was technically family, at least as far as DNA was concerned, Dave relented to the point of conceding one night's stay. Plus, he didn't want to look at that hairy naked body any more than absolutely necessary. Less, actually.

He closed the door, went to his own bedroom, took a shower, and got dressed. In the study, he printed directions to the bus station on East Koenig. Then Dave unlocked the glass case and saw the stacks of foreign coins on the shelf in front of the albums.

Hensley had been in the case. Wasn't the cash Dave had thrown at him enough? He brushed the coins aside, pulled out a folder, and flipped it open. Nothing missing. He grabbed a box and transferred the folders to it, checking each one. Hensley hadn't taken anything. He'd found the collection and left the coins inside the glass, evidently banking on a decades-old appeal to sentimental value, unaware that the only value left in the red and green folders was strictly financial. It wasn't Hensley's first mistake and probably wouldn't be his last.

ACKNOWLEDGEMENTS

Thanks to Dad for turning me on to Wodehouse decades ago and to Daniel for reading all the Sackett novels in his youth.

Thanks to Ian Rogers for brainstorming on this project seven years ago. You were in on the ground floor.

Thanks to Gene Naftulyev for pythonic advice.

Thanks to critique groups NIP and El Gee for feedback.

Thanks to the newsletter subscribers for providing feedback on draft four.

Thanks to Rebecca Leach for making the inside better, and Hilary Combs for making the outside look good.

— BRAD WHITTINGTON —

Sign up for the newsletter to get other sneak peeks and freebies.

BradWhittington.com

ABOUT THE AUTHOR

Brad Whittington was born in Fort Worth, Texas, on James Taylor's eighth birthday and Jack Kerouac's thirty-fourth birthday and is old enough to know better. He lives in Austin, Texas with The Woman. Previously he has been known to inhabit Hawaii, Ohio, South Carolina, Arizona, and Colorado, annoying people as a janitor, math teacher, field hand, computer programmer, brick-yard worker, editor, resident Gentile in a Conservative synagogue, IT director, weed-cutter, and in a number of influential positions in other less notable professions. He is greatly loved and admired by all right-thinking citizens and enjoys a complete absence of cats and dogs at home.

BradWhittington.com